A WOMAN IN
SHEIK'S
CLOTHING

TERROR TARGETS
LONDON

CLIVE WARNER

ISBN (Print): 978-1-950464-20-3
ISBN (eBook): 978-1-950464-21-0

OffBeat

Publishing

"Islam will wear out as color on a garment wears out, until no one will know what fasting, prayer, Hajj and charity (zakaah) are. The Book of Allah, may He be glorified and exalted, will be taken away at night, and not one verse of it will be left on earth. And there will be some people left, old men and old women, who will say: We saw our fathers saying these words, Laa ilaaha ill-Allah, so we say them, too."

— The hadith of Hudhayfah ibn al-Yamaan
(may Allah be pleased with him)

ONE

They met in the refectory of an old manor house. It had once been the grand residence of a lord, who, having gambled away the family fortune, had sold the house to a hotel chain. Unable to make a profit on it, the chain sold the increasingly dilapidated house, and now it was the Abu Afifa Madrassa. Supposedly it was a secondary-education facility for Islamic students. Actually, it was the UK base of the Haz ut-Tahrir, an extremist jihadi organization.

It was still dark as Hasan arrived. He pushed through the heavy oak door, leaving a trail of footprints wet from the dew. His rubber-soled combat boots squeaked on the varnished pine floor as he crossed to one of the benches and sat down.

Three minutes later, Zafir walked in, carrying an ungainly bundle of three war-surplus gas masks. Like Hasan, he wore black denim jeans and a black Barbour jacket. The jackets had hoods that left their faces in shadow.

"We're a bit early," Hasan said. The place had the acoustics of a crypt; it made him want to speak in a whisper.

"Better be early on Allah's business, especially dealing with spies,"

Zafir replied roughly, as if challenging the silence of these early morning hours.

Zafir went over to Hasan, placed the masks on the table, and sat down. Hasan saw that Zafir wore a military-style belt with carry loops. Tucked into the belt were an aerosol can and a leather sheath, from which the bone handle of a combat knife protruded. Hasan's own belt was of a simpler design. A pair of gunmetal handcuffs dangled from it, and nothing else.

Zafir stared at Hasan. "Now we'll deal with that snake. I can't understand why we didn't suss him earlier. He's a Jew. I bet Mohamed is not his real name."

Hasan thought about the man who called himself Mohamed Malik. He had been with them about three months, living at the madrassa, doing the work allotted to him, causing no trouble. Probably they would never have suspected him but for a new member who arrived in the past week: an eighteen-year-old who'd been in trouble with the law.

The new guy took one look at Malik, then asked to see the sheik.

Malik had been seen leaving a Jewish club. Now they knew what he was: a spy. When Malik was out of his room, Hasan and Zafir searched it thoroughly and found a tiny digital recorder.

Hasan looked up. Six minutes to five. From outside came a faint rustle, and then the door opened. A chill passed through him, and he shivered. The Sheik filled the doorway. He was just over six feet in height. Deep grooves ran from his nostrils down past the corners of his mouth. His face carried the lines of one who expects to be obeyed, not one who laughs at life.

"Hasan, my brother," he said in his deep baritone voice. "Are you prepared for jihad? And you, Zafir? Are you ready?"

"Yes, Sheik," they replied almost as one, rising from the bench to a position of attention. The Sheik crossed the floor, appearing to glide over it in his black robe. He stood in front of them and gazed into their faces, giving Hasan the unpleasant feeling that his doubt stood nakedly revealed.

"Have no doubts, and the strength of Allah will be with you," the Sheik said in his clear, strong voice. "Zafir, you will use the pepper spray," he continued. "You must be very quick. Take no chances. This yahoodi will no doubt be skilled in the arts of defense. Allah hu akbar." He reached out and took a gas mask, then turned for the door. Zafir and Hasan did likewise.

They took a winding path of smooth asphalt that led past ornamental shrubberies to the dormitory huts. The crescent moon provided just enough light to see by.

Hasan quietly entered Malik's hut.

Zafir and the Sheik followed him.

The three of them took up position in front of Malik's bedroom door. Hasan looked at the Sheik, who nodded his head, then back at Zafir. He pulled the mask over his face and settled it in place. It stank of old rubber.

Zafir touched his arm to get his attention, and gestured. Hasan nodded. Someone was beating a muffled drum somewhere; then he realized it was his own heartbeat, amplified by the mask. They braced themselves against the wall and raised their booted feet, then kicked hard.

The flimsy wooden door splintered and crashed to the floor.

Zafir leaped into the room.

Hasan followed. He saw Malik flip like an acrobat off the bed, land on the floor in a horse-riding stance, hands and feet seeking targets, then Zafir, arm outstretched, shot him with the aerosol spray. Malik went down, heaving and choking.

Zafir gave him another shot.

Hasan watched for a moment as the Jew writhed helplessly on the floor, clawing at his eyes. Hasan took a large syringe from his pocket, bent down, and jabbed the needle into Malik's side, below the rib cage, then pressed the plunger, hard.

Malik began to spasm.

When Hasan brought the syringe back out of him, he saw half the needle was missing.

The Sheik, standing just outside the door, lifted the edge of his mask for a moment to speak clearly: "Get him up. Bring him to the penitents' cell."

"I broke the needle off in him, master," Hasan said with difficulty through his mask.

"It won't matter. Be quick!"

Zafir and Hasan pulled Malik to his feet.

The Sheik gripped the man's jaw, tipped his head back, and peered into his dark-brown eyes. They stared back, blankly unfocused, their pupils dilated. A trail of saliva flowed from his thin-lipped mouth; his breath rasped in his throat. The Sheik nodded and they pulled Malik out of the room.

"Prepare him," the Sheik said. "We will put him to the test at nine."

Hasan and Zafir dragged Malik across a lawn of manicured grass, along a graveled drive, over several yards of stone paving slabs, then down a flight of steps at the side of the grand country house, the headquarters of the madrassa. His heels trailed along the rough stone.

Zafir shouldered open a door of varnished oak, and they half-carried Malik down an echoing corridor, arriving at a small door of studded pine.

Hasan saw that Malik's heels had left blood on the floor and made a mental note to clean the tiles later.

Freeing one arm, Hasan searched his pockets, then pulled out an old-fashioned cast-iron key and fitted it into the lock. He pushed the door open, reached inside, and clicked a switch. Fluorescent lamp starters chattered, then the tubes flooded the space with light. The room inside was like a monk's cell: stark whitewashed brick, quarry-tiled floor, ten feet deep, barely six feet high, and eight feet wide.

Bare of furniture. Originally it had been the wine cellar, but all traces of that had long been expunged.

"Get him over to the wall, Hasan. Quick, dammit, he'll be coming round soon," Zafir said. Oily ringlets of black hair showed at the sides of his hood, but his face was in shadow.

Hasan said nothing, merely nodded. Between them they manhandled Malik to the far wall and propped him against it, Hasan pushing on his chest to keep him upright while Zafir fastened the Jew's left wrist, then the right, into rubber split-blocks. Hasan checked his work, then pinioned Malik's head in a heavy brace with a rubber strap.

They bent down and secured his ankles with stainless steel manacles.

"Just as the Sheik wanted," Hasan said, surveying the prisoner. The Sheik would be pleased. Malik was spread-eagled on the wall like a butterfly in a collection.

Zafir nodded.

Silently, the two men left the room. Outside, birds sang their dawn chorus as the eastern horizon brightened with the new day.

Hasan checked his watch and turned to Zafir.

"Don't be late. Nine sharp."

"Late? You're joking. I'm looking forward to it," Zafir replied.

Hasan returned to his bedroom garret in the lodge. Unable to sleep, he went into his tiny bathroom and scrubbed his face until it was raw, to get rid of the stink of old rubber left by the mask. Traces of the spray still clung to his clothes, and he coughed harshly as he breathed it in. He stripped off his jeans and jacket and flung them into the bath, then poured water on them until they were saturated.

He lay on his hard bed in his underpants, staring at the water stains on the ceiling and wondering what the Sheik planned. In particular, he worried about the needle.

Hasan drifted off, and when he woke, his alarm clock read eight thirty-seven. He swung his legs off the bed, then dressed in his brown day robe. The Sheik did not tolerate lateness.

Zafir was waiting for him outside the penitent's cell. Moments later the Sheik arrived carrying a green canvas bag under one arm. He brought out the antique key and fitted it into the lock.

INSIDE THE CELL, MALIK HEARD A GRATING NOISE AS THE KEY TURNED. His thoughts had been racing furiously since he recovered consciousness and found himself pinned to the wall. He had a splitting headache, his heels hurt like the devil, and there was a sharp pain in his side every time he moved.

They were coming in.

"Ahh. There we are," the Sheik said. "You have nowhere to go. Speak now, speak. Who sent you here?"

Malik stared at them. He would not show fear to these bastards. They were an odd trio, he thought.

The thick-set, squat disciple with oily black hair was a third-generation Pakistani immigrant, born and educated in Britain but sent somewhere in Pakistan regularly. His madrasa name was Zafir, but originally he had been Jaffir. A nasty piece of work.

The other one, Hasan, the son of a Somali asylum-seeker, was built like a runner, tough and wiry, with razor-cut hair. He was one of the recruiters, spending most of his time in the city looking for runaway teenagers, the younger the better.

Malik brought his gaze back to the calm, black-robed man with the leonine face and full head of silver hair. He watched as the Sheik reached into a green bag.

He brought out a small towel, reached inside again, and produced a two-liter plastic soda bottle full of water. The two disciples moved forward until they stood in front of him on each side, then the black-gowned imam advanced on Malik, holding the towel by its top corners.

Malik's world turned white as the Sheik draped the towel carefully over his face, tucking the edge into the stout rubber clamp that pinioned his temples.

A gush of water saturated the cloth, plastering it to his skin. His nostrils filled with moisture and he opened his mouth to breathe, but the wet cloth stopped the passage of air. The harder he tried, the more it sealed itself around his lips.

He knew no one would save him. Khawdash Haganah, the UK Jewish paramilitary group named after the World War II Jewish resistance, had left him in no doubt of it. And he was a month overdue to report. There'd been no opportunity to slip away.

His lungs were on fire. His legs shook and he began a little dance with himself, all courage forgotten as his body screamed for oxygen. A gray mist rose up before him and he moved thankfully towards it, then someone snatched away the cloth and he filled his lungs with a painful gasp.

"It can be over so soon. Who sent you here?" The Sheik waited, but Malik stared dully back at him, his chest heaving as he sucked air. "This will not stop. You are not James Bond, and no one is coming to save you."

Zafir caught the Sheik's slight nod and dropped the cloth over the prisoner's face again, leaned sideways, and tipped the bottle to saturate the cloth. This time they waited longer, until the spasms passed their peak.

Zafir peeled the cloth away from the prisoner's face. Malik took a while to come round. He glared wildly at the Sheik, unable to turn his head to the side so he could see his other tormentors.

"Who sent you? Who? It can all be over," the Sheik said. "Who sent you?"

Malik knew they would not stop. He had to tell them something … something credible. No! Don't tell them anything, don't even think the name, someone would come for him, had to come for him. … But no, he was deep cover, always deep. This was not a movie.

The cloth came back again, again, and always after the choking, lungs burning, stomach twisted into a knot, there was the Sheik's face before him. He felt the hand at his head. No, not again!

The Sheik turned and opened the door of a small white cabinet on the wall. It bore the red cross symbol of a first-aid box. Reaching inside, he removed a syringe, sterile needle, and a small brown bottle sealed with wax. Upending the container, he pulled back on the plunger and watched the syringe fill with a pale amber fluid.

"Have you ever heard of a pretty little plant called the Blue Rush, you filthy Jew? It grows in the high deserts of Afghanistan," the Sheik said. "No? What a pity. You will be feeling quite different soon. Like a new man." He bent forward and pushed the hypodermic needle into Malik's neck just above the collarbone, angling it down, then pressed the plunger.

Malik heard him say, "We'll start with two hundred volts."

He peered at the man in the black robe. The room spun gently and everything took on a pink sheen.

Here came the face again. It looked very odd. Then he realized: It was the devil.

With his last moments of free will, he moved his jaw to oppose two teeth, and bit hard.

Not enough force.

Harder … harder.

Just when he thought the dental implant had failed, the false cap collapsed, releasing a lethal dose of fentanyl.

Grateful, he swallowed.

TWO

Hasan stood at the edge of a patio that adjoined the manor house, gazing over a low wall. In the distance, he saw some of the students tending the formal gardens. From behind came the sound of someone running in bare feet. As he turned toward the sound, Anisa swung round him as if he were a post and, with only hot stones to stand on, hopped onto his Reeboks and grasped his shoulders.

"Is it true, Hasan?" Anisa looked up into his eyes. "That most everyone in England is descended from a crusader?"

She asks such simple questions. "They are kuffars, and thus, to kill them is merciful and brings Allah's approval. And many must be descended from crusaders. This is obvious. You have been here nearly four months, but you haven't progressed in learning the Holy Quran. And you should be helping bring new students in."

She frowned at him.

Hasan cast his mind back, remembering one of his expeditions to London, four months ago.

It was a wet February day when he found Anisa. Euston Station at its dreariest, fine mists of drizzle blowing in like curtains. He did a

9

quick sweep on the lower level where the taxis pulled in; sometimes you found one or two strays trying for a few coins from the passengers.

He climbed the steps two at a time and went past the buffet room and the fast-food joints; not too fast, not too slow, eyes sweeping left and right. There she was. The look of northern Pakistan about her.

A young station porter had her; the man's face scowled. His right hand gripped the girl by the upper arm. Tears welled in her eyes as she stood on tip-toe, her thin shell-suit snagged on a broken wire in the wastebasket.

Hasan thought her hand was bleeding, but it was tomato sauce oozing from the half-eaten hamburger she'd taken. There was cigarette ash stuck to one side. The drizzle had plastered her black hair to her face, and mascara ran down her cheeks. The lightweight nylon jacket gave her little protection; dark patches showed where the rain had soaked through.

"Let me go! Let — me — go!" She panted, struggling to free her arm from the basket, but the man tightened his grip.

"You'll have to come with me, little missy. To the station master's office." The porter's East End accent carried sadistic overtones.

"Why? I haven't done anything. Let go of me!" She struggled harder.

Hasan hesitated. He didn't want to tangle with anyone who might call the authorities. It wasn't worth it; another mark would come along later. The chickie looked nice though, with her petite figure, tan complexion, and big black eyes. Hasan saw her freshness shining through the grime. He stepped forward, reached out, and grasped the porter's elbow.

"You like picking on young girls, do you?" Hasan smiled, but the smile wasn't reflected in his eyes. Up close, he saw that the porter had taken a blade down the side of his face at some time.

The porter tightened his hold. "You asking for trouble? I'll call the transport police if you don't beat it."

The smile froze on Hasan's face. "Don't do that." He flexed his fingers, one of them sinking into the pain point on the inside of the porter's elbow.

The porter grunted, his face twisting in pain. He let go of the girl and sank to his knees.

Hasan followed him down and grabbed two fingers of the porter's hand in his fist. He bent them back sharply and forced the man flat onto the platform.

"Ahh—" the porter mouthed.

"That's better. Now be good, or I'll have to talk to you later." He gave the kuffar's hand a final tweak, ignoring his sharp yelp, then turned to the girl, who stood with her mouth open.

"Come on, they might be watching on CCTV. I'll get you something better to eat than this crap. I'm with a Muslim group that feeds hungry teenagers. There's a Dormobile with some friends of mine parked over at King's Cross station. "

He paused, watching her. She was wary, but she'd go. For a moment he felt sorry for ensnaring these kids. But jihad was jihad.

They were soaked by the time they reached the plain white van parked at the back of King's Cross station.

The girls fussed over Anisa. Mo put her arm around Anisa's shoulders, her voice warm and sympathetic.

"They can be real bastards at Euston. Do you have any money, Luv?" Mo was twenty-one but dressed as if she was several years younger. She was nearly as tall as Hasan and would have been pretty if the acne she'd suffered in her teens hadn't left her cheeks looking like a battlefield.

"No. I lost it in the tube station. I was trying to read the map and someone snatched my purse from behind. It was crowded—" She started sobbing.

"Never mind. Here's some food." Hasan brought her a shiny plastic bowl full of vegetarian stew and a soup spoon.

"This your first time in London?" asked Najat, a dumpy, clumsy girl with big feet.

"Yes. No, I came here once before, with my stepfather. To see lawyers. I was seven, I can't remember much, except the tube. I fell on the escalator."

"We're all friends here," Hasan said, grinning. "Me, I dropped out of school at fourteen, my parents didn't give a shit. They were better off with me outta the way. The old man was drinking, well haram he was, and me mum, well, mother's little helpers were taking care of her. Mandies, twice a day, from the local GP. Well gone on it. I came down here, ran out of bread after a few nights, and ended up back of the arches, a place called Camden."

Anisa finished off the stew. She wiped half-dried tears from her face with her hand.

"Some parts of Camden are … well, you know, full o' methies, needle freaks, all kinds of garbage. The Sheik found me, took me in. Later he bought the Grange."

"The Grange?" She scraped the last bits off the side of the bowl and licked the spoon.

"Used to be called that. Now it's the Abu Afifa Madrassa. It's a big old country house. We all live there, one happy family." He looked at Anisa's empty bowl. "Like some more?"

She nodded.

They left her in silence to think things over. Mo hung Anisa's soaked jacket over the back of one of the seats to dry out.

Anisa curled up like a cat at one end of the Dormobile.

Najat and Hasan left the van to look for more prospects, but the rain was getting worse and all they found were a couple of hard-faced rent boys looking for partners. By eight o'clock, Najat and Hasan were back.

Anisa sat up, glancing from one to the other.

"We've gotta go, Anisa. It's been nice talking to you." Hasan saw the panic in her eyes. "D'you have somewhere to stay?" He was sure she hadn't; he had tagged her as a runaway the moment he spotted her.

"No. What should I do? You used to live in this area, didn't you? Is there anywhere I could sleep? Maybe I can find a job tomorrow."

The rain hammered on the roof, making it ring like a tin drum.

"Anisa, this area will be full of working girls and their men in another hour. Some big dark guy is goin' to take a fancy to a nice fresh young thing like you. Why don't you hang around with us for a few days?"

She hesitated, then, almost in a whisper, said, "I can leave any time I like, can't I?"

"Of course. Just try it for a few days. I'm sure you'll love it," he lied.

And at first, of course, she had.

―――――

THE WAY HASAN LOOKED RIGHT THROUGH HER, ANISA WONDERED, *Does he remember when we met?* After they left the station, she hadn't been able to keep her eyes off him and almost walked into a lamp post. Five feet ten, she estimated, and when he slipped his arm around her, she had felt his strength.

It was as clear in her mind as yesterday. Early February, the rain pissing down, her purse stolen, and — no doubt — her abusing step-father getting set to track her down. If she returned home, they'd ship her off to Pakistan, where she'd be forced to marry a man three times her age.

That rainy night. ... She remembered passing a video store. When she'd seen the televisions flashing inside, she realized who Hasan reminded her of. It was the boy in the Levi Jeans commercial: long-legged, narrow hips, even narrower waist, no hint of a beer gut. Wide shoulders, too, but the face had a sensuality not entirely masculine.

Hasan's hair had been cropped close to the scalp. *Why does he want it so short? But it does set off his pale blue eyes.* She'd hung back to get a peek at his rear. Strong muscles under the tight denim. Was it haram to think these thoughts?

Anisa remembered arriving at the white van, but after, the events of the night blurred together: headlights in the rain, the hiss of tires on the street, the van climbing up a winding path, and sleep, blessed sleep.

Now, with the early summer sun beating down, it all seemed a long time ago. Hasan had a strange look in his eyes.

"Hasan, I'd do anything for you. Anything. You know that."

"Would you, Anisa?" he asked.

She opened her mouth to reply, but Flaxen shouted from the other side of the patio wall.

"Anisa! You'll be late! It's half past one already!" Flaxen was a blond fourteen-year-old girl who'd joined the school a few weeks ago. She hadn't been given a Muslim name yet.

Anisa let go of Hasan and sprinted back to the house. She slipped on her tennis shoes, went into a corridor, and ran into a high-walled courtyard. On the far side, she stopped, combed her hair with her fingers, then pushed a green door open and walked into a long room that once had been the refectory. The other workers had already returned from lunch.

"Come on, Anisa. You'll get us in trouble!" It was Salma, another of the young girls. She laughed to say she didn't really mean it. Or only half meant it, maybe.

Anisa wondered what drew the rest of them together here, in the Grange. For herself, it had been, and still was, Hasan, although nowadays he virtually ignored her. "Doing Allah's work," he said, explaining his frequent absences, but was he really?

Several more young girls had arrived recently, quite good-look-ing, too, and she'd seen him eyeing them at the communal meal-times. The rest of the time the men and women were separated, working at their various tasks in a collection of outbuildings dotted around the grounds, or reciting the Quran.

She thought about the rumor. An unpleasant story had gone around all week, that someone — nobody was sure who — had seen dark figures dragging a body across the lawn.

"Salma, why did you come to the madrassa? I'd not have thought you a religious type."

"Religion's not so bad. The food's okay, an' after all, I got no place to go right now."

True enough, Anisa thought. Salma couldn't be more than fifteen years old, though she looked more; her figure was already well developed, although her face still bore the puppy fat of childhood.

"How much can you recite?"

"Not enough," Salma replied. Salma sat on Anisa's left, then Farah, who'd got her name from the Sheik like many of them. No one knew who her parents were.

Farah made her hands into fists, then opened and closed them several times.

A high-pitched squeak of rusty hinges cut through the air.

Anisa turned as the door opened. Her heart sank as she saw Rais framed in the space. He stepped into the room and walked slowly to her end of the table. Rais had only been with them for a few weeks, but in that time he'd decided Anisa was for him.

She guessed he was perhaps a year older, but he was hopelessly shy. A shock of unruly brown hair plus his upturned nose and freckled face made him look, well, maybe fifteen, she decided. Cute, and mixed-race. If it weren't for Hasan, she might have been interested.

"The Sheik sent me for the pamphlets, Anisa. I'll bring you an empty box in a minute. Anyway, it's close to break time, isn't it? You, er —" Rais hesitated, and Anisa bit her lip as she saw a blush spreading from his ears. She looked down, and he found the courage to continue. "You wouldn't like to go for a walk in the garden, I s'pose?"

She knew him well enough already to know he'd probably agonized for an hour or more before getting up the nerve to ask her.

"Maybe another time, Rais. We have to get another hundred of these pamphlets done by this afternoon."

She saw him wince, his face drooping, and felt sorry for him.

Rais bent quickly and picked up the box, turned toward the door, and there was Hasan, broad where Rais was slim, and Anisa's breath caught in her throat.

"What are you waiting for, Rais? The Sheik gave you a task — d'you need half the morning to do it?" Hasan stepped into the room and gave him a shove. Rais staggered toward the door, his face flushed.

Hasan moved next to Anisa and draped his right arm over her shoulder, allowing the palm of his hand to lie on her right breast.

Now it was Anisa's turn to blush. If the Sheik saw!

A sequence of fury, hate, and jealousy flew across Rais's face as he paused briefly in the doorway before stamping off down the hall.

THREE

Detective Chief Inspector Gordon Strange was on his way home when the request came in: corpse retrieval. The coroner and the local police needed assistance at the riverside, and no one else of suitable rank was available.

Strange notified his superior, Commander Imran Ashraf, head of the West Midlands Anti-Terror Group, that he was headed there.

He arrived just as the dive team put a tarp under the body, pulled it from the river Avon through some low scrub, and laid it in a body bag on the footpath.

Strange had seen dead bodies before. He'd seen the stabbed, the hanged, and the overdosed; but he hadn't seen one retrieved from the water. As he approached the scene, he smelled the stench of putrefaction.

The body had begun to bloat. The stomach was swollen; the thighs puffy; the skin colored blue, green, and violet in places; and above all, wrinkles everywhere. It was difficult to tell if it had been a man or a woman.

The coroner, who'd arrived in his personal vehicle, began his preliminary examination. Beside him, there were five in the team:

Strange; the two police divers, now busy stripping off their gear and loading it into their van; and from the local team, Sergeant James and a police constable.

Ten minutes after Strange arrived, a Citroen people-carrier came down the road and braked to a stop.

Strange watched as the constable went over to it, and heard him tell the driver it was a crime scene and to bugger off. Then the passenger door opened, and a woman he knew from Independent TV News walked around the front of the vehicle, down the footpath, and placed a soft hand on his arm.

Her legs provided most of her height. She had a heart-shaped face, auburn hair, and amber-flecked green eyes that shone with the light of intelligence. She'd have been flawless except for a slight mark above her left eyebrow: a scar or birthmark shaped like a question mark.

She smiled at him. "Excuse me. Are you in charge here, officer?"

Strange looked past her and saw a man with a video camera.

"This is a crime scene. You can't video here," he said politely but forcefully. He saw Sergeant James a little way off making a perimeter of crime scene tape.

"Sergeant!"

James peered back at him. He hooked the tape around a metal railing and came running.

"Sergeant, will you explain to these people that they are invading a crime scene and obstructing an investigation."

James knew exactly what the word "explain" meant. "Certainly, sir." He stretched out his arms and advanced on them.

The woman kept her hand on Strange's arm. "I'm Vicky Wallis, from Heartland Television," she said brightly. "Do you think you could spare a moment for our viewers, detective—"?

How the hell had this crew appeared from nowhere? God, she was a nice looker, though. "Would you mind telling me how come you suddenly arrived here, Miz Wallis?"

Sergeant James budged the cameraman out of the way.

Strange took a quick look at the Citroen. The thing was covered in antennas. Boosted mobile phone, telescopic UHF point to point, and the conical shape of a scanner. "You haven't been listening in on police radio frequencies, by any chance, Miz Wallis? That's highly illegal, you know."

She tilted her head and gave him a smile that seemed brighter than an LED lamp. "You don't think we'd do that? Besides, it's encrypted. No, we have other sources; the public, for instance."

The cameraman climbed into the people carrier and sat there staring out moodily.

Wallis glanced over her shoulder, then turned back, her on-camera smile gone.

James produced another roll of the bright-yellow and black tape from under his uniform cape and strung a line across the street, just in front of the news vehicle.

She asked, "What's your name, sir? Just for the record."

"I'm not permitted to say. Now, if you don't mind, this *is* a crime scene and you need to leave."

"Then I suppose I'll have to look it up." She turned as if to leave. Almost as if it were an afterthought, she turned back to him. "The ten o'clock news. Catch it if you can. You never know. You might be on it." She handed him a business card, went back to the Citroen, and climbed in. It pulled away.

He stuck the card in his pocket without looking at it.

The people carrier turned the corner.

Sergeant James said, "Bit of all right, sir, that one."

At the far end of the street, a police car came round the corner, its flashing blue lights reflecting off the river in rippled color. Following it was the coroner's refrigerated van.

It wasn't long before the autopsy team found the small blue mark on the body's side, just beneath the ribs. The X-ray machine showed a metal sliver embedded there, and they soon extracted it. A number twenty hypodermic needle, or rather, half of one.

"I think it's rather unlikely this chap injected himself, sir," one of the team said in a dry voice.

"Take tissue samples from that area and send them to the lab for analysis, with the fragment."

The forensic dentist arrived. Within a minute he spotted the collapsed tooth.

"Look at this." He used the dental camera to display it clearly on the overhead screen. "This isn't caries. It's something else."

They X-rayed the jaw, and there it was: an implant.

They found a small tattoo, hidden under the short hair at the back of the corpse's head. A star of David with a curved dagger through it, surrounded by a circle. They took photos of it and copied them into the file.

The coroner was in his office working on the postmortem report when the bloodwork came back from the lab. It showed a very high level, many times the lethal dose, of fentanyl, and an unknown substance that required further analysis. And one of his ever-curious staff had found a match for the tattoo, using image search: the Haganah.

The coroner picked up the phone and called Strange's mobile number.

"Detective Chief Inspector? Sorry to bother you at home, but I thought you might like to know. I'm sending a preliminary report to Central. It's definitely foul play. Not drowning, there's hardly any water in the lungs. Drug overdose, but at such a high level, there's no way this chap got into the river by himself. We found a broken hypodermic needle in him. And a couple of other odd things, too."

FOUR

Zafir was a scavenger, the hand that tried the doorknob, the black shape in the black night. He shifted uncomfortably, cramped from the fifteen minutes he'd crouched behind the old hospital waiting for the last vestiges of light to fade from the western sky. There didn't seem to be a watchman.

He slid over a low wall.

A sour smell hung in the air and caught in his throat. Had someone been burning something here? The place had been abandoned for months and should be a safe bet; safer anyway than the next target on the list, a chrome-plating plant.

Zafir stopped behind an outbuilding, listening. He took out his pry bar, jammed it into a door, and forced the lock.

He slipped through, pulled the door closed, and sneaked along a short passage and through an unlocked metal door.

He stowed the jimmy in its homemade leather sling and moved into a second corridor. This one seemed part of the main building, its age betrayed by the Victorian decor. Arsenic green tiles, suffused with a network of hairline cracks, came nearly halfway up the walls.

Above the tiles, mildewed cream plaster, relieved by a thin green line painted one inch below the ceiling.

Another twenty yards. A corridor branched off to the left. He paused at the junction, listening to the slight settling noises. His penlight showed a discolored patch of wall where there had once been a sign. The shadows were deeper in the left corridor; he turned into it and padded quickly forward.

Sluice … Day Room … a broom cupboard … the corridor ended in a T. The short right-hand branch led to a double door: Theater. He returned. Left, then right, a ten-yard dogleg. A biting smell hung in the air. Another door: Pathology. He looked around the room, hoping to find poisons, formaldehyde, perhaps; but the cupboards hung open and empty.

A little farther down the corridor, he found a dark shadow on the left. His flashlight revealed a stairwell going down in a clockwise spiral next to a hospital-sized elevator.

The pierced metal steps tapered on the inside edge to less than the length of his foot. He was tempted to rest a hand on the corroded metal banister — but no, the jagged surface might cut his latex gloves. He took the stairs carefully, keeping to the outside.

At the bottom, the well opened into a small vestibule. Clouds of dust rose in the stagnant air as he shuffled forward.

His knee came into sharp contact with a solid object.

Stumbling, Zafir uttered a muffled curse. Unseen in the murk, a low table had caught his knee. Recovering, he shone the light down and noted with interest two moldering magazines.

He picked one up. Small flakes of decayed paper fell onto the table. Using his light, he could see the title: "Woman's Own." He tried to open the magazine, but the damp had stuck the pages together. Nobody had been here for a long time.

He raised the light, saw a door in the opposite wall, and passed through.

The flashlight glowed on bulks of machinery, festooned with heavy cables and hoses. He pulled at one; flakes of rubber broke off in his hand. A conduit came away easily; someone had severed the connections with a saw.

It didn't take him more than a minute to discover that the place had been stripped. No mercury or platinum, just scrap lead and copper. Not worth the risk of hauling it away.

He took a final look around and discovered a storage cubicle against the wall, its heavy metal panel secured with a Yale lock. In the center of the door, faded yellow decals clung to flakes of rust. It was hard to make out what they might have meant.

He tried the number three Yale skeleton in the lock, but it was seized solid.

Zafir took out the pry bar again. The panel yielded reluctantly, a shriek of metal against metal echoing into the distant corridors as he forced its rusted hinges open.

Inside stood a squat cylinder eight inches in diameter and a foot high, dull gray in the beam of the pocket torch. It bore the same yellow decals as the panel, but these were bright and undimmed with age. Underneath the symbol:

"Cobalt 60 nuclear source. Handle only with suitable protection."

Cobalt. He liked the sound of it.

For a moment, he was a little boy again, playing with his chemistry set in his mother's kitchen. He held up a beaker of a violet-colored solution to the light, waiting for the last crystals to dissolve.

"What's that?" asked his younger brother.

"Cherryade," he'd said, unable to stop himself.

"Can I have some?"

Not for the first time, he felt the presence of something dark hovering just behind his left shoulder. "Here, try it."

Smiling to himself he remembered his brother vomiting in the sink.

His father had beaten Zafir with a studded belt until blood ran down the back of his legs.

He looked again at the squat cylinder with the bright yellow trefoil. It wasn't platinum, or even mercury, but nuclear stuff. The Sheik would be pleased.

FIVE

Zafir glanced at the filing cabinet that stood in a corner of the workshop. He had locked the cobalt-60 cylinder inside. Only he and the Sheik had a key. And when the workshop was out of use, it was kept locked, too.

It stood alone, a small outbuilding at the back of the old house. Zafir had a key to the door; so did the Sheik, Hasan, and a couple of others, the most trusted ones.

He was still thinking about the cobalt. He could hardly take it out of its protective lead cylinder, mount it in the lathe, and machine it. He and the whole place would be irradiated. But he had to find a way to create small particles so as to do the most harm. That was when he thought about dissolving it.

He plugged a jihad music thumb drive into a grubby boombox. The sketch showed a plastic crate on Dexion shelf supports. It wouldn't be strong enough, though. Not once he'd wrapped it in the lead sheeting that he'd ripped from a roof. He doubled up on the supports, bolted them together, and mounted a bathroom mirror over the crate, set at forty-five degrees. He still needed to make some long tongs of a rather strange design.

The acid would have to wait. A brother who worked in a chemical wholesaler was getting it, but it had to be brought in person. In the meantime, he would get on with making mush.

The door opened and Hasan walked in. "The Sheik said you needed help."

"Yeah. I need you to stir." Zafir pointed to a narrow garden spade that he'd borrowed from the estate gardening tools. He picked up a fifty-five-pound bag of fertilizer, cut open the end, and poured it into a wheelie garbage bin.

Zafir folded the empty bag and put it to one side. He took a can of metal powder and added the contents. "OK, stir away, habibi. And stir it well."

Hasan put the spade into the mixture and began working it around.

Zafir took a five-gallon can of diesel and poured it slowly into the bin. Next, he added the filler/binder.

"I'm tired." Hasan stopped stirring and rubbed his arms.

Zafir took over. "It won't take too long now. Go and check the mailbox. I'm waiting for some electronic stuff from China."

SIX

Commander Imran Ashraf, leader of the West Midlands anti-terror group, was mopping up his Aloo Gosht with naan bread when the call came in to his mobile phone. An unknown number. An informant?

"Hello?"

"Commander Imran?"

"Who's that?" The voice sounded familiar.

"Have you forgotten already? Remember, last year, that incident at the shopping center?"

"Oh, yes. Now I remember." A chill passed through him. It was the Khawdash Haganah on the line, a deep cover Israeli team based in London but responsible to the Mossad in Tel Aviv. If it hadn't been for their tip-off, half of Bullring Shopping Centre would have been blown to rubble. "So, what now?"

"We're a man down. Local police came to the house yesterday. Our man was running a deep penetration against the Haz ut-Tahrir. They've opened a madrassa near Evesham. It's a cover for an ISIL jihad operation. Lots of money behind it — they bought the estate, it used to be a stately home, then a hotel, but —"

"Yes, I know the place." Imran had driven past it several times but had never had cause to visit.

"And do you know what goes on there? Surface activity, copying propaganda. Reciting the book. Housekeeping. But there's another level. There's a video room where they show jihadi videos from Syria and Iraq. And an electromechanical workshop. Where are the funds coming from? Saudi? The UAE? Tehran? It's run by a man who calls himself the Sheik. I don't think he's from the UK. We'd like to know his real name. And we want to know what happened to our man. He was going by the name of Malik."

Ashraf sighed. "I'll see what I can do. My number two, Detective Chief Inspector Strange, attended the retrieval. Malik was found in the River Avon. The coroner said the body had been in the water for four or five days. Not drowned; an opiate overdose. You have a number I can call?"

"Can I call you back tomorrow at the same time?"

"Sure."

The phone disconnected.

"Who was that?" his wife, Shafilea, asked in Urdu.

"Could you speak in English, please? Sixteen years since you came to England, and you're still struggling with the language. You need to get out more. Integrate." There were times when he wished he'd married a local girl. But his parents had insisted.

"But who was it?" Still in Urdu.

"Work." She was crazy jealous of him. She suspected every phone call of being another woman. As if he needed another woman in his life. Between her and work, he had hardly a minute to spare. And now this new pakhana, this new shit, near Evesham. The Haz ut-Tahrir organization. Very bad indeed.

He reviewed his options. Likely this wouldn't be his baby to deal with, not for long. MI5 would get in on it soon enough. If he could get in first and gather some information, it could be a stepping stone. But he'd have to avoid giving away his back channel.

He went upstairs into their bedroom and closed the door. But why? Did he not trust his wife? Feeling guilty, he opened it again. He heard her downstairs, arguing with his daughter, Naz.

Taking out his phone, he dialed the direct line to MI5 in London. Tomorrow he'd talk to the murder squad at Birmingham Central. Find out exactly where they were with this case. He planned on paying a visit to the madrassa, but this was a tricky business, crossing the interests of his department, anti-terror, and the homicide squad. No doubt they might argue. Perhaps the best solution would be a joint visit.

His contact at "5" answered. Yes, they knew about the madrassa. Nobody had paid it a visit yet. "Multicultural sensitivity" was the reason given. *Well, fuck that.*

He went downstairs.

Shafilea immediately accosted him. "Naz is so disrespectful. Why don't you discipline her? She leaves the house without her hijab."

"Shaf, not this argument again. She's still a kid. She grew up here. She wants to mix with a wider circle of friends. That's all."

"She wants to go out with kuffar boys. I won't have it, bringing disgrace on the family. They'll be talking about us at the mosque. And she hardly ever attends now. She's not a good Muslim. I would not be surprised if she's tried alcohol. Next thing she'll be smoking skunk."

"Shaf! Please! Don't say 'kuffar.' How can we get a good relationship with the community when you use names like that? We call them kuffars, they call us Paki bastards."

"It's a matter of honor. You know she's promised to my second cousin Ali."

"*I* didn't promise her. You did. And without asking — me, or her. Of course she doesn't want to marry him. He's thirty-four, only a year younger than I am. She's half his age! He's ugly — his face pitted, his teeth stained from chewing betel nut." He knew why she was raising this again. A contact in Peshawar had informed him that Ali Ahmed ran poppy for the Talibs. Risky business.

"But it's the family honor," she said.

"Kuti ka bacha! Fuck your honor! And I'm not having our daughter marrying an opium smuggler." There, he'd said it. The words had escaped and there was no taking them back.

He turned and walked out of the room, just in time to see Naz dodge into the parlor. She must have been listening. Well, he'd deal with that later. He was too furious to talk to her right now. The only thing to do was head back to his office. Otherwise, he'd be tempted to have a few drinks, another thing that Shafilea hated him for. Not for the first time, he wondered if the marriage would last. It seemed the longer they stayed together, the further they grew apart.

He picked up his keys from a hook on the wall. Ten past seven. The rush hour should be almost over. He'd try the coroner first, see what the autopsy said. Opiate poisoning? That's what Strange had reported.

SEVEN

Doctor Albert Newton had practiced in the same Victorian house in Upwood village for longer than most of the residents could remember.

He ran his nicotine-stained fingers through his thinning silver hair and shuffled through an untidy pile of patient records.

Someone was coming down the corridor. There was a hesitant knock, and then the face of a man in his early fifties showed round the edge of the door. Newton got to his feet and pasted a smile on his face.

"Ah, Mr. Emerson, isn't it? Tony Emerson? I can't remember the last time you were here. Quite awhile, I should think."

Emerson's suit showed patches of dandruff over the shoulders. Strange; Emerson had always had a reputation for his dapper appearance, though he could do with a change of style. There was one more thing, too; a slight smell about the man, like a whiff of decay.

"Take a seat," Newton said. It took him a minute to find Emerson's file. He peered at his own untidy writing through his bifocals, thinking that he'd mentally referred to Emerson as a middle-aged man as if the term carried a stigma, and here he was, still in practice, at an age when most men had already retired.

"The last time you came to see me was, let's see, three years ago. Slashed hand, gardening accident, wasn't it?"

Emerson nodded. He bent forward, coughed, then pressed a handkerchief to his mouth and spat something into it. The doctor waited patiently, wondering. He knew Emerson was a non-smoker and had been all his life. This was the fifth patient he'd seen this morning with what seemed to be combined lung and enteric symptoms. Yesterday had been even worse, with such a line outside that he'd had to send out for a locum, otherwise the house calls — and they'd been more than double the usual number, too — would have been impossible.

He pulled a silver pocket watch out and peered at it. Three minutes past eleven. Averaging a patient every seven minutes, he'd get through another dozen before the surgery closed at twelve-thirty. The doctors' dilemma: how to give attention to everybody and yet have enough time for proper diagnosis. He was always busy, but this was sheer overload.

"How long have you had that cough, Mr. Emerson?"

"The cough? A few days, I guess. I was sneezing all last week. No, it's not the cough, although that's bad enough, it's my stomach. I've been running to the toilet for the last three days. This morning I got up at five o'clock to be sick."

"I see." Newton reached into the desk drawer, withdrew an old-fashioned mercury thermometer, wiped it with an antiseptic swab, and handed it across the desk.

While he waited for the reading to settle, he made out the delivery slip for a small parcel sitting across the room. It contained a dozen samples of urine and stools from the morning patients. They were packed in ice, in a special container guaranteed to maintain the temperature at less than five degrees centigrade for up to twelve hours.

He took the thermometer from Emerson and examined the silvery capillary thread. Ninety-nine point three, nearly a degree up on normal, but nothing that could really be called a fever.

"You've got a slight temperature, but it's nothing to worry about. I'll give you a prescription that should help. If you're still having trouble tomorrow afternoon, come back again, will you?" Newton scribbled rapidly on a prescription pad. A packet of Imodium, a small bottle of kaolin and morphine, and a bottle of paracetamol 500 mg. That should do it. As he tore off the script, he realized that he'd dished out over a dozen prescriptions just like it the previous afternoon, and a dozen more in the morning session. He turned back to Emerson.

"Have you been eating out by any chance, Mr. Emerson? In the last few days, that is."

"No, I wouldn't say so. Just the odd packet of crisps down the pub, that's all. Do you think it could be something I ate?"

"If it was, then it was something half the village ate, by the look of it. No, there seems to be some sort of bug going around. Probably a virus. No doubt it'll all blow over in a few days."

He amazed himself, sometimes. His cheery voice, billowing around the surgery. He felt anything but cheery. Doctors were just like actors, disk jockeys, and television personalities, he thought. Politicians, too. People didn't want to know about their illnesses, their depressions, their failures. They wanted to hear from happy, successful folk. Newton sometimes got fed up pretending to be cheery.

By twelve-thirty he had seen the remaining dozen patients, seven of whom reported symptoms similar to Emerson's, to a greater or lesser degree. Could it be rotavirus? Norovirus? A list of possibles rotated through his mind's eye, but none of them quite fit. Salmonellosis sounded right for symptoms, but there was no common food source. Not paratyphoid either — that started with constipation. The violent stomach cramps of amoebic or bacillary dysentery were missing to a large degree. No, it looked like a virus rather than a larger organism. Well, the public health laboratory would do cultures and test for antigens. With luck, they'd have some results soon.

He sighed. Half an hour for lunch and then the afternoon house calls. One of which would be his wife, Barbara, who had spent most of the night in the bathroom. First, though, he'd call the same-day courier and get these samples off to the lab in Birmingham.

EIGHT

Anisa had been standing at the window for the last two hours watching the twilight fade from the western sky. It wouldn't be long before the red of the shepherds' sunset was replaced by the distant glow of Birmingham's lights on the horizon.

Finally, she saw what she'd been waiting for: Hasan came out the door of the main lodge and strolled down the gravel path. It would take him past the bathroom and round the edge of a croquet lawn in front of Anisa's hut. Normally she shared her quarters with Salma and Lamya, but tonight they were both on the rota for the van at King's Cross and wouldn't be back until late.

She lifted the latch and grabbed the side of the door, taking some of the weight off the hinges to avoid the penetrating squeak they made. Leaving the door ajar, she slipped down the side of the hut, keeping behind the shrubs that lined the gravel path. Early dew wetted her feet. She tried to breathe slowly to calm herself as she waited, but it didn't work.

She heard the sound of his boots crunching the gravel.

HASAN WALKED ALONG, A MEDLEY OF THOUGHTS IN HIS HEAD. He seemed to be losing favor with the master, especially since Zafir had gone out on some kind of special night mission.

Bloody Zafir. Hasan kicked irritably at the gravel, spraying it at the bushes. Idly, he wondered: If it came to hand-to-hand combat, which of them would walk away from it? He thought of the jihad videos they watched every evening. He would sever Zafir's head with the zombie knife.

He smelled a waft of perfume in the air. It probably came from the rose bushes farther down the path.

"Ssst!"

A shadowy figure beckoned to him from behind the shrubs. "Anisa! What are you doing out at this time? It's against the rules. You'll be in real trouble if anyone sees you. Me, too. I can't talk now. Flirting! It's haram."

She grabbed him by the arm just above the elbow.

He resisted, trying to pull free.

"Hasan, I had to see you. I've been waiting for hours. You don't talk to me anymore."

What to say? Her voice wavered, full of unshed tears. She clung to him and he resisted the temptation to pry her loose with his free hand.

"Anisa, we don't have much to talk about. Don't you think you should be looking for someone your own age?"

"Hasan, I—"

Gravel crunched farther along the path. She grabbed his arm with renewed strength.

The Sheik turned the corner and saw them.

"Anisa, you should be in your bed. Hasan, I'd like to talk to you, please. Now." He spun on his heel and walked off.

Anisa let her hand drop and turned back to the door of her hut. Hasan hurried to catch up with the Sheik, trying to ignore her sobs.

"Hasan," said the Sheik, "That girl is infatuated with you. You shouldn't lead her on. And it's wrong. It's haram."

They reached the Sheik's quarters. Hasan waited while he unlocked the door, then followed him inside. The Sheik sat down and gestured to a chair opposite. His private meeting room was sparsely furnished, the chairs basic, fashioned from rough pine; they would not have been out of place in a seventeenth-century alehouse or monastery.

"Sheik, I have tried to discourage her. She clings like a leech." And maybe you fancy her yourself, Hasan thought irreverently.

"There were no newspapers in the days when the Prophet, peace be upon him, walked the Earth, let alone television. Word of mouth and his deeds were enough. Now, though, no one believes unless it is on the magic box that takes so much of their attention every day. Or on the computer, that other spawn of Satan."

Hasan nodded slowly.

"They will call us many things. Your brother Zafir, he has taken up the sword against the kuffar. A mighty blow, Hasan. And we are preparing another. When the day comes — and it is coming soon — will you stand by me?"

"Of course, Sheik," he said.

NINE

Doctor Albert Newton tossed and turned in his rumpled bed. He squinted at the window; a faint peach bloom outlined the dark treetops, announcing dawn's arrival.

A pervasive drone, like badly synchronized generators, set his teeth on edge. The very air oppressed him with its humidity. A migraine coming on? Close by, his wife, Barbara, stirred and mumbled in her sleep. He listened but her words were unintelligible.

Without disturbing her, he slipped out of bed, padded across the carpet to the wardrobe, put on a pale-cream dressing gown, and crept downstairs. He turned left into the kitchen and switched on the light. The LEDs came on and he winced, screwing up his eyes.

He felt cooler here but still opened the window the few inches allowed by the security catch.

In the distance, he heard a distinct rhythmic thudding. For a minute or two it disappeared, but then it came back louder. And even louder. He peered through the window, but because of the kitchen lights, he couldn't make out anything.

An intense blast of sound sent him reeling. Massive low-frequency waves beat at him, overlaid by the shriek of high-powered turbines.

A helicopter lofted over the line of trees at the end of his garden and lit it like a football stadium.

Newton clapped his hands over his ears, stunned.

The helicopter passed overhead, engine subsonics playing with the house, rattling doors and cupboards.

One of the doors of the Welsh dresser burst open. A cavalcade of his wife's Lladro porcelain marched like lemmings across the glass shelves and fell to their destruction.

There'll be hell to pay for that.

The din receded slightly, then steadied again. After a few moments, it began to wind down.

Christ, it's landing in the field on the other side of the road. He scrambled for the stairs.

Barbara burst out of the bedroom door just as he reached it.

He jerked back, narrowly avoiding a collision, and took hold of her shoulders to steady her.

"Albert, what's going on? I thought a plane was crashing on the house."

"One nearly did — a helicopter, one of those big transport jobs. I think it came down in the field behind the road." He made for the wardrobe, almost shouting the last words over the continuing racket of rotor blades. Where were his glasses? Finally, he found them.

As fast as he could, he dressed in trousers, a shirt, and shoes.

Barbara peered out of the bedroom window.

"I can't see anything except a lot of light over there."

Together, they made their way down the stairs into the hall.

His wife turned into the kitchen, while he walked to the front door.

The doorbell jangled.

He took a step forward and tried to release the catch; it was stuck. Irritated, he hammered at it with his fist.

The door sprang open on him and he staggered backward, arms windmilling. *It's an astronaut. No, that's ridiculous, it can't be.* Strange what the mind comes up with when faced with a radically new experience. It was as if he stood beside himself, commenting sarcastically on his own inadequacies.

He took in the detail: hoarse breathing, a white rubber suit, a man's face behind the tinted visor. The hands carried some kind of instrument.

Monosyllabic grunts came from the suited figure. "In. Now."

More of them came through the door. One half-dragged Barbara from the kitchen; Newton saw that she was almost in hysterics. None spoke except one-word commands. One of them pointed a metal tube at his wife, and he heard a rattling sound.

Newton began noting more details. Including that they all had badges on their suits.

A horn sounded outside. The man in front gestured for him to get out.

The doctor made his way to the doorway, to find two more of them waiting.

One gestured at a large white van standing with its rear doors open. "Get in."

More vans were coming down the street, coming from the main road that ran through the village.

He got in the van, and Barbara joined him. The doors slammed shut. There were no windows. A dim light in the center of the roof provided their only relief from the darkness.

The van started moving with a sudden jolt. The vehicle twisted and turned, stopping occasionally. He lost track of time and distance.

He heard the driver change down a gear, then the van tilted, climbing. A bump jolted him, then the van leveled out, coasting to a stop as the driver cut the engine.

Without warning, the doors flew open.

A white-suited figure said, "Follow me, please. Both of you." The doctor saw, now, the suits must be military issue, for CBW: chemical and biological warfare.

Newton and his wife followed the man down a corridor lit by old-fashioned fluorescent lights. The doctor heard footsteps following, and raised voices. He turned and saw a group of people he knew from the village, guided by more of the CBW men.

"To your right." The man in the CBW suit opened a door for him.

"Doctor Newton?" The voice was deep, authoritative, from a woman in her mid-fifties perhaps; it was hard to tell. She wore a surgical mask with a plastic head cover, a rubber gown, and incongruous pink rubber boots.

Newton opened his mouth, but she put out her right hand, gloved palm toward him.

"I'll answer your questions shortly, doctor. We've very little time. I'm sorry you and your wife were treated so rudely, but you will soon discover why. Now, please step over to one of the cubicles you see there."

The wall opposite had three identical doors, like a public toilet.

"There is a steel bin inside. Take your clothes off, put them in the bin, and walk into the shower. You will see an instruction plate on the wall. Read the instructions and then press the black button below the plate."

He stared at her. "Where the hell are we? I want to know what's going on!"

"We have no time, Doctor. Please, I will explain later.

Newton strode off stiffly toward the cubicles. *This is a bloody disgrace. This is England, for God's sake, not some banana republic where people disappear mysteriously in the night. Someone will suffer for this, this—*

He opened the door.

A recessed fluorescent tube flickered to life as he went in. He wasn't surprised to discover that the inside door face had no handle.

As he entered the tiny cubicle, the stifling sensation of claustrophobia attacked him. To his left stood a utilitarian steel bin. Directly opposite, set into the wall, was a galvanized steel door. Riveted to it was an enameled steel notice, which bore a set of simple instructions:

Decontamination

Remove all clothing and place in receptacle
Step up to the door
Press the black button
Enter shower

Newton lifted the lid of the bin to place his clothes inside and discovered a small pack of disposable paper towels. The black button being his only option, he pressed it, then walked into the tiny shower. His feet shrank from the bare galvanized steel. The electric lock clicked behind him.

He looked up and saw a large crude-looking metal sprayer. Air roared from it, causing him to blink, and then, just as he looked away, it blasted him with freezing cold water.

He shouted involuntarily, a quick "Ah!"

Just as he was turning into pure gooseflesh, the gush turned boiling hot in a matter of seconds. The pipe gurgled and spat, and the tiny cubicle became a steam box. He pounded on the door, to no effect. *Are they trying to boil me alive?* His skin turned the color of cooked lobster.

Finally, the water cut off, and the door clicked. He pushed it open and dried himself with the paper towels. They were hopelessly inadequate. Wondering where to put them, he opened the bin again, to find that his clothes had been taken. Another click; the main door had released. It swung open.

In a foul temper, Newton stepped through the opening and

found the female doctor outside. Now that she had taken off her protective gear, he saw a stout white-coated woman in her mid-forties. Laughter lines around her eyes belied her stern expression. Silently she held out a thin white garment.

Newton took it and slipped it over his head. It was a hospital gown.

"That bloody shower damn near boiled me alive," he complained.

"I'm sorry about that. It hasn't been used in quite awhile. Walk over to cubicle B in the corner, please." She spoke in a dry West Country accent.

The door to another of the showers clicked, and he saw his wife walk out, trying to cover herself with her arms and hands.

"Just a moment, doctor." The woman doctor took a gown from a rack and handed it to his wife. "Please, Mrs. Newton, cubicle A." She pointed.

They followed the woman to the cubicles.

She opened the first door and gestured. "Stand in the painted circle, and close the door, please."

He did as instructed. A polished steel shaft rose vertically to the ceiling. Slowly, a black ring about two and a half feet in diameter descended, passing down his body, until it reached the floor. He guessed it was a whole-body scanner. A dull clicking sounded intermittently from a grille set in the wall. When the ring stopped moving, a buzzer sounded and a green lamp lit up.

He opened the door and walked out. From the buzzing sound coming from the next cubicle, he guessed that his wife was being scanned. There was no sign of the woman doctor. The floor was cold underfoot, and his feet were cramping.

The door to the next cubicle clicked and Barbara came out. "What's going on? It scanned me twice. I got a red light."

The woman doctor came back, two pairs of carpet slippers in her hand. In her other hand, she held a couple of printed slips of paper. "Would you mind coming with me, Doctor?" She turned to

Barbara. "Please wait here, Mrs. Newton. Someone will be along in a minute."

Newton put the slippers on. They were a sloppy fit. He followed the doctor down a short corridor into what appeared to be a changing room.

She said, "I'm sorry, but I have bad news for you. You're almost free of contamination, but your wife is registering a heavy dose. More than two sieverts. Do you understand that, or shall I explain?"

Newton paled. *This is a nightmare. It must be.* He felt numb. He'd wake up in a minute. "Radiation? What bloody radiation? There are no nuclear plants within fifty miles of here," he said loudly, glaring at her. "It's because of those samples I sent off, isn't it?"

"Yes, Doctor. Which brings us to the problem. There's been an incident. If we were to allow your wife and the other patients to go freely about, we would expose the public to radiation."

"Other patients?"

"Most of the village, it seems."

"But what's happened?"

"We don't know yet. The army has been called in. They're trying to find out. But right now, we have to deal with it the best we can. The more serious cases will be quarantined. We'll treat them to reduce the internal contamination; chelated minerals, amino acids — we're trying everything. It's cobalt-60 nitrate. Some have received a lethal dose. The government is very concerned."

"What's the bottom line, Doctor? How long do you expect my wife will be in quarantine, and where, may I ask?" How odd; he felt almost no emotion. Delayed shock, no doubt.

"Your wife? You're a fellow doctor, and I have to warn you, I'm terribly sorry, but your wife may not get through this. Not with a dose of two sieverts. How long? I can't say right now. Where? Well, that's another problem. You know, we have nearly three hundred from the village in the same situation. Right now, we're putting them in tents, courtesy of the armed forces that are securing the area. We're making them as comfortable as possible, I assure you."

"Tents. I can imagine," he said. His face took up a grin, like a rictus he couldn't budge. *God, what's the matter with me?*

"Doctor Newton. I understand how you must feel. I'd like to request your help." She steepled her hands, and he picked up on the body language straight away: steep hill, something tough is coming. He managed to shift the inappropriate grin. It took an attempt that was almost painful.

"We need a good GP to deal with the quarantined patients on a day-to-day basis. If you help us, my department will provide every possible assistance. Of course, you will be able to stay with your wife."

"And if I choose not to cooperate?" Her hands were still steepled, he saw.

"That might be unwise. I'll have to ask you to sign the Official Secrets Act, of course, and everything to do with this incident is regarded as covered under its terms. I'm sure you understand?"

He understood too well. "But what has happened? How—"

"Our guess is that it's in the water supply. And we suspect a terror attack."

"Very well, I'll do it. Now what?" His mouth tasted of metal.

"We'll return your clothes when they have been cleaned and checked. That takes a few hours. You'll need a film badge to record your daily exposure. In the meantime, please come with me." She inclined her head toward the exit.

"Where the hell are we anyway?" Newton found his confidence returning, but his voice squeaked disconcertingly on the word "we." The woman looked at him dispassionately, and then a smile unexpectedly lit up her face. Now she looked, perhaps, thirty-something.

"You'd never guess. You're beneath the Town Hall."

Newton gaped in disbelief.

"It's a civil defense relic, doctor. It dates back to the fifties. You remember, when the government issued those stupid notices advising people to whitewash their windows in the event of a nuclear attack. As if that would have been of any use. Well, the council spent cash from some fund they'd stashed away for a rainy day, and converted the cellars. It's all totally obsolete, of course — I wouldn't want to open any of the canned food, for a start — but the basic kit, surprisingly, is still in perfect order."

She took his arm.

"We've got a lot to do, Doctor."

TEN

Commander Imran arrived at his office to find the department fully staffed despite the hour. "Why all the activity?"

His second in command, Gordon Strange, looked up, saw him, and put the phone down. "Was just calling you. Complete horror show going on in ..." he looked down at a paper on his desk, "a place called Upwood. Village of about three hundred souls, very touristic, apparently."

"What do you mean, horror show? Be specific."

"The Nuclear Directorate's been on the phone. Outbreak of mass radiation poisoning. Cobalt 60. No way it's an accident — that stuff is only found in hospitals and certain industrial sites, and none's been reported missing."

"Any ideas?"

"The army has taken over, the whole area cordoned off, road-blocks in place. Seems to be in the water supply."

A medley of thoughts whirled through Imran's head: *The Russians are sabotaging the water supplies. Those polonium poisonings. The Novichok case. But no, those were targeted killings, not mass terror.*

"Any indication of what, or who, we're dealing with?" Imran asked. "Political? Islamic? Right-wing?"

"No, I've checked with Special Branch, the Nuclear Inspectorate, the two intelligence arms — five and six. Nothing yet. It's a hot one."

Imran grimaced.

"Sorry for the pun," Strange said. "They've got two hundred and eighty-seven people in isolation. Many aren't expected to make it. Most are so hot that the medics are wearing anti-rad suits. They've set up a tent town for the villagers. It's just as well the weather's good, but what to do next? The health department says it can't have people wandering about in public with cobalt 60 sloshing about their innards. You can see their point."

Imran nodded, so Strange continued.

"The village is completely off-limits. The phones, too, except for the local bobby's house — we're using it as a command center. The telecom companies have already asked why the systems are down. We've told them it's an exercise."

"That won't hold for long. We must release a story to the media around noon. You're it, Strange. Talk to Leavey at the Home Office. You've got nearly two hours to dream something up."

"Something? Like what?"

"I don't care, as long as it's convincing. Just don't blurb it like you did with that baby-food poisoner. The manufacturer lost half of his business after that hit the screens."

Strange bit his lip instead of replying with the fact: Kids could have died if he hadn't gone public.

Imran winked slightly to show it was a joke.

"Come on, Strange. Increase your exposure. The Conservative Party conference is next week. Party of law and order, yes? Well. I'm sure you'll handle it with tact. Yes, tact. Oh, by the way, the body in the Avon. I have some news. I'll be in my office. Give me five minutes."

Strange wrote the communique and checked it with Imran. He'd begin with the BBC, then call Heartland Television News.

His mobile rang.

"Hello?"

"Is that you, Gordon?" Oh, shit, he thought. His ex-wife.

"Yes, Denise."

"I'm still waiting for a reply to that letter I sent you. Are you going to send the extra money?"

"Look, Denise, I don't think it's a good idea to send Julie to a boarding school. She needs a home life." Images of his six-year-old daughter, laughing and smiling, came into his mind. His ex-wife had won custody. "Mental cruelty," she'd alleged, citing the long hours he'd been away.

Her penetrating voice came back at him: "Well, I'm not prepared to give up my career and live on the pittance you send me. I have my life to live, too." The images of his daughter dissolved and were replaced by one of his ex.

"You're her mother, Denise. She needs you. It's not fair to Julie, sending her away to one of those places. And when would I get to see her? Last weekend I turned up and you'd taken her out somewhere. I want reasonable access, Denise. I am her father."

"And a fine father you made. Never home, always off in some place or other for days at a time."

"For Christ's sake, Denise, let's not start all that again. You married a copper, what the hell did you expect?"

"A man with the guts to stand up to his bosses rather than spend all his life out on the street."

Strange breathed deeply. *She'd never understood.* It hadn't been easy in the early years. He'd seen the looks on people's faces when they'd asked his ex-wife, "And what does your husband do?"

"Well?" Denise's voice pierced his thoughts. *How did I ever find her attractive? I wish she'd break out in a plague of boils.*

"Well what?" he said in exasperation. "I'm busy with a major crime scene. Haven't got time now!"

"Are you going to send the money, or aren't you?"

"No, I'm bloody not. If that's all you want to know. And I don't want our daughter exiled to any boarding school, either."

"So that's your last word, is it?"

"Yes," Strange replied, feeling a dull thudding sensation in his temples. *Easy, easy, take deep breaths.*

"All right then. If that's the way you want it. You'll be hearing from my solicitor."

She hung up abruptly. He winced. *If she wants a fight, she'll get one.*

It took him a moment to collect his thoughts. The press release. He'd have to clear it with the Home Office first. No doubt the COBRA team would be meeting at 10 Downing Street.

ELEVEN

Doctor Newton put his right foot deep into a rut full of black filth and swore under his breath. His shoe squelched when he pulled it out. The muck worked its way down, toward his toes. *How the hell do they expect me to practice medicine in these conditions?*

He came up to tent thirty-seven. "Mrs. Williams? Are you there?"

A feeble cry came from inside.

Newton pulled back the entrance flap. The canvas walls cast a greenish light over everything. *Even so, that's not enough to account for the color of my patient's face.*

She lay on her side on a foam mattress, clutching her abdomen. On the ground next to her stood a large bowl, half-filled with something so rank that disinfectant hadn't killed the stench.

He breathed through his mouth, trying not to gag.

"Mrs. Williams?" Newton kneeled on the flysheet and pulled on a pair of surgical gloves. *Thank God this is the last patient on my afternoon round. No — there's still my wife.* How much more of this could he take? How much more could *they* take?

The middle-aged woman looked up at him and grinned weakly.

"I'm a mess, aren't I, Doctor? And it's worse every day. I wish I could just die and have done with it."

"Don't talk like that, please, Mrs. Williams. There's always hope." He palpated her liver, noticing its enlargement. It felt mushy. He took a small black leather notebook from an inside pocket and jotted a quick entry.

"It's bedlam, doctor. The moaning, all around, it never stops. And the shouting."

Newton nodded, then wrapped the flexible cuff of a blood pressure meter around her upper arm.

"At night we get the drunks, staggering back from the NAAFI tent. And the babies, God help them, but they won't stop screaming."

He pumped up the cuff and placed the end of his stethoscope over the vein inside her elbow. Slowly he released the pressure, listening. *Ninety-seven over fifty-two. And still dropping. What to do?*

Someone nearby turned on a radio, far too loud, and Newton scowled.

"When are they going to let us out of here, Doctor? Take us to a proper hospital? Oh, I'm sorry, I know you are doing your best, I didn't mean anything by it—"

"No, it's all right, Mrs. Williams. I'm sure they'll move us really soon," he said, wishing he could believe it. He packed his instruments into his bag and crouched over her. "I'll bring you something later to make you more comfortable." He took one of her hands and squeezed it gently, then ducked through the entrance flap and stood up, gazing down the tent rows toward the entrance. Mrs. Williams had been his patient for more than thirty years; this was simply awful.

Newton sniffed the air, hoping the light breeze wouldn't change and bring the smell of fermenting urine and feces from overflowing latrines at the far edge of the field. He stepped carefully to avoid the mud, and finally entered his own tent.

Barbara lay there snoring, eyes half closed. Her waking moments had been filled with pain for the past week, and her urine was pink that morning. She'd have to go for scans, and he dreaded the prognosis.

They slept on air mattresses. She had hot spots inside her. The army people had told him to move to a separate tent, but he had stared them down.

He took her pulse, noted the reading on the folding chart, and sat on his mattress, head in hands. You could fight bacteria with antibiotics. Soluble Cobalt-60 was a different matter. The government report had come in: gamma radiation poisoning. *If hell exists, then this is purgatory. Damn the bastards who had done this.*

For more than thirty minutes he sat there, too sad to move, as shadows cast by oak trees slowly lengthened across the canvas.

A man's voice called from outside, "Doctor? Are you awake?"

Newton pushed the flap to one side and eased through. It was Billy Stepton, handyman, a slim, bony man in his mid-thirties with the face of a sad beagle.

"The same old argument, is it?" Newton asked. Stepton was desperate to get out of the camp.

"Doc, we've gotta do something. They've even taken our phones. We can't sit here forever."

"Come on Billy, you know very well no one would allow you through the gate in your condition. Anyway, the government is paying compensation."

"Come on, Doc, I only took a little bit of cobalt. Hardly anything really."

"You wouldn't want to go around contaminating folk outside now, would you?"

"I'm not going to go aroun' spittin' on people. It doesn't come out in my sweat, does it?"

"Who knows where it comes out, Billy."

He understood why Billy was fed up. His wife had divorced him not more than six months ago, and what woman would look at him if they knew what he carried?

"Look, Billy. There's nothing I can do about it. Go and get yourself a beer from the NAAFI tent, why don't you?"

"I don't want a beer, Doc. Nor any of those happy-time tablets they hand out with the lunch. Anyway, I'm out of tokens, the fuckin' tokens only last till Tuesday."

The way you drink, they do, but then Billy grabbed Doc's arm.

"Come on, Doc. There's a meeting. You got to go. That's what they said. I'm sorry. Are you comin'?"

"Okay, Billy. Quiet, please, Barbara's asleep, and she gets precious little rest. I'll come and listen to what you have to say."

They had taken over the catering tent, fifty of the villagers crammed inside, he estimated. Six men stood on low benches made from cut-off tables. The babble of conversation rose as the two entered, then one of the men on the benches spoke over the chatter.

"Quiet, please! Quiet! Thank you. I shouldn't have to warn you, the military doesn't like us gathering together — there's liable to be trouble if they catch on. Right. I see Doctor Newton has honored us with his presence. Doctor, welcome to the Democratic Action Committee."

The speaker, a sandy-haired heavyset man of about thirty, waved left and right. Newton remembered seeing him about the village but couldn't recall him ever coming into the office.

Grim laughter came from the back.

The other men standing on the tabletops bowed toward the doctor, but with an air of mockery rather than respect. The doctor recognized three of them: Ed Crowell, Eric Woolman, and Tony Emerson. He'd enjoyed a few games of darts in the pub with Woolman: a decent sort, if a little boisterous. Woolman looked embarrassed to be standing on the top of a cut-off table, then hardened his features.

The sandy-haired man carried on in a loud voice. "My name is —

well, most of you know who I am. We'd like to know who you work for, Doc. Whose side are you on? And, Doc, I'm to tell you there'll be no nasty stuff if it turns out you work for them."

The last word was spoken with a degree of scorn, Newton thought.

"Provided, that is, you tell us now. Later, well, I couldn't speak for your safety."

"I'm not sure who you mean by 'them,'" Newton said.

The sandy-haired man stared at him.

"Well, it's a bit hard to say, isn't it? The bloody army keeps us here penned in, living in these terrible tents, but who gives the orders? The government, that's what we guess. Who did this to us? And why?"

"I don't think they know who did it."

"We've been left here to die, haven't we? I suppose at the end of it all, the bulldozers will arrive and we'll be shoveled under."

"That's not true," Newton countered, but his voice wavered slightly. The speaker picked up on it straight away.

"Are you with them, Doc? Maybe you'd better leave now, and I don't need to tell you to keep your gob shut, do I?"

The muttering in the crowd didn't sound friendly. "Don't tell me whose side I'm on," Newton snapped, color rising to his cheeks. "Not when my wife's sick. She'll be lucky if she lasts three months."

Saying this, he felt as if something had risen into his throat, and he turned away, wiping at his eyes with the back of his hand.

"I'm doing the best I can," he said, facing them again. "What d'you want, man, you think that people with radioactive isotopes in them can just go down to the pub? You think they'd let us walk in the streets without bells and signs around our necks? You know what the signs would say? 'Unclean,' that's what they would say."

The men on the stage looked uncomfortable, but the crowd was getting louder and more aggressive. The speaker stamped on the table and shouted over them.

"We should be taken to proper hospitals, Doc, not kept penned in here like animals. They won't talk to us. All we get is claptrap from that brown job Captain that comes round in the morning. Well, we've had enough. I say we get out."

Shouts came from the crowd:

"Cockroaches and beetles in the food."

"The flies are everywhere."

Newton gave them a minute to calm down, then raised his voice.

"You'll get hurt, I'm telling you. Let me talk to them. For the record, I agree with you; it's time something better than this was organized. Okay?"

The speaker turned to the others on the bench. They nodded. He looked back at Newton.

"We'll see, Doc. Best o' luck."

TWELVE

Strange arrived at Heartland TV and checked his phone. A little before eleven a.m. — he was early. He showed his warrant card, and security waved him through the door.

"Straight ahead, sir. Through the double doors."

Strange waded along a corridor through heavy carpet in gold and white. The same motif was on the walls and ceiling.

He passed an alcove with a massive old-style camera. Its turret lens system looked as if it could launch grenades. Above it, an engraved plate read: "Marconi Mk. V."

Someone had fashioned a lifelike dummy operator for it. The machine dwarfed the hunched figure. A red sign glowed brightly, announcing "On air."

Immediately ahead, a set of double doors swung open. A young man with a professional smile pushed through, his hand outstretched. He wore a lilac shirt with gold stripes.

"Gordon Strange, dahling, how nice to see you." The man's prominent Adam's apple bobbed up and down as he spoke. He pumped Strange's hand vigorously.

"I'm Freddy. Assistant producer. I saw you on the Beeb this morning. You looked very butch." He laughed, moving through the doors into the hospitality room.

A babble of noise came from an excited group of youngsters in one corner of the spacious lounge.

"Quiz show," Freddy said, deftly steering Strange toward the bar. "What'll it be?" Freddy waved at an array of bottles on polished glass shelves. "I'll serve you myself — the regular man doesn't come on until four."

"I see you've got your own licensing laws around here," Strange commented dryly. "I'll have a coffee, please."

Freddy went behind the bar. "You're sure you won't have something stronger? I do a very good G and T. Vicky's with Andy. They won't be long."

"Andy?"

"Andy Beeston. Producer for news and comment. The spot starts at one, with fifteen minutes of national networked news from Independent Television News. At a quarter past, there's a commercial break, then we take over for the last fifteen minutes." Freddy produced a glass coffee decanter from below the counter. "How do you like it?"

"Milk, no sugar, thanks."

A producer came in and shepherded the quiz show kids away, leaving Strange alone with Freddy.

Freddy left the carafe in front of Strange, then came out from behind the bar. "I'll just tell the producer you're here." He headed for what appeared to be a blank wall, then opened a barely visible door, cunningly decorated so as to blend in with the Conrad wallpaper.

IN THE DRESSING ROOM, THE MAKEUP GIRL APPLIED A FINAL DUSTING of powder to Vicky's nose and forehead, then inspected the result. "You're all set."

A man's voice said over the intercom, "Ready, loves? We're getting into position. Vicky, your guest is in the lounge."

"Be right there," she replied.

Vicky popped into the lounge for a moment. "Hello."

Strange raised his head at the sound of her voice, his face breaking into a smile that lit up his brown eyes. "I remember you," he said. "I'm sorry it couldn't have been under happier circumstances."

She shook hands with him. "Yes, indeed. What happened with that case, by the way?"

"I shouldn't say, but off the record?"

She nodded.

"It's murder. The case has been passed to homicide."

"Oh. Sorry, but I have to rush off; I'll see you in the studio."

A technician glanced up as she arrived in the News Room.

She gave him a friendly nod and turned to Andy Beeston, who waited with a small folder.

"How's our guest looking, then?" Beeston asked.

"Uniform, one of those flat hats with the checkered band," Vicky replied soberly.

"What?" Beeston's eyebrows elevated, and his mouth opened in a surprised O.

"Just joking," Vicky said, showing the dimples in her cheeks. "Smart suit. Serious. Good-looking. The housewives will love him. Bit of a James Bond. He's thirty-eight."

"Oh." Beeston's eyebrows descended again. "Okay. Usual network sign-off, then we'll slip Strange in during the break. Have to be fast, it's only ninety seconds. Then two minutes before we run the video. Watch the monitor for the corner blip and time yourself."

"Video? What video?"

"Just came in. We got a guy near enough to the village with a thousand-milli lens. He shot a good hour. We've edited the best stuff into a ninety-second slot. Just go with the teleprompter. You'll walk it."

Vicky, her face pinched, stared at him. Bastard. No time left to preview it or warn Strange.

"Then interview for a couple of minutes, wrap it up, and hand it over to Martin."

That had to be at twenty-seven past the hour, give or take a few seconds. The weather was on for three minutes, then the network soap.

Beeston flashed his fake Rolex. "You've got four minutes."

She threaded past trailing cables, sparing a brief "Hello, Pat" for camera two's operator. Her comfortable executive chair was an old friend. She sat, put the talkback plug into her ear, and exchanged a few words with Martin.

Thirty kilowatts of mixed LED and discharge lighting fired up on the overhead gantries, turning gloom into day.

Vicky glanced at her camera, number two. It was still off. A red light glowed on the front of camera one, her co-presenter Martin's.

In her ear, a ghost voice squeaked, "Three, two, one, go!"

Martin came to life, looking straight into the lens. "Good afternoon. On Heartland News today—"

A minute later he cut over, and Vicky launched into the local news, starting with a savage assault on an old lady. There were three video clips in eight minutes.

During the last item, Beeston came to the side of the rostrum, out of camera view, winding an imaginary handle in the air.

She gave the camera a big smile. The scene on her monitor cut to a Quantel Paintbox animation: the news desk rolled up into a tube, revealing a woman getting into a car. The Peugeot commercial.

The red lights on both cameras were out. The brutes on the

gantry faded, leaving one small floodlight. A grip came in pushing a chair like hers. He was closely followed by Strange, who was being fitted with a lapel radio microphone. The grip positioned the chair, and Strange sat down.

The gantry lights came on again. Strange flinched.

Beeston hovered nervously.

Straight out of the break, she went into the rush item. "Two nights ago, the small village of Upwood, near Worcester, was sealed off by the army. Heartland has the latest information on the incident, and we have with us in the studio Chief Inspector Gordon Strange, from West Midlands Police."

The red light glowed on camera four. Her inset screen showed a brief cutaway to Strange, sitting with a neutral expression on his face. He looked fine. The camera returned to her. She carried on with the teleprompt, giving a quick outline of the few facts.

Beeston gesticulated to her as the text rolled toward the single large word "INTERVIEW."

Strange's camera lit up, and she turned toward him. On a large monitor off-rostrum, the view broadened to include both Strange and herself, as camera two reverse-zoomed.

"Good afternoon, Detective Chief Inspector, and thank you for coming to the studio." She smiled warmly. "Can you tell us what is happening in Upwood?" The official line, straight off her prompter, was that an epidemic had broken out.

"It has been necessary to seal off the village because the water supply appears to be contaminated," Strange began. "The health department is investigating."

Vicky noticed camera one dollying into position for a close-up of Strange's face. In the top right corner of her monitor, a small flickering square appeared. The thirty-second video warning.

"So you can't tell us why this whole village has been sealed off? Or why the Upwood telephone system seems to be out of order?"

"We expect to release a bulletin shortly. In the meantime ..." —

Strange extracted a small piece of paper from his jacket — "anyone with relatives in Upwood should call this number for information." He slowly read a Birmingham number.

Vicky knew that in the control room there would be frenzied activity as the Paintbox operator typed the numbers into an overlay. Within seconds, the number appeared on the monitor, superimposed across the front of the news desk. The VT prompt flickered faster now; they'd cut to the report in less than ten seconds.

"Thank you, Inspector," she said and repeated the number. "One of our reporters has just returned from Upwood with live film."

Camera two zoomed back in until it filled the screen with her head and shoulders. A second later her image disappeared, replaced by a view of the main road into Upwood. It was taken from a position to one side; Vicky suspected the reporter had been hiding behind a hedge or in a ditch.

The studio lights dimmed and the "On air" sign went out.

Strange was taken aback. "No one mentioned a tape!"

"They sprang it on me at the last minute. Sorry, there was no time to tell you."

The monitor showed a close-up of a barrier across the road. Several vehicles in army camouflage sat on the grass verge. Antennas festooned one of them; a command truck. A thick cable ran from it and disappeared into the adjacent hedge. Just beyond the hedgerow, a satellite dish pointed into the sky.

"This is the main road into Upwood. All vehicles are being turned back at the roadblock," the reporter commented.

Birds twittered in the background. The camera cut to another scene. This time the viewpoint was elevated. The reporter had found a tree to climb or some other vantage point.

A wall blocked the lower half of the view, but beyond that appeared part of the main street. An army tow truck was removing a parked car. Only two other cars were in the street, both in dull army green. The nearest store was the village's small supermarket. The doors opened and two bulky figures appeared, dressed in white biosuits. The screen flared white as the sun reflected off the visor of one. They had some kind of instrument, like an old-fashioned hair dryer with a long snout.

The camera panned slowly, wobbling. It zoomed out even further, focusing on a Victorian brick structure, eighty feet or so in height. A termite nest had been disturbed: white-suited figures milled about. Several large vehicles clustered nearby.

The camera cut again, to a closeup of the reporter. "These pictures were taken at ten o'clock today, on the outskirts of Upwood. The village appears to be deserted except for the army. No one is being allowed in. Why are soldiers here, dressed in what appear to be biohazard suits?" He waved an arm to his right. "Transport helicopters are landing every half hour."

He paused for dramatic effect. "What happened to the people? This is Rick Hamilton reporting for Heartland Television, from the village of Upwood, in Worcestershire."

Beeston's voice crackled over the talkback. "Give me a closeup, one."

Strange's face filled the screen, at nearly double magnification. Vicky watched the monitor from the corner of her eye. Every bead of sweat on the poor man's face stood out. She wanted to reach out and touch his arm.

Vicky turned to Strange, reminding herself that they were both professionals. She used her "serious" look. "Where are the residents of Upwood, Inspector?"

"I'm afraid I really don't have any more information right now," Strange parried. "Anyone who has relatives or friends in Upwood should call the information line that I gave you earlier."

The desk engineer overlaid the image of the emergency number on the screen again.

"Can you at least tell us the nature of the problem, Inspector? Why are all those army people wearing chemical warfare suits?"

"It's standard procedure, I believe, when it's possible that an outbreak of infectious disease has occurred."

"You're saying that it's an epidemic, Inspector?"

"I'm not in possession of that information, I'm afraid," Strange commented mildly.

Vicky wouldn't let go. "Can't or won't, Inspector?" But time was against her. Even as Strange replied, "I'm sure the situation is under control," Beeston's disembodied voice came thinly over the talkback link. "Thirty seconds, darling, wrap it up."

She just had time to exit cleanly, get a five-second outro from Martin, and link into the weather. The clocks in the control room read 01:27:25 as the gantry lights cut, the daylight discharge lamps still glowing dull red in the dark.

Vicky turned to Strange with an apologetic smile as soon as the lights went down. She checked that no cameras were live. "I'm terribly sorry. The tape arrived when I had three minutes to air time. No chance to warn you." She felt embarrassed.

Strange glared at her. "That wasn't very nice."

Damn Beeston. You shouldn't put James Bond in an embarrassing situation. "Go through into the hospitality room and have a drink. You've earned it. I'll be along in a minute."

As they got up, a man made his way across the rostrum toward them. Andy Beeston, her producer.

Vicky turned to Strange and gave him her best smile. "I won't be long."

———

STILL FUMING, STRANGE GOT UP QUICKLY FROM THE CHAIR AND EXITED the rostrum.

A sound engineer approached and detached his wireless microphone.

He made his way back to the corridor, and then to the now-deserted lounge. High up in one corner, a large monitor played, soundlessly, the daily one-thirty soap.

Strange's mouth felt bone-dry, and it wasn't just because of the lights. He went behind the bar and opened the door of the large refrigerator. Rows of beers and mixers welcomed him. The Beck's foamed as he poured it down the side of the glass.

"Jesus H. Christ," he muttered, grateful that the interview had finished when it did. The beer went down in one swallow. He stashed the empty bottle in the trash and helped himself to another.

Vicky came in just as he raised the glass to his lips. He looked her up and down, trying to be discreet about it. God, she looked terrific in her tight dress. She reminded him of the famous Mexican weather girls he'd seen on YouTube. "Christ, I must have looked like an idiot."

She walked over and sat down on the stool next to him. "I'm really sorry about that video. My producer sprang it on me at the last minute. You handled it very well."

It was impossible to remain irritated with her. "Did I?" What scent was she wearing? His hormones were running wild.

"No, really, you were fine. Is that a beer?"

"Beck's. I helped myself. Freddy not being around. It's my day off, the first in weeks. Can I get you something?"

"A low-alcohol beer. Heineken."

He poured the beer into a goblet, then came round from behind the bar and sat down next to her. He felt like a tongue-tied teenager again. Nothing like this had happened to him in a very long time.

"Vicky, would—"

"Have you—"

He stopped, embarrassed at the word clash, both of them speaking at once, then said:

"I'm sorry. First, call me Gordon, for God's sake. I'm wondering, maybe, if you've eaten? Would you consider having lunch with a humble copper?" Well, there it was.

Her face went neutral for long moments, then she smiled. "Okay, Gordon it is, then. And, yes, why not."

THIRTEEN

They seemed to be the wine bar's only customers except for a pinstripe-suited man hidden behind the Financial Times. Vicky, perched on a hard half-barrel seat, knew she'd soon have pins and needles in her bum. She tugged at her skirt to avoid showing too much leg.

Strange sat on another half-barrel chair. The gnarly old plastic tree-trunk table was edged with real bark. He tested the table with his fingers and easily broke off a piece. The ceiling loudspeakers were playing nineties Britpop. They seated themselves to the tune "Girls and Boys" by Blur.

The wine waiter finished mopping his counter, then found his way through the barrel maze to their table. Strange evidently knew him.

"Hi, Rick. How about a glass of something a bit better than that vinegar you call the house white?"

Rick smiled with thin lips. When he spoke, Vicky discerned an Australian accent. "Got a nice Semillon, from Argentina."

"I've never heard of it," Strange said.

Vicky liked the way the corners of his mouth turned up.

"Naturally," Rick replied. "You were too young to appreciate it when it was last popular."

"And when was that?"

"Thirty years ago. Wiped out by botrytis. It's making a comeback."

"What would you like?" Strange asked her.

"I'll have the same, thanks. But just one glass."

Rick sauntered back behind the bar and disappeared.

"What do you think of the place?" Strange asked.

"Not bad. A bit overdone," she replied, listening to Rick rummaging through bottles. "Are you a regular here? He seems to know you very well."

"I know him from another vocation," Strange said with a laugh. "I've only been here a few times, but I thought it would appeal."

Rick reappeared and poured the wine.

Strange sniffed it. "Mmm." He took a sip and nodded. "Nice." He said, "You have to forgive me, it's been a very long time since I invited a beautiful young woman on a date. Where do we start?"

Vicky thought that was quite sweet. "I'll start. I can't apologize enough for that videotape." She reached out and touched his hand. "Beeston, my boss, loves to spring traps like that. It rebounds, though, and he doesn't see it. The next time I try to get the same person in front of the cameras, wild horses couldn't drag them." He frowned, and she guessed he'd been thinking the same. "Were you terribly embarrassed?"

"At first. But I've been thinking of you ever since we met by the riverside. I can't get you out of my head."

This was getting too serious. She squirmed on the hard barrel seat. "This is a little too deep for me, Gordon. Do you mind if I change the subject?"

"What would you like to talk about?" He leaned toward her.

"You."

He toyed with his glass for a moment. He was a bit old to be unmarried, and that worried her most of all, but he wore no ring. With men, however, that was not much to go on.

"The tape. I thought I would turn to stone."

"I'm sorry. Really. Damn Beeston, anyway."

He looked into her eyes. "How long have you been with Heartland TV?"

"It must be, let's see, nearly three years. Not nearly so much of a meteoric rise as your career, Detective Chief Inspector." She emphasized the word "chief" with an arch tone. "Just eight months after joining SO10. Impressive." Perhaps she'd said too much.

Strange sat back, his jaw dropped slightly, and his eyebrows rose. "I thought we were talking about you. How come you know so much about me?"

She laughed. "I'm in news, Gordon Strange. You caught the maniac who put ground glass in the baby food."

"Oh. You remember?"

"It was good for quite a few prime-time news minutes while the chase was on. I grabbed that story and ran with it. It cost the manufacturers a lot. Most packaging has changed; safer, tamper-proof. You had a lot of responsibility for that." She put her hand over his. "You seemed cold and somber that time I found you at the riverside."

"I had already put in a full day's work and was heading home, but no one else was available. And it wasn't the kind of thing people should see. Especially on television."

She thought she should change the direction of this conversation. "I'm starving. Didn't you mention lunch? What kind of food do they serve here?"

"There's not a lot of choices, but what they do have is good. I usually have a French loaf filled with roast pork, stuffing, and applesauce. There's a veggie option. The menu's over there." He pointed to a large blackboard.

She squinted at it. "I'll just have a salad."

The baguette, when it came, looked delicious. She wished she had ordered one instead of the salad. But no; a moment on the lips, a month on the hips.

Vicky told Strange how she started off typing teleprompter scripts and running errands for the newsroom at a station way up in the north.

"It might as well have been the Outer Hebrides," she said. "Imagine! But it was a job in TV. What about you? Were you always in the police?"

"I left university with a degree in sociology. It was during the recession, and I ended up with two choices: teacher or police. The police job paid better. After the first two years, the force became my life."

"Your whole life? No room for a wife, then?"

"Divorced. I can't blame her. Being married to a police officer can be difficult. You tend to end up with only police friends. My boss has the same problem with his marriage, but it's worse for him: he's Muslim, and there are people in his community who think he's their enemy. But I'd rather talk about you. How difficult was it to get on the air?"

"Oh, the anchorwoman had an accident, no one was available, they gave me a chance. It turned into a regular feature." She grinned and added, "Somehow a tape got back to Heartland. They hadn't been on the air long; it was a new franchise."

He was easy to talk to, Vicky thought, but then so were all the men who'd assumed that she'd be happy to jump into bed with them after a few glasses of wine. *Please don't let him be like that.*

"No kids?"

Strange leaned back and raised his eyebrows. "I have a daughter. She's six. My ex wants to send her to boarding school. I don't."

She guessed it might be better not to pursue that topic. "Can you tell me more about the village of Upwood? There's obviously a lot more going on than we're being told."

"I was afraid you were going to ask me that." Strange frowned.

"I'm not a 'jobsworth,' but if I say anything more, it might really be more than my job's worth."

"Off the record, then?" She had finished half the salad but didn't fancy anymore.

"Hmm. It would really need to be off the record. Seriously. There are issues of public confidence, possible mass panic."

"All right then. Seriously off the record. My ears only." She pushed the salad plate away.

"It's a terror attack. At first, we weren't sure, it could have been an industrial accident, but now ... we've identified the source. Someone poisoned the local water supply. Hundreds of people affected."

"Oh, my God. Hundreds?"

"Yes. And the nature of the contamination ... well, the military has made the village a no-go area. It's sealed off."

"What kind of contamination?" She leaned forward.

"I can't tell you that. Really I can't."

"All right. But I hope you'll keep me first in the loop for news on this. What happened to the people who lived there?"

"With the army involved, and other departments, that information is outside my brief."

"Oh."

He finished his baguette.

She checked her phone. "I need to run. I've enjoyed myself. You're not like I expected."

"I'm very attracted to you, Vicky," Strange said. "I'd very much like to see you again."

She examined his open, honest face. The wall was coming down. "I'd like that, too. I must fly. I've got to get ready for the five o'clock."

Strange checked his watch. "It's only three forty-seven. You've got plenty of time. And I have the afternoon free. I haven't had any time off for months. The government austerity program, we've lost so many officers."

"Sorry. There's a lot to be done before the evening news. I'll show you sometime."

"Is that a promise?" Strange asked.

"Thanks for the afternoon, Gordon Strange. And yes, it is a promise. Call me when you've got the time. Before ten a.m., though." She took out her mobile and called an Uber.

Strange scribbled in the air with an invisible pen, causing Rick to materialize with the bill. Vicky pretended not to look as Strange paid with his contactless card and left a rather large tip in cash.

They stood up, and he took her arm to escort her to the door. Outside, he turned to face her, hesitated, and then it was too late.

She bent forward and gave him a peck on the cheek just as the Uber pulled up. She climbed in. Through the rear window, she saw him standing there like a lost boy, watching as the vehicle drove her away.

FOURTEEN

Years of repainting had turned the rungs of the water tower's wrought-iron ladder into fat German sausages. Irregular patches of fingerprint powder covered them. Strange had difficulty holding on, wet as they were with the morning dew.

He lost his grip. Vertigo. Bile surged into his throat and he gagged at the sight of the ground, eighty feet below.

"Ooof!" With a violent jerk the safety harness bit into his stomach, his feet swung over his head and he was bobbing like a pendulum, arms windmilling air. A hand came into view, then the upside-down face of a sergeant from the Worcester police. "Lucky for you someone rigged those safety lines eh, sir?"

Strange laughed, but the sharply gusting wind tore it from his lips. In truth, he was scared shitless. At ground level, the gusts had been a gentle breeze. He waited for the ladder to come within reach and grabbed it, then swung himself upright again, gasping.

He kept his eyes on the sergeant, climbing just above. One glance at the ground below had been enough. This was the first time the army had allowed access to the civilian police force, but now he regretted his decision to climb the side of the Upwood village water tower.

At the top, the ladder swan-necked one-eighty degrees. The sergeant swung himself over and onto the flat roof. Strange followed.

"I thought there was a ladder inside the building," Strange grunted. "What was that small door down there, the green one?"

"There is a ladder behind that door, but that's not how our bird gained entry," the sergeant replied. The exertion appeared to have had no effect on him. "The locksmith told us no one's been through that ground-level door for years. It was practically rusted solid."

"Any prints?"

"No, sir. Boot prints on the rungs. Just partials."

The roof was a flat circle some forty feet in diameter, its graveled bitumen surface overgrown with moss and straggly grass. On the other side, Strange saw a low object like a small hut. It, too, was covered in tar, with a rusty iron access door set in the front.

They made their way to the portal, the wind tugging spitefully at them as they went. A padlock and hasp had secured the tiny door, but the broken hasp now hung uselessly to one side. The rusted metal bore fresh scratches like claw marks.

Strange pointed at it. "So this is where our mystery poisoner got in." He pulled at the door and it opened outward, complaining on its rusty hinges.

Strange stooped through the entrance and made his way carefully down a short flight of perforated metal stairs. At the bottom, he stepped onto a circular path of ochre brick, waiting for his eyes to adjust to the gloom. The sergeant joined him. Around the perimeter of the wall, five feet from the floor and several feet apart, window slits pierced the brickwork. These let in enough light to form a dull gloom.

Strange wrinkled his nose in disgust. "Smells like something died in here," he said, peering around. The sergeant nodded. Wind gusted from the slits behind Strange, blowing his hair into his eyes.

The narrow path extended right around the inside of the structure. Almost flush with it was the black, painted metal surface of the giant water tank. Strange moved out across the top. Seized by a childish impulse, he stamped one foot on the surface. The tank reverberated with a hollow boom like an immense kettle drum.

"Steady on, sir!" the sergeant called in alarm.

"Sorry," Strange replied, "but it should be ok. They built things to last in those days."

He saw three raised manholes that sat like iron toadstools. One of them was larger than the others. Its crude lid bore a pair of steel handles. Strange bent down and examined a label someone had attached with wire. It was a note from forensics, announcing that the lid had been checked for fingerprints.

"So this is where he — or she — dumped the stuff in," Strange said, then added: "But mass killers are usually men."

He tried to lift the lid. One side came up, but then it stuck.

The sergeant, a small, wiry man, raised an eyebrow. "Not supposed to lift this, sir. Risky. And we're only allowed to stay five minutes, even though it's been drained and flushed. That's the safe limit. Well … we're wearing dosimeters." He put his hand under the rim and heaved. The top finally came off with a grating sound, and the two of them moved it to one side.

"Well, I guess that proves something," Strange commented. "Either a bloody strong woman, a man and a woman, more than one woman, or a fairly strong man. That lid must weigh about a hundred and forty pounds."

Strange peered into the tank. Inside was inky blackness, except where dim light came through the opening. He fumbled in his pocket and brought out a flashlight, and shone it into the tank.

"There's a ladder," Strange noted. "I'm glad I don't live near here. I don't think the folk hereabouts will ever drink from the water main again. At least not unless a completely new system is installed. How could you ever tell that some particle isn't waiting to be released into your cup of tea?" He gestured to the sergeant, then they reached over and replaced the cover.

"I've organized lunch at the village pub," the sergeant remarked. He laughed at the look that Strange gave him. "No, not the one in the village center. The water there came from this tank. There's another pub, on the new housing estate. It's connected to the same main as the houses on the estate, and we know that's clean."

Strange's leg muscles were complaining by the time the two of them reached the ground. After stowing the belts and shackles in the Range Rover, Strange took the wheel and drove the vehicle around the parking lot to the entrance. A sign read:

SEVERN TRENT WATER

NO UNAUTHORIZED ENTRY

A policeman came and opened the gates for them. He wore a bulky dark-blue jacket that looked like it might be lined with Kevlar, and carried a Heckler & Koch nine-millimeter machine pistol. On each side of the gates, a chain-link fence four feet high marked the perimeter of the pumping station.

"It would have been easy enough to get in, sir," the sergeant commented.

Strange glanced at him and nodded but remained silent. He couldn't help thinking of things that had no bearing on the case. Would his old Jaguar car pass its road safety test? It was becoming prohibitively expensive to keep it running. Why hadn't he made a more determined pass at Vicky? After all, neither of them were teenagers.

He moved off, turned onto the main road, and headed for the newer part of Upwood.

First, they had to go through the old village. It was an eerie experience to see how fast things decayed without people to maintain them. Litter blew along the deserted main street. Windows stared blankly from abandoned cottages. Some panes were broken. Shops were shuttered or had been boarded up. Frayed yellow curtains fluttered from one house, like ships' flag signals: "Keep away. Fever."

Two soldiers patrolled the street. They wore full combat dress, masks over their faces, and carried NATO assault rifles. They stopped to watch the police Range Rover as Strange drove by. He was glad when he reached the outskirts and left the houses behind. In the distance, he saw the army's roadblock.

Once past the checkpoint, Strange threaded the Range Rover down the narrow lane, made even narrower by lines of vehicles parked on the grass verges. They included a BBC outside broadcast unit, two more from independent TV companies, another from ITN, and several news cars from radio stations.

The O.B. units were running their generators; a haze of diesel fumes hung in the air. At the front sat the Heartland TV van. An engineer was adjusting a parabolic antenna on its roof.

When Strange saw the logo, Vicky came into his mind. He looked about nervously, expecting to see someone pointing a camera at him.

"It's just a mile and a half sir, and then you turn left at the crossroads, onto the new estate," the sergeant said. "You can't miss it. It's right on the main road. The Galleon."

FIFTEEN

Doctor Newton sat in his tent as the last of the twilight faded from the western horizon, typing his case notes into a tablet. Mrs. Williams had died that morning. Mr. Williams had interrupted him on his rounds.

"Doctor, please, come quickly. It's my wife."

Newton had followed Mr. Williams through the tents and stopped at one that bore a small sign: "Williams. 078." Around the tent, someone had planted a pathetic row of flowering weeds, an English cottage garden of desperation and longing.

Mrs. Williams lay gray-faced on her camp bed. She seemed to be asleep.

Newton bent down and checked her pulse — fluttering at ninety-seven per minute — and then her drip. A half-full bottle of blood hung from a stand at the head of the bed.

"Mrs. Williams," he said to her. No response. Louder, "Wake up, Mrs. Williams." He squeezed her upper arm. The imprints of his fingers stayed in her flesh as if it had been Playdoh.

Her husband knelt at her other side. "I can't get her to wake up. I tried for five minutes, then I ran to get you."

Newton nodded. "I'm going to call the team."

Shortly after, another doctor and two nurses arrived in a small motorized vehicle that was not unlike an electric golf cart, and pushed their way inside.

Newton looked up.

"Mr. Williams?" the new doctor asked.

He nodded.

"Could you wait outside? We need room to work."

"Take her to a proper hospital, for God's sake!" Williams replied, his voice cracking.

"That's what we're here to check, Mr. Williams," the new doctor said.

Williams got up, shaking his head, and was halfway through the canvas door when a harsh rattling came from the woman on the camp bed.

Her breathing had stopped. "Ventilator!" Newton yelled.

The team went into a crash routine. From the electric car came a defibrillator machine, adrenalin, and oxygen.

Mrs. Williams bounced up from the bed every time they hit her with a charge from the defibrillator.

Finally, they had to admit defeat. The portable heart monitor flat-lined. Newton tried to hide his distaste as a rank smell filled the air; the dead woman's sphincters had relaxed, voiding her bowels.

Her husband stood in the doorway, broken, tears running down his face.

Newton went over to him and put a hand on his arm.

Mr. Williams threw it off violently. "Get off me, you quack!" he half cried, half shouted. "Why couldn't she be taken to a proper hospital? Bastards, keep us penned up, out of sight, out of bloody mind. ... Bastards!" he cried again, plunging through the canvas door.

Newton shook his head, back in the relentless present. This bloody place, this camp. When would the authorities admit them to a hospital?

He saved the case notes file and checked the time. It was nearly eleven o'clock at night. The wind was getting up. Between gusts, drunken singing drifted from the men over at the NAAFI beer tent.

Private Anders stamped his feet on the wooden slats of the small guard hut outside the front gate, trying to get the feeling back in his toes. *Looks like I'm in for a rough night.* A dog patrol passed him on its way along the eight-foot reinforced fence that surrounded the tent village. It was a long perimeter.

He'd seen seagulls flying inland in the afternoon, and now he smelt damp in the freshening wind. There had been a bit of activity at half past eleven when a medic team had come to deal with a collapsed drunk.

He checked his watch. Eight minutes to one, six hours before his relief would turn up.

"Hey! We want to talk to you!" someone shouted from the compound.

Private Anders came out of his hut and walked to the gate, rifle at port position, facing several of the male residents. Bright-white LED flood lamps mounted on the perimeter fence threw their shadows like stilt men.

"Yes?" he asked, making his voice carry. He was sick of this diseased lot. They would come to the gate, moan about the conditions, then ask to see a senior officer. No fucking chance. In the end, he'd get pissed off and tell them to come back in the morning.

"We want to see the warrant officer," said a man with wiry sand-colored hair, his hands on his hips, his face set like stone.

Anders consulted his watch. "Gentlemen, it's nearly midnight.

Why don't you go and get some sleep, and we'll see about this in the morning?"

The full moon shone briefly before hiding again behind ragged clouds. In the extra light it seemed there were more residents than he'd first thought.

"Hey, fella, we want to see your boss right now. Why don't you get on the phone, eh? Go on, will you."

Anders moved forward to get a better view and glanced over the small crowd. There must be what, a couple of dozen? Damned if he was going to bother the warrant officer though. The captain was a martinet. Anders knew he'd be cleaning the shitters for a week if he brought the captain out at this time of night. He glanced back down the gravel road to where the army post lights gleamed in the distance.

"Sorry, no can do. Not at this time of night."

"Okay. We'll see you tomorrow, then," the sandy-haired man replied. The group drifted away toward the tents.

Well, that was easier than usual. Except that two of them were arguing now. The wind was in their direction, so all he could make out were phrases between the gusts.

"No way, no way! Gotta—" "— Fuck you too, man—" And then suddenly one of the men flung a punch, slipped, went down, and both of them were scrabbling in the muck.

"Kill ya, muthafu—" the sentry heard, and then there was a strangling sound as the big guy started choking the life out of the smaller one.

Anders grabbed a radio. "Main gate, Anders here, condition blue. A fight. Get some men — yes, Anders; that's what I said, over."

A villager brandishing a tree branch arrived. He couldn't dislodge the big fellow.

Anders didn't want a murder happening during his watch.

"Help! Help me get him off, he's killing Bernie!" the man with the branch shouted at Anders. The big fellow heaved the branch guy off and went back to choking Bernie, the little guy.

"Help. For God's sake, help!" pleaded the third guy, now at the gate. The tree branch drooped from his hands.

The radio crackled. "Anders? Are you there? Over."

"Anders here." Shit, it was the warrant officer. "Over," he added.

Anders started toward the gate, pulling the key from his belt.

A large raindrop came from out of the dark and splashed in his eye. Another struck him on the cheek. In the distance, he saw a stroke of forked lightning.

Static blared from the radio, then the captain: "Anders, what's the situation? Over."

"Two men, sir. One's in a bad way. A third guy's trying to separate them. Over." A patter of rain lashed into his face, and he turned instinctively to avoid it, hunching his shoulders.

"We'll send a squad. Four men be enough? Over."

"Should be, sir. I need them fast. Over."

"Right away. Over and out."

The fight continued. Where were they getting the energy? The men were completely covered in mud now.

Anders fumbled with the key in the lock. He couldn't put his rifle down. How could he deal with the big fellow? A kick in the balls would stop the drunken sod.

The gate came open.

He ran over to the fighting men and drew his foot back.

AN OVER-REVVING LAND ROVER DISCOVERY SWEPT AROUND THE curve of the track and slithered to a stop next to the sentry box. Arriving in the teeth of the storm, Sergeant Parry — with Privates Simms, Leen, and Luff — was just in time to see Eric Woolman rise up out of the darkness, slip the branch over Anders' head and drag him backward.

The two men on the ground rolled apart and sprang to their feet.

A lightning bolt cracked into the ground nearby, followed by a deafening bang of colliding air.

Sergeant Parry flinched.

The wind was moaning through the perimeter wire, and a loose canvas thrashed and slapped in the gusts. Rain was trying to come again, but the wind wouldn't let it.

The squad jumped from their vehicle and ran for the gate, carrying their compact Nato issue point two-two-three assault rifles.

Sergeant Parry saw that Anders had both fists clenched around the branch in a futile effort to push it away from his throat. His feet thrashed uselessly and he made gurgling sounds as he was dragged toward the tents.

Another lightning strike. A drum roll of thunder echoed across the fields. Even before it died, lightning struck again, nearer still, filling the air with the biting tang of ozone.

Sergeant Parry shouted over the rising wind: "Quick! Simms, Leen, take the left and right. Luff, secure the gate. I'm going to fire warning shots."

The sergeant raised his weapon and fired three rounds into the air. The flat cracks banged across the fields and died in the distance. He wondered if it would be enough, and thumbed the selector to fully automatic. He'd send a few over their heads if he had to. The captain had left him in no doubt: no one was to get out of the compound.

Lights came on.

Trees in a nearby copse rustled loudly, precursors of a squall that whipped into the tents seconds later.

Trash flew and canvas snapped and drummed.

Shouts came on the wind.

DOCTOR NEWTON, WOKEN BY THE STORM, HEARD FEET THUDDING PAST his tent. He peered out to see why, then the first shots split the air.

His wife, Barbara, twitched in her sleep then woke, sat up, and pulled the blanket to her throat.

Rain beat against the tent roof, and the canvas wall bellied in as the wind pushed against it.

"Darling, what is it? Something woke me up—"

"Don't worry, dear. It's some kind of disturbance. I'll go and see."

Newton pulled on his clothes and stooped to get out. It was just forty yards to the gate, but the mud made it seem a lot farther, and it was slightly downhill. As he got closer, he heard shouts, then spotted the melee. Oh, God, he thought, Williams has been stirring up people.

Two bolts of lightning cracked into the trees on the far side of the fence. An ear-splitting double bang followed. Newton saw the soldiers at the gate flinch, hesitate for a moment, and then the villagers were upon them.

The doctor ran forward, shouting: "No! Don't!"

From behind the mass of struggling men, the sergeant appeared, brandishing a rifle. He backed away, lifted the weapon, and took aim into the sky, above the heads of the mob.

Newton watched helplessly as two fighting men crashed into the sergeant.

The sergeant nose-dived. His legs folded and he fell forward. A burst of fire rang out.

Screams from the tents.

This can't be happening, Newton thought. Can't be happening, can't. Got to move.

With difficulty, he freed one foot from the mud and took a step. His eyes were fixed on the struggle at the gate.

The men on the ground froze after the shots, and one of the

soldiers took advantage of the respite. "Back off! Back off, you bastards!" the man bellowed, waving his rifle at them.

The mob disentangled itself like an amoeba disengaging from a noxious prey.

Approaching headlights threw dancing shadows over the tents. One soldier remained on the ground, one of his legs bent at an odd angle. Another soldier retreated, limping slowly toward the gate.

The full storm broke. Curtains of rain marched across the fields and turned the already muddy ground into a bog. The magnesium glare of a lightning stroke lit up Doctor Newton like a statue; he stood over the prone men with arms out and fists clenched.

"Animals! Bastards!" he howled at the fleeing villagers and retreating soldiers, but the storm tore the words from his mouth and threw them back in his face.

SIXTEEN

At exactly nine o'clock, Commander Imran's phone rang. It was Leavey, the parliamentary private secretary to the minister for Home Affairs. Leavey had been in his present position for seven years and seen Home Office ministers come and go.

"Good morning, Commander. Or is it?"

They had crossed paths once before, to Imran's disadvantage. Best to treat the question as rhetorical and wait the man out.

"Have you seen the newspapers, Commander?"

On Imran's desk lay several newspapers. The one on top, the most popular tabloid daily, had a screaming headline in eighty-point type:

ATOM SCARE — ENTIRE VILLAGE DISAPPEARS!

The other papers were more restrained, but the story had made all the dailies. Only the Times relegated it to page two.

"Yes. I've seen them." He wished he hadn't.

"Well, then, old chap, may I ask precisely who, or what, we're dealing with here? The press are quite persistent," Leavey said in his clipped Eton College voice.

"Not yet sure, sir. Cobalt-60 was the agent, crudely prepared, according to forensics." Imran glanced at the lab report. "Dissolved in nitric acid. Half-life, about two and a half years."

"MI5 says it's terrorism. The P.M. is going to face some awkward points at question time today. He wants answers. The whole village water network was contaminated. Cleaning is not a realistic possibility. Would you like a cup of Upwood tea, Imran? Add a few sparks to your plumbing, eh? It's in the wastewater treatment plant, and all the drains."

"Detective Chief Inspector Strange has just paid a visit, sir."

"I know. I had the army on the line. He drove down High Street with no protective suit. Past contaminated houses. Contaminated gardens. Contaminated sewers. We're looking at twenty-five years before the isotope decays. The residents will never move back. Many will not survive."

"And the incident at the holding camp. That doesn't look good. Do I need to remind you that we are the party of law and order? The next question time promises to be most difficult. May I say that we expect an arrest shortly, Commander?"

"I wouldn't go so far as that, sir," Imran said. "We're following some good leads."

"Your man, what's his name? Strange? The one I saw on the television news when this thing first went public?"

"Gordon Strange, sir."

"Yes. Our unhappy masters are taking an interest in his future. It won't be my name on the bullet if it all goes wrong. Put Strange in the hot seat, Imran," Leavey said. "And do it fast." He hung up.

Imran put the phone down and pressed an intercom button. "Strange? Come to my office, please." He picked up one of the newspapers. The front page had an image of Upwood taken from above. Some reporter had got a drone past the security perimeter.

The army roadblocks could clearly be seen on the only road in and out.

Strange knocked on the door and entered. He looked stressed out.

"Take a seat, please, Chief Inspector." Imran slapped the newspaper on the desk.

"The Home Office is taking a direct interest in this. Questions are being asked in the House. The prime minister's got sod-all for a majority and, I don't need to remind you, they made a big play on the law and order issue at the party conference."

"Quite so, sir."

"Did you get anything from the crime scene?" Imran asked.

"Not much. I climbed the tower, had a good look around. Wouldn't be here save for the safety line. Lost my grip." Strange winced. "Forensic got partial boot prints off the ladder, size nine Reeboks. Huge numbers of that model sold in the last year. No fingerprints."

"Security?" Imran tapped his fingers on the desk.

"The water tower was unattended. It would have been easy to gain access. The CCTV was broken."

"Have you heard the news this morning? It didn't make these early-morning papers." Imran shuffled the newspapers together. The pile's irregular edge annoyed him, so he began to organize it by width.

"The shooting? I caught part of it on the car radio."

"Some of the villagers tried to make a break for it last night. It got nasty."

"How nasty?" Strange leaned forward.

"One of the soldiers fell. Fired his weapon into the tents. The wife of the village doctor was shot dead. An accident, of course, though that won't make any difference to her. Two other villagers wounded, one seriously, and two soldiers injured."

The width of the news pile tapered perfectly, but the other axis was ragged. Tearing his attention from the annoyance, Imran continued, "It's gone political. They're moving the Upwood victims to a hospital in London before the media can turn it into a civil rights thing. And the opposition party wants an independent inquiry."

"I see," Strange said. "The inquest on the man who was found in the Avon, sir. I will have to attend, as the first senior officer at the scene. And he's part of this, isn't he?"

"Yes, he is. I want these bastards caught, and fast. Don't forget, tomorrow we're going to visit a madrassa near Evesham. We'll be taking an inspector from Homicide with us. And a drone operator." Imran scooped up the pile of newsprint and dropped it into his paper recyclables bin. But the damn lid wouldn't go on.

SEVENTEEN

Imran and Strange left early in a police vehicle, needing the extra space for the drone equipment and its operator. Homicide had not had the manpower to send one of their officers. Or so they had claimed. Imran frowned, remembering how they had waited until the last minute to tell him.

By nine a.m. they had worked their way through the early-morning traffic and were on the narrow "B" road that led past the madrassa and its extensive grounds. Soon its tall metal gates came into view.

"Keep driving Strange, there's a lay-by a couple of hundred yards farther along."

Strange drove past the gate with its CCTV cameras, continued a couple of hundred yards, then pulled the vehicle off the road and got out.

Imran took in the view, which reminded him of the bucolic simplicity of a Constable watercolor. *So peaceful here.*

"Shall I get the bird up now, sir?" the drone technician asked.

"How long is it good for?"

"About twenty minutes, but I've got spare batteries if you need more time."

"How much noise does it make? They'll spot it, won't they?"

"Not at three hundred feet, sir. I doubt they'll notice. The camera can pick up a fly on a leaf from that altitude."

"We'll wait until we finish the interview, see what kind of rat scurrying goes on."

"Right, sir."

Imran and Strange walked back down the road and approached the tall black-iron double gates. A CCTV camera tracked their approach.

"Body cameras on, Inspector," Imran said, making sure that his own was recording. "And remember, officially, we're here about Malik. But this has a bad smell about it."

He loved and hated the first approach to the suspect.

Imran pressed the call button on an intercom box attached to one of the gate support pillars.

A clicking and crackling came from the loudspeaker, then a scratchy voice. "Yes?"

"Good morning." Imran put a smile on his face for the benefit of the TV camera. "West Midlands police. I'd like to have a chat with the person in charge of the madrassa, please. May we come in?"

Silence for a moment. The silence lengthened, then a new voice came over the intercom. "Is this official business? What is it about?"

"Just routine inquiries, sir. It will be easier to explain if we can sit down and talk to the person responsible for this, umm, school? It is a school, isn't it? This won't take long."

The scratchy intercom became silent.

Imran became aware once again of the birds chattering in the trees, the touch of the gentle breeze on his face, and the faint smell of decaying leaves.

After a short while, a young man came to the gate and let them in.

Imran introduced himself. "And this is Detective Chief Inspector Strange," he added, offering his warrant card for inspection.

"I'm sure you are who you say you are, Commander. I'll take you to see Sheik Maulan, our teacher. Please … " — he pointed to a pastel-blue electric golf cart — "It's a little way."

The tarmac drive curved through the wooded grounds for a hundred yards and debouched onto the sandstone-flagged parking lot at one side of the Edwardian manor house.

Imran and Strange followed the young man through the front door and into a corridor, then were shown through a door on the right into a small library.

"Please make yourself comfortable. Sheik Maulan will be here shortly."

Soft old-fashioned leather chairs surrounded a large table. Bookshelves lined the walls from knee height almost to the ceiling, with leather-bound books crammed end to end, but these were not in English, as they saw from the gold titling in cursive script.

Imran ran his gaze over the row nearest to him. He'd forgotten most of his father's teachings, preferring to become a modern Englishman rather than carry on the traditions of his first-generation grandparents, but he recognized several different editions of the Holy Quran, and these, here, must be the Sunnah. The others would be volumes of fatwas, Islamic histories, and so on. Quite a collection.

He felt uneasy about this visit. How could he justify it if his superiors asked him why this particular place? He could hardly mention his source of information. There'd be no more cooperation if he did. Not to mention if it leaked to the Muslim community.

Strange sat in one of the chairs, tapping his fingers on the table. After examining the books, Imran sat in the chair next to him.

The door opened and Sheik Maulan walked in.

He wasn't at all what Imran had expected: no robe, no religious trappings at all. He was dressed in a pin-striped dark-blue suit, immaculately tailored; expensive shoes; a short, well-kept beard.

He would fit right in to the boardroom of a major financial company. It must take a lot of cash to run this place. Where was the money coming from? A prickling of the skin on the back of his neck.

Imran and Strange rose from their seats.

Mualan gave a short bow. "As-salaam-alaikum."

Imran replied automatically, "Wa-alaikum-salaam."

The Sheik gestured at the chairs. "Please, gentlemen, tafaddal; take a seat." He sat down opposite them and drew up his chair. "To what do I owe the pleasure of this visit?"

"I'm Commander Imran, and this is Detective Chief Inspector Strange. Do you have any objection to our body cameras? It saves having to scribble in notebooks."

"Not at all. But what is this about?"

"Routine inquiries regarding a Mr. Mohamed Malik. Do you remember him?"

"Malik? Oh, yes. He stayed with us for a while, a little over a month? Said he was recovering from domestic problems and preferred to stay at an Islamic center. Quiet person. Why do you ask?"

Strange replied, "Mr. Malik was found dead in the River Avon a little while ago. I attended the scene. We're trying to trace his movements. Could you tell us exactly when he left your facility?"

"I'm not sure, but I'll check. Just a moment." He took out a mobile phone. "Brother Hasan, please check our records for Mohamed Malik, his time of arrival and leaving. Yes. The library. Thank you." The Sheik put the phone away.

Imran glanced at the loaded shelves. "You have a very impressive library here."

"Some books would not be out of place in a museum, Commander. Are you Muslim?"

"I am of the Ummah, yes."

"I see. You will understand that the closer to the source of knowledge, the better, difficult as it is to read these early works. The Arabic of today is not as the Arabic of then."

"I'm sure." This was not a line he wanted to continue.

Someone knocked on the door.

The Sheik called, "Enter."

A young man walked in. "The information you asked for, Sheik." He placed a sheet of paper on the table, gave them a short bow, and left.

The Sheik examined the paper. "Here are the dates, Commander. I have no information as to where he went, however."

"Do you mind if I keep this?"

"Not at all. I'm glad to be of assistance. How did Malik die?"

"I'm not at liberty to say. It's an active investigation."

"I am sorry to hear of his death. He did seem somewhat depressed. But drowning is a bad way to die. Is there anything more I can do for you?"

Strange glanced at Imran, and said, "I'd like to see where he lived."

"Certainly. Although there is nothing much to see, I'm sure." He took out his phone again. "Hasan? Please show our visitors the room that Mr. Malik occupied during his time with us."

Imran folded the paper and placed it in his notebook. Possibly forensics could get a print or DNA trace from it. "Did Malik have any friends here?"

"No. He was a quiet person. Very private."

The Sheik opened the door and showed them out. Hasan was waiting for them.

"Hasan will show you the place. Now, if there is anything else?"

"I believe that will be all. Shukran."

They were shown a neatly made-up bed in a spartan dormitory. There was a basic wooden chair, a small wardrobe, and a small folding table. The wardrobe was empty, with no personal posses-sions of any kind. There was no telling if Malik had even been here. As Imran suspected, anything of interest would be well hidden.

After finishing their inspection, the young man, Hasan, accompanied them to the front gate. It locked behind them with a loud clack.

They stood there for a minute, looking around, then walked down the road to their van, where the drone operator waited with his device, now fully assembled and ready to go.

"All right. Let's get this thing in the air and see what we can see. Approach from the west and keep it high enough not to attract attention."

"Yes, Commander." The operator dismounted from the van holding the drone above his head and tapped a button on his remote control.

The rotors came to life with a fierce buzz. The operator released his grip and it rose quickly into the air.

It flew along the road so as to clear the boundaries of the madrassa, then climbed rapidly until it was barely a dot.

"Got a great view, Commander." The operator swiveled the hand-held monitor so they could all see. The screen reminded Imran of a Google satellite view, but much more detailed.

"I'll pan over to the main building."

The view became more three-dimensional as the camera angle changed. Someone was walking toward the front door. The operator zoomed in on the target's face.

"It's Hasan," Imran said. "Isn't it?"

"Yes. Reporting that we've been escorted off the premises," Strange said.

"You're recording, right?" Imran asked the operator.

"Yes, sir. Stills, too, if you'd like."

"Let's have some. A general view up to the boundaries, then the buildings, and go around the edges. Let's see what access is like if we want to pay them a visit without asking first."

The operator began maneuvering the drone.

Imran turned to Strange and said, "He killed Malik, I'm sure. Proving it will be another matter."

"Why are you so sure, sir? Is there something you're not telling me?"

Imran blew out his cheeks. "Personal contact. You know. Malik was an operative in deep cover. Not one of our people, you understand. You mustn't mention that. Let homicide deal with it."

He turned to the drone operator. "We'll leave as soon as you've finished." Then to Strange, "I'll file the report for Homicide. Let's get back."

EIGHTEEN

Vicky took longer than usual to redo her makeup after her last appearance, wanting it to be perfect for her first real date with the detective. She picked a lipstick to contrast with her dress, chose a smoky eyeshadow, and tried on three pairs of shoes before realizing the first pair was perfect. Would he notice the designer bag? She could hope.

Freddy was still hanging around when she finally emerged from the dressing room. Even though she made it clear that she'd finished her day's work, he followed her down the corridor, jabbering away:

"—simply must do the ten a.m. in that way, dahling, think of the impact it would have. And the lighting, it's drying up your skin, we'll—"

Vicky rounded the corner of the corridor and clutched her bag. Strange was at the door talking to the security guard. She hurried toward him with a smile, leaving Freddy talking to the air.

"Hello!" she called.

Strange turned. His face lit up. The suit he wore obviously wasn't one that he used for the office. It was a very deep blue with faint pinstripes, fitted him perfectly, and was in the latest style.

He was shy, or nursing old wounds perhaps, from his failed marriage. Their lunch date had told her that.

"Well, really!" came Freddy's voice from where she'd left him standing.

Vicky linked arms with Strange, and they went out into the street. It had rained earlier, and the wet pavement struck silver reflections from the street lights. The air, heavy with humidity, smelled fresh.

She was glad she had chosen the burnt-orange sheath. The color popped against Strange's dark blue and touched her curves in exactly the right places. It left her shoulders bare and was cut low in front, even lower at the back. Around her neck, she wore a single strand of real pearls, a twenty-first birthday present from her mother. In her black patent-leather high heels, she was nearly as tall as he was.

He said, "You look terrific! I'm sorry I'm a bit late, I had trouble finding a parking spot."

"Thank you! What's wrong with over there?" she asked, pointing to a space.

"Not big enough," Strange said, somewhat smugly she thought.

"For what?"

"You'll see. It's just around the corner. Only a minute's walk."

What was it with men and their cars? Some treated them with more respect than their friends, lovers, or wives. She hoped he wasn't one of those types.

"You've had your hair done," he noted.

"Oh, you noticed. Do you like it?" He'd better. It had cost a fortune.

He smiled at her. "Smashing."

They turned the corner and she saw a line of parked cars: a tatty Mini, a nearly new Ford, a slightly battered Mercedes, a vintage but pristine dark-blue Jaguar, and a sparkling white sports car. Which was his? The sporty one, she guessed. She would have come to a stop at the white car, but Strange pulled her along to the next one, the Jaguar, and she saw the sign in the window: Police.

"This is yours?" she asked, making an effort to keep her voice neutral. If her friends saw her in this!

"Yes," he replied, pride gleaming in his eyes as he opened the door for her.

A strong smell of vintage leather wafted out. For a moment, it transported her back to when she was little when she liked to hide behind the sofa at her grandfather's house. She would never forget that smell.

"My God, how old is it?" she blurted before she could stop herself.

A hurt expression crossed his face. "It was made in fifty-nine. XK-150SSS, same as the one that won the Le Mans motor race five times in the nineteen-fifties. Forerunner of the E-Type." He reached across and helped her with the seat belt. "Of course, I had to have seat belts installed. They weren't compulsory until sixty-five."

The pleated leather seat fit her like an old shoe.

Strange heaved at the ungainly steering wheel as he drove backward, then forward, to get out. "No power steering," he explained. "Wouldn't suit most men, not these days. But I care for things from this period."

He got the Jag's nose out into the street and put his foot down. The rear of the car dipped and Vicky was pinned to her seat by the surge of raw power. Strange braked hard as he came up to the main road and the safety belt bit into her.

Was she going to regret this? She gritted her teeth.

Strange went on about technical specifications while she started to think her worst fears about the Jag would be realized. How could she ever compete with the love of his life? "The three-point-eight engine was in production until recently, so there's no problem with spare parts. It costs a fortune to maintain, though. Really advanced for its time, the engine being all alloy and twin overhead cam … walnut dash. …" He touched the wood. Finally, he ran out of steam. "I'm babbling, aren't I?" he said.

"A bit." She looked out to see where they were headed. They were passing through a mixed area. Normally she wouldn't venture here, but she felt reassured by Strange's presence.

"We'll be there in a minute. Do you like South American food?"

"I've never tried it," she admitted. "What's it like?" It sounded spicy, or would it be a meat place? She hoped not.

"Actually, I'm not sure. A friend recommended this place." He maneuvered the big car through a narrow passageway and parked it with some difficulty.

He held the door open while she climbed out.

She stumbled on the cobblestone yard and he caught her by the elbow.

"Thanks." Above, a red neon sign announced "La Doñita."

Strange pushed open the door.

Vicky walked through the entrance into a babble of conversations, clinking cutlery, and, in the background, the type of pan pipes music popularly associated with the high Andes. She stood looking around while Strange closed the door behind him. A couple of dozen tables spread with cheerful printed cloth, mostly occupied by couples and foursomes. Rustic brick walls, unglazed clay wine bottles, odd-looking musical instruments, woven blankets, zig-zag stripes. At the far end of the room, servers came and went.

A slim young man with jet-black hair and olive skin came up to them from the far end of the room. "Buenas noches, good evening. Do you have a reservation, sir and madam?"

His grin was infectious, and Vicky found herself smiling in response. Perhaps her nervousness was unwarranted.

"For eight o'clock," Strange replied, then checked his watch. "We're a bit late. Sorry."

"No importa," the waiter said, still smiling. "If you will please to follow me?" On the way to their table, he bumped into a chair but caught it before it fell over. He straightened the cloth on their table but nearly upset the table candle.

Strange pulled out her chair before seating himself next to her. An old-fashioned gentleman. Well, nothing wrong with that.

They ordered nachos as a starter. The dish came with a large bowl of corn tortilla chips, a smaller bowl of cheese dip, and a plate of pickled green jalapeños. For the main course, Strange decided on chicken and a puree based on sweetcorn, with fried plantain, while she tried stuffed green peppers with picadillo.

The food was too greasy for her liking, but she didn't want to leave a mountain on her plate. She bit into a green vegetable of some kind that had been lurking inside a pile of overdone minced beef and went "mmf" as red hot fire lanced through her mouth. She swallowed it before she could stop herself.

To her embarrassment, the people at the next table were watching her with undisguised amusement.

"You don't care for the food, do you? I'm sorry. I thought it would be a change," Strange said. "Let's head off somewhere quieter for coffee, what do you think?"

"La Bamba" came from the ceiling loudspeakers. Over in one corner, a large group of people had pushed three tables together. Now they began singing along with the music in loud, happy, drunken voices. The servers hurried past the tables, giving the group nervous looks.

"I think I'd better ask for the bill." Strange inclined his head slightly in the direction of the singing.

There was a lot left in the bottle of Californian white wine on their table. Maybe it would put out the fire in her mouth. She filled her glass and gulped it while Strange gestured with increasing irritation for a server. Eventually one came over and he asked for the bill.

"La Bamba" had stopped, and now Trini Lopez sang of how

down in the cantina they were serving green beans and something or other she couldn't quite make out.

Strange paid for the meal, then turned to Vicky and opened his mouth to say something, when a female voice half-shouted, "No! Stop!"

Strange rose out of his seat.

It was the mob in the corner. One of the men had snared a passing server and dragged her onto his lap. She had a tray full of plates and tried to keep hold of it, then the drunk fondled her with his free hand and the tray went up in the air, plates crashing to the floor.

"I'll deal with it. It won't take a moment," Strange said, grim-faced.

Before she could say a word, he left the table and set off across the room. Was this really happening?

Vicky got to her feet and looked toward the commotion in the corner just in time to see the man who'd had the server on his lap throw a pint of beer over Strange.

The double doors to the servery opened, and a man in chef's clothes came out, then headed toward the troublemaker's table.

At that moment, her stomach began churning, and she could swear it had a voice: "Out! Out!" She grabbed her handbag and fled to the bathroom.

She barely made it. Ripping paper from the roll and throwing it on the floor to protect her knees, she got down and vomited into the bowl. After wiping her face with more paper, she got to her feet, but caught the hem of her dress on her heel and ripped it.

Vicky made it out of the stall and to the mirror, where she wiped off her smeared mascara and reapplied her lipstick.

Thanking her stars there had been no one to see her distress, she fixed her hair as best she could and went back into the restaurant, where she found Strange at their table, talking to the restaurant manager. He was holding a paper napkin to a cut over his eye, and his suit was soaked in beer. There was no sign of the drunks who had caused the trouble.

The manager said, "I'm sorry for your bad experience. There is no charge for anything. We will be glad to serve you any time you'd like to return."

Strange turned to her. "Vicky. I'm terribly sorry. Those louts have gone."

"It wasn't your fault. You stood up for that server. Thank you for that. A lot of men would have looked the other way." His suit jacket looked pretty much ruined. "My place isn't far, and we're both a real mess; we need a bit of TLC. If you like—"

"I'd like that very much."

As they made their way out, a pop group from the fifties or sixties was singing "Tequila!"

Strange knew the city so well that she hardly needed to give directions. Traffic was light, and the journey to her flat took only ten minutes.

Vicky lived in the bottom half of a big, old Victorian house on Pershore Road. A batty old woman shared the top floor with a tribe of cocker spaniels. As Vicky and Strange entered, the dogs started barking.

"Sorry! I've got used to it. They belong to my upstairs neighbor, the dog lady. There's only one bathroom, so I'll go first. But take your jacket off. I won't be too long."

She went into her bathroom and took a shower.

Fresh powder and her silk robe restored her self-esteem. A large spoonful of antacid put her stomach at rest. Then she found a spare dressing-gown for Strange; it had been a freebie from some hotel.

She came back and handed the robe to Strange. "There you go. I left a towel for you."

Rain pattered against the windows as she sat in what had been the drawing-room of the old house, surrounded by awards and mementos. She turned the stereo on, loaded a Janni album, and brushed her hair out, letting it tumble around her shoulders.

The album finished, and moments later Strange came through the door wearing the robe.

NINETEEN

"That's a lot better! You smelled like a brewery accident," Vicky said.

Strange laughed, delighting in the sound of her voice. "I imagine so!"

"You'll have to take that suit to a dry cleaner first thing tomorrow. If it can be rescued, that is."

"Tomorrow?"

"You didn't think I was going to let you go now, did you?" She turned her emerald green eyes up to him, then took a step forward and delicately stroked his wet cheek. "That cut over your eye looks worse than it is, I think."

"I hope so."

"So what happened? I saw you rush in to save the lady's honor."

Strange winced. "I told him to keep his hands to himself, then the other idiot shoved me. Then the first one punched me in the face."

"So you arrested him?"

"No, the waitress said she wouldn't make a complaint. And all the paperwork. ... The manager threw them out, then I thought for a minute that you'd left. I wouldn't have blamed you." He gently held her shoulders.

"My knight in shining armor, rushing to save distressed damsels." Vicky grinned at him. "Do you see yourself as Lancelot, Gordon? I've always loved that name. I wonder what they did after the tournaments." She laughed and batted her eyelashes at him.

"I can imagine. A dropped hanky, a sideways look, a fluttering fan. ...." She moved into his arms, and pressed herself to him. "Mmm. Why, Gordon, I do believe you would have enjoyed living in those times. Lancelot, indeed!"

"Vicky, I'm not used to dating. It's been a long time—"

"Shhh." She kissed him gently.

He kissed back awkwardly, putting his arm around her waist.

She took his hand and pulled him gently along the hallway.

He followed, aroused by the way her buttocks moved under the shimmering silk of her robe. My ex never once took the lead, he thought. They passed a door to the left, then came to another.

Vicky turned the handle and pushed it open. Warm yellow light spilled from inside. She pulled him into her bedroom. A delicate scent arose from a large vase full of white roses. Their petals reminded him of the curves of her face.

She reached out, threw her arms about his waist, and pulled him into her. He took her face in his hands, his breath deepening. She turned her face upward to him. Her eyes were wide. Their lips met, parted, and his tongue felt the first inquisitive touch of hers. He trembled like a teenager on his first date, slipping out of control, falling. Their lips parted again and he took a ragged breath.

His hands fell to her shoulders. Delicately, he parted the robe, then explored her soft skin with his fingertips, running them down her neck and tracing her collarbones.

She reached up and removed his tie, then undid his shirt, button by button.

He reached down, trembling more, and brought his right hand to the small of her back, bringing her close. He felt her breasts against his chest.

Vicky sighed, then moved her hands downward out of sight. He felt her shoulders move as she did something with her hands, then her robe fell open. Her hands caressed the back of his neck. She sank down until she was sitting on her bed.

Strange sat next to her, gazing into her face. Her eyes held mysteries for him. He reached out with his right hand, cupped her breast, teased the nipple. An electric current flowed through his blood, pulsing, hot.

He kissed her again, this time more strongly, exploring her mouth. Vicky's breath drew in sharply, catching briefly in her throat, as she ran the edge of her nails down his back, then pulled his shirt open. Strange moved his mouth from her lips to her neck, breathed into her ear, and nibbled delicately at her satin skin. He was having difficulty controlling his breathing.

"Wait, wait a moment," she whispered. "The bathroom's over there. Top drawer, the black box. Don't take too long."

When he came back to her, she had turned the bedside lamp down. His breath caught in his throat at the sight of her golden-skinned body. He sank down beside her, then they kissed again, deeply, exploring each other.

The touch of her skin felt like white fire on his body when she linked one of her long, firm, thighs with his. His breath came in harsh gasps as he tried to maintain control, and a small groan escaped from his lips as he cupped her breasts. He groaned again as her fingers squeezed him. She followed his contours with the tips of her fingers.

Then it was her turn. Strange took her nipples into his lips, traced overlapping damp circles with his tongue, stroked his finger-tips down the satin skin of her thighs, converged on her center. He gave her no mercy, teasing her until he felt her shudder violently and cry out.

They made love gently, delighting in each other, knowing there would be no time more special than the first, savoring the moments, holding back, until Strange could resist no longer and it was his turn to shout.

Afterward, it seemed to Strange that the very air around them had to take time to settle. He hugged her to him, gazed into her eyes.

"You've been in my thoughts so much, I can't do my job properly," he murmured.

"I had my doubts about dating a cop, you know. I mean, it's not the kind of job people associate with romance. But not anymore."

"You wouldn't have been the first. To have doubts, I mean." He tried to keep the bitterness out of his voice.

"She hurt you very badly, didn't she?"

"I miss my daughter. My ex-wife works things so I hardly ever get to see her."

"You can start taking that wall down, now, Gordon. Don't worry. Everything will be all right, you'll see."

———

DAWN LIGHT SHOWED AROUND THE EDGES OF THE CURTAINS WHEN Strange awoke. For a moment he was disoriented, but then he heard the shower running, and it all came back to him. His temple throbbed painfully. He explored the cut over his eye and winced. Careful not to make a sound, he padded across the soft carpet to the door of her bathroom, tested it, and found it unlocked.

He eased the door open and joined her in the steam. She shrieked playfully, turned, grabbed him round the waist, then in other places. His hands roamed her calves, her thighs, her narrow waist, her breasts.

Afterward, he sponged the worst of the stains off his suit while she made a quick breakfast of croissants with thick-cut Chivers marmalade and Kenya Blue Mountain coffee.

At eight, they hugged each other in the doorway, lingering over their goodbye kiss.

"I love you so much," he said.

"The first time we met, I had the feeling you were special. Take care of yourself. For me."

Strange climbed back into the Jaguar. He wound the window down and leaned out, holding the car with his foot on the clutch.

"I'll find a better restaurant the next time we go out," he joked.

"No," she replied seriously. "I'll choose the restaurant next time. … Gordon, call me. Or I'll call you. Like, this afternoon!"

"You can bet on that," he said, blowing her a kiss. Gently, so as not to spray gravel, he let out the clutch and pulled away.

TWENTY

It was a perfect day for mayhem.

Zafir and Hasan, with Zafir driving, took the stripped van up B roads, to avoid cameras, and then up the M40, via the M5, to the M6, and the North-West. They both wore baseball caps and sunglasses so as not to leave useful images on CCTV.

Hasan bought the van from a web ad especially for the trip, providing fake information to the seller. Then, in the madrassa workshop, Zafir and Rais used an angle-grinder on the chassis and engine serial numbers and removed the VIN.

The cargo area now held two backpacks. One contained thirty kilograms of sulfur, potassium chlorate, accelerant, ignition devices, ammo, and two gas masks. The other, heavier due to the sheet lead protection, concealed a plastic bottle of cobalt-60 nitrate. A Winchester pump-action shotgun, illegally modified to allow a larger magazine, lay between the backpacks wrapped in a blanket.

Zafir suspected that the lead shielding would be insufficient but didn't care; Hasan would lug it for the last stretch.

At five-fifty a.m., Zafir joined the M58 but turned off after three exits, down a series of country lanes that he'd studied on Google

Street View. He was heading for an abandoned plastics factory located on the bank of a river, more than a mile north.

At six forty-seven, Zafir parked the van on the grass verge of the access road that led to an abandoned factory.

The sun peeked above a bank of clouds on the eastern horizon. A hint of brine from the estuary drifted in on the light breeze.

"How did you find this place?" Hasan asked.

"A brother. He's in DEFRA, the ministry. He has a list of abandoned and disused buildings — and their hazards."

Hasan got out, carrying a battery-powered angle grinder. He walked to the gate.

Zafir watched Hasan cut off the padlock, worrying about the shriek of the disc cutter, but it didn't last long.

The gate swung open.

Zafir put the van in gear and drove through.

Hasan secured the gate with some rusty steel wire and climbed back in for the short ride from the gate to the factory.

Zafir drove the van around the side of the factory and parked it next to a loading bay. They both got out and walked down the side, toward the back. As they rounded the corner, Zafir grabbed Hasan's arm and pulled him into the shadow of the wall.

About sixty feet away, a thin column of dirty gray smoke was rising from the stovepipe of a watchman's hut.

The door opened. An old man hobbled out and gazed into the sunrise. He wore the kind of clothes found in a jumble sale: pin-stripe trousers from some city gent, stained and two sizes too large; old-fashioned black boots with string for laces; and a sweater brightly patterned in zigzag lines. He stretched, yawned, and went back in, closing the door behind him.

"There's just him, I reckon," Hasan said.

"Yeah. I think you're right. Let's do the bastard."

"Why? I don't think the Sheik would want that." Hasan shook his head.

"How could *you* know what he'd want? I know. It's just another kuffar." Zafir pulled out the stainless thirty-eight revolver stuck in his belt, thinking, Hasan is so fuckin' stupid sometimes. "Right, let's go. We'll leave everything in the van for now. We'll have to be quick."

"Wait a sec. I've got an idea." Hasan scuttled to one side and dug around in the pile of waste. He pulled a lump of cotton waste out of the junk.

They ran across the waste ground as fast as they could, avoiding tangles of wire and scrap. Once at the hut, Zafir offered his clasped hands and boosted Hasan silently onto the roof.

Hasan took the lump of greasy cotton waste and stuffed it firmly into the top of the stove pipe, then crept to the edge and let himself back down.

Zafir flattened himself against the wall next to the door.

It didn't take long. Zafir heard the sound of chair legs scraping on a wooden floor, then the hut vibrated with footsteps and the door banged open.

Zafir pulled the trigger and shot him in the face. The shot seemed incredibly loud. Blood and bits sprayed from the back of the watchman's head, and he collapsed backward into the hut.

Close behind the hut, a steep grassy slope fell away into the muddy brown water of the river Smolt. The water gurgled and slapped as it rushed by. It was on the ebb, and just after high tide.

A swathe of flotsam, wooden beams, discolored plastic toys, used condoms, bottles of every description, and matted vegetation, formed an irregular border on the lower edge of the bank. It stank of decayed plant matter. Chunks of white polystyrene foam that had escaped from the factory formed a large part of the litter. Nearby, large blocks of the stuff lay scattered on the ground.

"Right, that's it. In with him." Zafir gestured toward the river. He grabbed one of the dead man's feet. Hasan grabbed the other. They towed the body to the bank and rolled it over the edge, then watched as the current took it downstream.

"Right. Now for the factory," Zafir said.

"We have to unload the van first."

THEY LUGGED THE BACKPACKS TO THE FACTORY'S MAIN DELIVERY portal. It was a massive affair, made of rusty, accordion-pleated steel, with an employee entrance door set into one side.

Zafir grinned happily and reached inside his jacket, then with a flourish produced a short jimmy. He rammed the sharpened end into the top of the door, next to one of the hinges, and put his weight on the bar. The top of the door bowed, and he heard a sharp snap as the hinge pin broke.

Once inside, they explored the process equipment quickly and came to the place where the raw stock was melted down.

"Look at that. There's got to be a hundred gallons of plastic in there," Hasan said.

"Yeah. We need to start a fire, get it good and hot, lots of smoke. The sulfur should burn, make a toxic cloud, carry the radiation."

The power was off. If it hadn't been for that, and the musty smell of decay hanging in the stale air, Zafir could have believed that the equipment was ready to start up. A giant steel vat sat like a huge mop bucket next to a furnace.

Zafir climbed a ladder up a storage bin that sat against the wall of the building. He shouted down to Hasan. "It's half full of small plastic bricks. Just what we need."

He pulled a handle on the side of the bin. A torrent of cubes poured out of the bottom of the bin, onto the floor.

Zafir sprang off the ladder. "Let's get going. Cram the furnace with these plastic bricks. Put the backpack in there, too. Then pour half of the accelerant on it. I'll take the sulfur; that's our insurance."

Zafir took a can of gas out of the first backpack and handed it to Hasan, then headed out the back door with the other items still in the pack. He began just outside the door, pouring a thick trail of sulfur mixed with chlorate, walking steadily away, until thirty or forty feet from the door he came to the factory's dump, a clutter of decaying cardboard boxes, polystyrene waste, discarded wood pallets, and other junk. Here he concentrated his efforts, dumping the rest of the sulfur and oxidizer in a heap.

He threw the backpack on top and was halfway to the factory when he caught movement out of the corner of his eye.

Zafir turned. A police patrol car pulled up at the gate.

Damn. Zafir was exposed in the open.

"Hey! You, over there!"

A second cop got out of the car, looking straight at Zafir.

"What?" Zafir shouted.

"Come over here, sonny!"

"Yes, sir. Be right there!"

The cop at the gate said something to the other — Zafir couldn't quite catch what — and began untwisting the wire from the gate. The other one jumped back in the car.

Zafir sprinted to the back door, threw it open, and dived inside.

Hasan had finished the preparations and was standing a respectable distance from the cobalt backpack.

"It's the police! Out the front!" Zafir grabbed the shotgun and ran for the front door. Over his shoulder, he shouted, "Light the fire!"

TWENTY-ONE

Strange eased off the accelerator and moved into the near-side lane of the A45 Coventry Road, slowing from over eighty to fifty-five. He had the blue lights and siren going. The interchange was coming up for Birmingham International Airport.

Commander Imran was sitting in the front passenger seat.

"How are we for time, sir?" Strange asked.

"Not bad. But it's already been nearly half an hour since the radiation alert."

"Half an hour? Christ." Strange drove as fast as he could through the perimeter roads to Monarch's engineering hangar, where he parked.

The Eurocopter EC135 began spooling up as Imran and Strange ran across the tarmac. Imran climbed in, and when Strange followed, he found the two tactical police officers already seated and checking out their equipment. He took his seat, fastened the safety belt, and put on the headset. Now he could talk to Imran without having to shout over the engine noise.

"Any updates, Commander?"

"Yes, just now. The wind, thank God, is taking the plume out to sea, to the northwest. Squires Gate RIMNET station is picking up a little, but there's a dangerous reading at Ronaldsway, building up by the minute. Gamma radiation. It will be over Northern Ireland soon — we'll get reports from Aldergrove and GlenAnne. Depending on wind speed."

"What d'you know about these monitoring stations?" Strange asked.

"There's about two hundred of them, mainly around the coastline. The first ones date back to the Windscale reactor fire, but most of 'em were built following the Chernobyl disaster in eighty-six."

"So, a bloody big fire, a plastics factory gone up, and gamma radiation? It's got to be—" Strange noticed that they were moving slowly forward. The civilian pilot came on the headset, requesting takeoff clearance from the tower.

The tower granted clearance, and their speed increased to a fast walk.

"Got to be what? The madrassa? That phony Sheik?" Imran said.

"Yes." Strange had flown on the chopper before but could never get used to the feeling of the ground dropping away, and everything on it rapidly dwindling. Not like a proper aircraft, where the Gs pushed you back in your seat.

The pilot came on to tell them their ETA at John Lennon Airport in Liverpool.

"Can we go directly to the scene, please?" Imran asked.

"Sir, we can't get that near because there's a national alert. That airspace is closed."

"Well, how near can you get?"

"Two kilometers east of the factory, there are fields there and a farm road."

"All right. Can you patch me through to the officer in charge, please?"

"Yes, just a moment."

The headsets went dead for a minute, then one of the two tactical officers came on. "Putting you through to Commander Carragher. He's your counterpart, North West ATG."

"Thanks. I've met him before."

The headset went quiet again, then a new voice came on. "Imran? That you?"

"Yes. Shaun, isn't it?"

"You remembered. What's your ETA?"

Imran checked his watch. "Thirty minutes. Can you update me, please?"

"Of course. A routine police patrol spotted a van parked next to the abandoned plastics factory. Thought scrap metal thieves. They went to take a look and were shot at. Then the fire started."

"And they're still in the building? The van's still there?"

"Oh, yes. My men have blocked the gate with their car. The fire brigade is on the scene but can't get near. And now we're evacuating and setting up an RMU, Radiation Monitoring Unit."

"I see. Can you have a car ready when we arrive?"

"Already done."

THE EUROCOPTER LANDED IN A MEADOW NEXT TO A SEWAGE FARM two miles from the burning factory. Imran thanked the crew and they took off immediately, because the CAA alert had increased in scope — the cloud of radioactive smoke was beginning to spread out.

A car from the local force took them to the scene. The road, not much more than a track, really, twisted and turned and then split into two. Strange held on to his seatbelt. The signpost to the left said the village of Allenby was one and a quarter miles distant. Already he saw a plume of black smoke hanging in the sky.

They drove past two fire appliances that had parked on the grass verge, then past the factory gate, and parked next to a police command car, where the road ended in waste ground.

Strange surveyed the scene. The lane ran east-west and was bordered by a chain-link fence. The fence gate now hung open. Beyond it, the narrow factory access road ran south for fifty yards, then curved around to the east to avoid a low earth mound. Ten or so yards after, the road curved back to the south, ending at a concrete patio that extended down both sides of the factory. The south side of the building was on the far side and out of his view.

Imran's counterpart, Carragher, a florid-faced man of about fifty, stepped forward. They shook hands. Carragher said, "The RIMNET station is monitoring the smoke. Right now, it's blowing out to sea, but if the wind turns, we'll be in real trouble. It's carrying some kind of lethal radioactive dust, they tell me. One last thing: I've got officers with assault carbines on the perimeter. This is my show, and you're here as observers."

Strange asked, "The far side of the factory. Have we got that covered?"

"Not yet. The ground drops away to the river. It's over ten feet deep, and twenty across. There's no bridge for miles. There's only one way in or out. They won't get away."

Thick black smoke was pouring from the factory chimney, high into the air, spreading out as it cooled until it formed the shape of a giant anvil fit for a devil's hammer.

A young constable from Allenby stood nearby talking into his radio. After a moment, he put the radio into his pocket and hurried toward them. He spoke to Carragher, but loud enough for Imran and Strange to hear.

"Sir, the chief constable was on the line. The RIMNET station reports high levels of radioactivity in that cloud. A shipping warning was issued, but the wind is changing. If it blows back inland .... We must put out the fire or there'll be a major disaster. People in the town are being told to stay indoors."

Strange asked, "How many are in there?"

"Commander Carragher believes two, sir. At least one is armed. There's little cover. We tried making a rush for it. Had a man down. Shotgun, and it wasn't small stuff; more like buckshot. Keep your head low, sir. We're out of range here."

"Can we get closer?"

"There's a dry ditch just here." The constable pointed. "It runs around the perimeter."

"Let's take a look," Strange replied. He glanced at Carragher. "OK with you, Commander?"

"Just don't get killed." Carragher turned to deal with one of the firefighters.

Strange got down in the ditch. The young Allenby copper and Imran crouched behind him. They crept along on their hands and knees, keeping their heads down.

They reached the end of the ditch, still thirty or forty yards from the factory. "Now what, constable?" Strange asked.

"It's a bit difficult, sir. We'll have to be quick. It's a bit of a scramble across this broken ground." He pointed ahead and to their left, where an earth berm partially concealed the factory. Two officers stood behind it, using it as cover.

"Yes, constable, I think we'll manage. I must remember to bring my walking frame next time, though," Imran said.

One at a time they ran, crouched, from the ditch to the berm. A clutter of equipment lay there: three heavy plastic riot shields, several smoke flares, a loud hailer, a coil of nylon rope, and a torn and bloodstained police jacket.

"It was Jones," one of the officers explained. "Had to be a bloody hero. Silly sod made a run for the factory. He only got ten yards. He's got buckshot pellets in him, but they reckon he'll be OK."

"Is this it? Just this team?" Strange asked.

"We've got a Transit riot van with four chaps inside, H&K machine pistols, ready to go. That should be plenty against a shotgun and maybe a pistol or two. There's a couple of heavy crews coming over from Chorley HQ. They should be here in half an hour."

"I doubt we've got time to wait. The wind's shifting. If we don't get this fire out, and fast, half the county will be contaminated. Of course, I'm only an observer." Strange imagined what Carragher, a tall, rangy man, was thinking: Should he put his crew up against the unknowns in the factory, or risk the wind shifting and not getting the fire out in time?

The officer's radio squelched, and Commander Carragher's voice came on the channel. "Foxtrot Four, Foxtrot Four, Echo control, over."

Another voice replied: "Foxtrot Four here, Echo."

"Foxtrot, go in now, we can't afford to wait."

"Roger, Echo. Moving off now."

"That's the team in the Transit, sir," the officer said.

Strange looked to his left. The Transit was through the gate and accelerating up the access road. It began rounding the curve.

Three shotgun blasts came from the factory.

Steam and boiling water exploded from the van's radiator. The second shot struck the windshield grille and ricocheted away. The third ripped through the anti-missile mesh as if it were gossamer and blew a hole in the polycarbonate screen. The van stalled, water pouring from its radiator.

Strange lifted his phone camera to get a view over the berm. They were about thirty yards from the right corner of the building. Although they were at a forty-degree angle to the front wall, he clearly saw the barrel of a weapon protruding from a small circular window near the top. The metal furnace chimney, farther back, glowed a dull red. It had set fire to tar on the roof; streams of molten bitumen were falling in graceful parabolas of yellow flame.

Imran took out his radio. "Carragher? Imran."

Carragher's voice replied, "Yes?"

"You need to get your team out of there. The van's had it."

Semi-automatic carbines opened fire from the main road. Strange held his phone up again and saw powdered brick exploding around the window. Someone inside pulled their weapon back in.

"That's got their attention." Strange half turned. "Smoke! Come on!"

Imran stooped to the equipment pile. He picked up two smoke flares and handed one to Strange. They pulled the rings and hurled them over the berm toward the factory.

Strange held up his phone again. Dense white smoke obscured the factory. The breeze was taking it away, toward the road. He looked around the left side of the berm, to see the Transit. Smoke enveloped it. The rear doors opened. Two officers in ballistic vests jumped out, then helped a third officer, whose arm hung uselessly. They ran down the road toward Carragher's group. He clenched his fists in anger at the twats in the factory, Carragher, the shit situation.

The two small factory windows overlooked thirty yards of bare ground littered with factory debris. No way to cover that distance, not against a shotgun. Not if he wanted to stay alive.

TWENTY-TWO

Z afir spun around from his position where, from one of the
two windows, he was raining shotgun slugs. "Hasan! I'm
running out of ammo. Time for the sulfur. Get over here.
Bring the respirators."

Hasan ran to retrieve the respirators, climbed the iron stairs, and
handed one to Zafir.

"Here." Zafir handed the shotgun to Hasan and took the pistol.
"Put your respirator on, keep the road covered. I'm going to light the
sulfur."

Just as Hasan was about to look out the window, several rifle
rounds slammed into the brickwork around it, and two or three
came through, ricocheting off the far wall.

Hasan flinched and dodged to the side.

"Keep the front covered, brother, this'll be a minute." Zafir
bounded down the stairs and ran to the side door where the sulfur
trail ended. He tugged the respirator over his face, grabbed a
cigarette lighter from his pocket, and ignited the trail.

The sulfur-chlorate flamed. A wave of combustion ran out the door, licked the waste ground, and sped to the dump. The large sulfur cache caught fire, and an eery, beautiful, deadly tongue of blue flame flared one, then two yards high.

Zafir smiled, satisfied that although he couldn't see it, the cloud of sulfur dioxide would be spreading rapidly in the light breeze toward the police positions.

"Allah hu akbar!" Zafir laughed and ran back up the stairs to where Hasan stood, covering the access road. "We'll see the results in a minute," he said, his voice muffled by the full-face plastic cover.

Hasan nodded. He looked out of the window, left and right.

Several more rifle rounds hit around the window. Zafir heard the sound of a marrow hit by a mallet. Pink matter spattered his respirator. As he wiped the face mask with his sleeve, the shotgun clattered to the ground outside. Hasan's body fell back, tipped over the guard rail, and fell to the floor below.

"Fuck. Should've kept your head down, bruv." Zafir leaped down the stairs, two at a time. Hasan's body lay nearby; the respirator had come off what was left of his head. The furnace was making a dull roaring sound. Waves of heat scorched him as he hurried past to the offices at the rear.

He waited there for the chemical attack to do its job. No chance now to escape in the van. The police would have the road covered, and anyway, there was only one way out. The river, though, gave him an idea.

Zafir stood at a rear side window and watched the police retreating in disorder. The sulfur had got to them, but it also was beginning to get through his respirator. Time to go.

He exited the back door, wormed his way across the concrete, and dropped into a drainage channel. Rifle fire cracked through the air over his head.

He wormed his way downslope, grabbing a slab of polystyrene waste along the way, until he reached the riverbank. The tide had turned and now flowed inland, toward the farms and town. The level had risen to a couple of feet below the edge of the bank. He slipped over the edge and into the dark water, resting his upper body on the buoyant slab. Steering with his feet, he let the tide carry him upstream, away from the spreading cloud of sulfur dioxide and cobalt plastic soot.

TWENTY-THREE

Crouched behind the earth mound, Strange spoke urgently into his mobile. "No, I don't care if he is with the minister. This is a life or death — yes, at Allenby."

A whiff of something horribly acrid caught at the back of his throat, and he reeled back, choking. "My God. What's that?"

Imran began coughing violently. "Chemicals! Get back, before we're poisoned!"

Strange didn't know Imran could run so fast. All the way to the police car they ran, with his lungs on fire and back muscles clenched, fearing a shot from behind. They dived in the car, then two other officers crammed in, and the driver took off down the lane, closely followed by the van carrying the police sniper team and Commander Carragher's command SUV.

Two miles down the road they braked to a halt. Imran lowered the window. No gas.

Imran flung the door open, staggered out of the car, and stood on the grass verge with tears streaming from his eyes, lungs heaving, coughing.

Carragher's car pulled up and slewed half across the verge. The passenger door opened and Carragher fell out onto his hands and knees. "Imran! Do something!" he gasped.

Imran pulled out his phone and dialed his headquarters in Birmingham.

"Hello? It's Commander Imran. Get me the Home Office. Now, dammit."

He put the mobile on speakerphone so Strange could hear. After a couple of minutes delay, Leavey came on the line. "Imran? Where's Carragher? I just stepped out of the COBRA committee meeting — the Prime Minister is chairing it."

"Commander Carragher is out of commission, sir." Imran stopped to cough and retch. "Some kind of chemical attack. We've had to evacuate. Fire brigade is on its way with self-contained breathing equipment."

Leavey's voice squawked over the tiny speaker. "You've got to get that fire out, Imran. If the wind direction changes—"

"I know, sir."

Movement caught Strange's gaze. He turned and saw a Fire Service Operational Support Vehicle edging along the narrow road.

"Strange!" Imran pointed at the OSV. "See if they have breathing apparatus!"

"Sir!" Still coughing, Strange stumbled a short distance down the road and held up his hand. The OSV stopped, and its doors opened. Firefighters climbed down.

"We've got to get in there to stop a sniper, but the air is full of some kind of gas," Strange explained. The firefighters ran to the side of the OSV and flung open a door. One of them helped Strange put on a breathing set, and another went running with a set for Imran.

The lead firefighter said, "There's a New Dimension Vehicle on the way. Maybe half an hour. Are you trained with this kit, sir?"

"No. But we can't send your men in. Active shooter." Strange examined the air supply regulator.

"You can't go in alone. Not wearing breathing apparatus. It's only good for thirty minutes, tops."

Strange glanced over to where Imran sat, still coughing and spluttering. Imran had given up trying to put the breathing set on. Mucous was running from his nose.

The firefighter said, "He can't drive. We've got to put this out. I'll drive."

"Drive what?" Strange pointed at the Operational Support Vehicle. "That?"

"No. The light pump." The firefighter pointed down the lane, to where a medium-size truck was approaching. "Two armed officers can hang on the back; we'll need to get them kitted up with air."

Carragher made his way to Imran. His eyes were bright red and he was crying. "Strange! We've got to put out—" He bent over and had a coughing fit, unable to finish.

"Get me two armed support officers," Strange told him. Observer status, sure. Carragher was going to be out of commission for the foreseeable future. Not that he felt that good himself.

The truck pulled up, and two more firefighters got out.

Strange had an idea. "You've got any strong tape? Duct?"

"Yes, sure." One of them rolled up a side shutter, delved in, and produced a large roll of gray tape.

"Good. Get two vests from those officers there." Strange pointed at the armed support group. "Tape them onto the windshield, leave a slit to look out of. Meanwhile," he looked at the firefighter helping him with the breathing apparatus, "Train me to use this. In two minutes."

IT WAS CLOSER TO FIVE MINUTES WHEN STRANGE AND HIS SQUAD began their approach. The truck butted through the mesh factory gate, and they set off up the drive that ended at the factory loading bay. Two AROs, armed response officers, hung off the rear of the vehicle, using it for cover. Each wore full armor and breathing equipment, and carried a SIG Sauer SIG516 rifle.

Strange had his nine-millimeter SIG226 service pistol ready and the passenger side window rolled down, in case he needed to lean out and fire.

The lead firefighter, once they were through the gate, accelerated the truck to thirty miles an hour.

They arrived at the loading bay without incident. The two AROs secured the immediate area. The side door hung slightly open, with a broken padlock dangling.

Strange flattened himself to one side and took out his phone. Camera on. Put his hand and phone through the door — video mode — quick one-eighty and out. He checked the video. No one to be seen in the smoky murk.

One of the AROs shouted, "Sir!"

Strange glanced to where the officer stood against the wall, at the front corner of the building. "Yes?" It was difficult to speak through the respirator mask.

The officer ran over. "Shotgun, sir. On the ground in front."

"Maybe that's why we took no fire on the approach. Right. Let's take a look."

The two AROs went in, took a brief look, and came out. One said, "Sir, there's a body. The place is full of smoke. Nobody can be in there, not without portable air."

"You're right. Let's get some backup." He turned to the firefighter. "Can you make a start on that fire? I'm going to take a look at the body."

He tapped one of the AROs on the arm and signaled his intention.

Strange moved to the front corner and stuck his phone around the wall. Nothing on the camera. He exchanged the phone for his pistol and moved around the corner in a crouch.

It seemed all clear. The body of a man lay about four feet from the wall. He must have fallen from the window above. Part of the head was missing. The face lay in a pool of blood. The arms flung carelessly, the leg bent sharp.

He heard an engine. Strange looked up and saw the larger fire appliance moving up the approach road, flanked by several police officers wearing portable air.

Seized with a fit of sudden enormous anger at all of this pure *shite*, Strange needed to identify the body. He pulled out his mobile and took some pictures. Then he bent down, took hold of an arm, and turned the body over.

What was left of the man's face had been distorted by the energy of the rifle round. Masked in blood, the top of the skull was missing, the brain exposed. He took a photo.

Strange looked around and spotted a piece of cotton waste. He used it to wipe the congealing blood from the body's face. It looked familiar.

With a shock, he realized it was the young man who had welcomed them to the madrassa.

TWENTY-FOUR

Strange and Imran took the tube to Euston and then the express train to Birmingham.

"That was a hell of a roasting the COBRA committee gave us." Imran said quietly, even though no one else was sitting nearby. "So *Amaq* is claiming it as one of theirs. Do we wait for forensics? I don't think so."

Strange pulled down the window blind. "It was him, I'm sure. The guy at the madrassa."

"Your eyes were messed up with that gas, which is why we're taking the train. If you think it was him, despite his head being half demolished, and if the madrassa is a base for Daesh, how many of them are there?" Imran leaned forward. "It's wooded, the old house is substantial, grounds are extensive, we'll have to call on other departments."

Strange said, "And firearms? Forensics said the solid shot was some kind of amateur — but effective — armor-piercing shotgun round. Lead, cast around a half-inch masonry drill bit. Flutes carved into it, to make it spin. Proper workshop job. And pistol fire."

"Full tactical gear. We'll need to block the road on both sides. In fact, let's get a patrol out there right now, to keep an eye out. Discrete. Out of range of the cameras at the entrance."

Strange gazed out the window while Imran spoke to HQ on his mobile. Graffiti on the walls. A freight train, sitting stationary in a siding. Plastered in paint. Not a square centimeter left untagged. Fucking gang activity.

"Done." Imran put his phone away. "They've not caught that other one."

Strange looked at Imran. "How long did Leavey say it would be before the radiation clears?"

"Years, probably. We're lucky most of it went out to sea and came down before crossing land again. Bloody lucky the wind was in the right direction." Imran shook his head. "National media going mad. Carragher's going to wait a long time for his next promotion. Be lucky if he's not promoted to patrolling the public toilets. What a mess."

Strange nodded. "It could have been worse."

"Yes. That was quick thinking. But you took a big risk exposing yourself like that." Imran tapped his fingers on the tabletop. "How much of a dose was it?"

"Not a lot more than you. The firefighters got the worst."

"Speaking of the media, I hear you've been seen with that news-woman. About time you got out and about. Socially I mean. Just be careful what you say."

"Of course, sir." Strange glanced out the window. Fifteen minutes out of London and they were passing through leafy suburbs and, increasingly, farmland. Black and white cows grazing in a field, a water trough, wooden fences, whizzing by at a hundred miles per hour.

Imran frowned. "And we'll need specialists. Nuclear specialists. There could be another incident. But if we're too slow and there is— This is going to take time to organize."

"We should bring the army in," Strange said.

"Not for us to decide. Between us, though, I agree." Imran rubbed his chin. "We'll need air support. Have to bring the Fire Service in, just in case. One of their New Dimension Vehicles."

"And a radiation monitoring unit. It's not going to be easy keeping all this out of sight before we go in." Strange remembered the narrowness of the two-lane road that ran past the madrassa's entrance. "And ambulances, they'll need the MTFA protocol." Yeah. Marauding Terrorist Firearms Attack. Carragher hadn't even organized ambulance backup.

"Suppose they make a run for it out the back?"

"There's no road. Only a cart track. We'll have the helicopter." Strange felt uneasy, though. "It's a pretty big perimeter."

"There's only about six of them. Males, that is. And a few females."

"How do you know there's not more?" Strange felt aggrieved; was his boss withholding information?

"I had a phone call last night. My C.I. — confidential informer. The same as before."

"Six or sixty, we'll need to grab the lot of them, sir. Or it won't just be Commander Carragher patrolling the lavvies."

Two young women came through the inter-carriage door and sat nearby.

Imran put his finger to his lips and shook his head imperceptibly.

Strange took out his phone and started the browser app. He began scanning the newspaper headlines.

ATOM SCARE
COBALT HORROR
UK JIHAD

Enough. Still, when they got to Birmingham, he could stop being a policeman until tomorrow.

THE EXPRESS PULLED INTO BIRMINGHAM NEW STREET. IMRAN TOOK an Uber to his office, to chase up a search warrant. Strange headed home to shower and change. He'd already been working twelve hours straight. On the way, he called Vicky. "Hi. I've just got in. New Street."

"Where've you been?"

"London. Security committee meeting. Look — I need a shower, and to take off my suit. Are you free in an hour?"

"Make it an hour and a half, and yes. Where?"

"Wagamama?"

"All right. See you later."

WAGAMAMA WAS RELATIVELY QUIET. A GROUP OF TOURISTS SAT IN ONE corner, finishing their smoothies.

Strange was finishing his tomato juice when Vicky walked in. He went to her, admiring her face. And other parts, too. Strange took her hands in his, leaned forward, and air-kissed her. She wore a smartly tailored knee-length skirt in a light-gray fabric, with a matching jacket. Strange suddenly felt dowdy in his jeans and open-neck shirt. He'd done some hard thinking. "You look amazing."

She flushed pink like a schoolgirl. "You're not wearing a pint of beer today."

"I think about you all the time," Strange said. "I'm sorry I didn't have time to call you before I left for that incident up north."

"I guessed you were involved. I read the news reports." She kept her voice low. "Your eyes are pink."

Strange pursed his lips. "Chemicals in the air."

"How was it, really?" she asked.

"On or off the record?"

"Look," she said, "I've been thinking. Let's make an agreement: Everything you say is off the record, and professionally I didn't hear it unless I say otherwise. Deal?"

"It's a deal. We'll have to be careful, that's all." He put his hand over hers. This was damnably difficult. He'd fallen in love with a woman who could be the death of his career if he let the wrong words slip. He decided to answer her question. "Off the record: one officer dead, another maimed with ruined lungs, a third in intensive care, sulfuric poisoning. And you know the rest, it's on the news. A whole housing estate evacuated on a panic basis. The authorities were caught flat-footed."

"And you've no idea who did it?" Vicky asked.

"My boss was chewed out well and truly by the Home Office," he replied, frowning. "Even though I wasn't the officer in charge. We do have a lead, and it's a good one. We're following it up right now, although I can't say anything officially."

Strange had the Katsu curry. He knew its coconut-based sauce and crispy chicken would fill him up; he hadn't eaten since seven that morning, and a horrible hollow feeling was taking over his stomach.

Vicky had the Bang Bang Cauliflower.

"What's that like?" Strange pointed to her dish.

"Spicy. But vegan."

"Are you vegan then?" He grinned to show it didn't matter to him.

"Experimenting." She laughed. "I was in Sainsbury and found this package of eggs that said 'vegetarian'. Ridiculous. So I finally found a manager. He said that it was because the chickens only ate vegetables."

Strange laughed. "I bet they probably manage to eat a few worms anyway." He frowned. "That's what I need to do right now. Eat a few human worms."

They were finishing the meal. "May I see you tonight?" Strange prayed that she'd say yes.

"I don't know. I'll try to get away by nine forty-five. I have a meeting with senior management. The Beeb is beating us in the ratings."

"Not for long, I'm sure. How was that cauliflower?"

"Terrible. I see you've eaten all your curry." She grinned.

"Fried chicken and junk sauce. But it wasn't that bad, and I was starving. I thought I would try this place. That's twice I've failed at eating out. Maybe I should live on doughnuts like American police do in the movies." Strange laughed. "This is me trying to be posh."

"I knew it was going to be bad, because all my friends at the studio have eaten here, but I had to find out for myself." Vicky gave him a quizzical look. "So if you're not trying to be posh, where would you eat?

"Lunch? Oh, I don't know. It depends. Dinner would be balti. Ideally, from one of those places in Ladypool Road." Strange helped Vicky with her jacket and was opening the door for her when his phone buzzed. He helped her through, then checked his mobile.

"Hang on a second, love." He glanced at the text.

"It's my boss. We're getting a search warrant. I'll have to run."

TWENTY-FIVE

Zafir and the Sheik were sitting in the madrassa library. Zafir disliked the place; he couldn't read Arabic, and so the books reminded him of his lack of education.

"A great blow, Zafir. You have brought fear into the kuffars' hearts. Amaq has already broadcast the news. Now the kuffar know us. Allah hu akbar."

"Allah hu akbar. But we lost Hasan."

"Hasan is a martyr now. That is not the problem. What if they identify him? No — they will identify him, the police aren't stupid. We must thank Allah that you escaped. Allah has other plans for you." Sheik Maulan tapped his fingers on the table. "Make ready. Observe the kuffar. And we will strike another blow yet. Be sure that one day you will go to paradise forever."

Zafir stood up, relieved to escape. He hurried through the corridor and up the stairs to the IT room and sat in a swivel chair in front of the largest computer screen. He started the remote camera app for the tower cameras and waited for the images to come up on the screen.

He'd installed the cameras on the roof of the tower himself. The structure was a folly, erected in 1898. About twelve feet in diameter and fifty feet high, built of red brick, weathered and mossy, it blended with the landscape. Situated on the hilltop, the tower perched among trees that hid the lower thirty feet, leaving the top sticking up as if from a green sea.

The four-camera view came up on the screen. Zafir selected camera A, pointed it toward the road gate, and panned it left, to cover as much of the road as possible before trees interrupted the view. Camera B covered the road to the right. He set motion alarms on both. The other two cameras he focused on the madrassa: camera C to the rear, although rising ground and trees limited the view; and camera D, on a small group of figures working close to the front gate.

He zoomed in and brought Anisa's face into focus. She bent down and her face was replaced by a side view of Salma, then Anisa pulled a weed, flung it into a large straw basket, and winced as she straightened up again, putting her hand to the small of her back.

He glanced back to A and B. On the road that ran past the main gate, there didn't seem to be any traffic, except for a couple of cyclists. They cycled past the madrassa's gate, heading west, away from the town. Zafir tracked them as they pedaled down a long slope that led to a tight corner, a T-junction with another B road that ran north-south. The cyclists laughed and gestured to each other, having a friendly race by the look of it, then as they slowed down for the junction … what?

A man with his arm raised walked into the road in front of the two, causing one of the cyclists to skid and nearly take a tumble. Zafir backed off the zoom, expanding the field of view. What was going on down there?

Zafir saw the guy arguing with the riders. They obviously wanted to carry on down the right-hand fork, but the big fellow pointed to the left. The riders moved off reluctantly; he saw they were exchanging words, glancing behind, then Zafir noticed a group of vehicles parked farther up the road. The cyclists passed them, peering sideways. A man exited one of the cars and strung a wide yellow tape across the road, with writing. He focused in on the tape, which waved and twisted in the breeze, and there it was, the word he hated most: POLICE.

He watched as a car stopped before the barrier. It had to turn down the other road instead of continuing on. He noticed that the cops didn't bother to inspect the car, just diverted it. Zafir couldn't pan left very far because of the heavy growth of trees that extended nearly as far as the town center, two miles distant. Nothing to be seen.

Well, it was enough to know that something could be in the wind. Yeah, in the wind, he thought. Like the factory. *That* went into the wind all right, except that the wind had changed to the wrong direction. Poor stupid bloody Hasan, but there was a bright side to that — at least he was out of the way, and things were more like the old days, with the Sheik paying him more attention.

A large white van came into view, pulled to one side, and then moved across the grass verge until it all but disappeared under over-hanging tree branches. Zafir counted three, no, four radio antennas of different types. This was enough for him. He picked up an internal telephone and dialed.

"Yes?"

"Sheik, this is Zafir. I picked up some police movements."

"Police movements? Explain."

Rapidly, Zafir outlined the activities at the T junction.

"Have you picked anything up in the other direction?"

"No, Sheik, can't see very far; the trees block the view. I can see some of our people working near the gate."

"Find out if they're at the other end of the road, too. Who's working near the gate?"

"Anisa, Salma, Rais, and Arno."

"I see. Come down here and get a bicycle from the shed. Take it down to the gate; no, wait a moment, do you have any cash on you?"

"Perhaps twenty pounds, Sheik."

"Right. Take the bicycle down there, give it to, let's see … give it to Rais. Ask him to go into the town. There's a small general store, the Indian one, on the corner just as you get past the crossroads. Ask him to buy two cartons of milk. Note the time he leaves. If he's not back in ten minutes, let me know."

"Of course, Sheik."

Zafir grinned at the thought of ordering Rais into town on a fool's errand, but then frowned uneasily. The bastards, putting their yellow tape across the road. They can't have anything solid, he thought, or they'd be banging on the gates by now. Well, he'd give them a few surprises.

TWENTY-SIX

"We won't have armed support in place until tomorrow morning."

Strange peered through the car window at the dark trees on their left. "Let's get off the road." He parked alongside two other police cars on the grass verge.

Strange closed the window, then he and Imran got out. They were a mile and a half from the madrassa.

Strange put a set of lightweight binoculars to his eyes and scanned the estate. There was some kind of building amid the trees near the top of the hill; a tower. A brief flash of polychromatic light came from it. Maybe the setting sun had struck a flint. Or a camera lens.

"The magistrates are sensitive about religious organizations; the potential for bad publicity ... cultural sensitivity. All we can do is wait and watch for the moment. You've got the drone pictures?" Imran asked.

"Yes. The area around the old house will be difficult if there's resistance — it's completely open, no cover at all." Strange pulled a folded paper from an inside pocket and spread it out on the hood of the car. "I got this map from the library in Evesham. It's a planning office copy. They had some extension work done a year ago. The Grange is a listed building, so they have to submit detailed plans for anything more than basic maintenance."

Imran ran his finger over the map. "Main entrance, here: just wide enough for two cars to pass. The road winds up through trees maybe two hundred yards, then breaks into this open space, half-moon shaped, with the Grange in the back edge there. Most of this open space is grass and rose beds, but here and here are buildings. Wood-built stuff. Back of the house, the ground rises again, quite steep, maybe another fifty yards or so to the crest. More trees."

"What's this?" Strange pointed at the plan. "I could make out some sort of building through the glasses. Looked like it might be a church spire."

Imran shook his head. "Not a church, a folly. The estates around this part of the world are full of them. Towers without stairs, little love nests, odd spires, and chimneys." He peered closely at the notes. "This one's a gothic tower with a room at the top that's too small even for a bed. Listed, like the house; grade two, so it has to be kept original come what may."

"And this?" Strange pointed.

Imran bent forward and peered closely at the plan. "A pillbox, Second World War."

"It's within easy reach of the access road, halfway up. If these jokers did the factory — and they put someone in there with small arms — it would be bloody awkward." Strange took his finger off the plan.

"Yes. A squad on each side? Just inside the tree line? Yes, that's right. To stop a break for open country."

"Yes, sir. Let's see: five, no, six, for the front door of the big house. Three men for the outbuildings to the left there, two more for that one on the right. Air support to monitor the rear. Every man with a respirator." Strange thought about the police van in front of the plastics factory. Maybe some anti-tank rockets.

Imran said, "Leave a couple of the lads here at the crossroads checking what comes through. Change them every four hours."

The radio in Strange's top pocket suddenly sounded, but the message wasn't decipherable. He held the radio up and fiddled with the volume. A loud hiss sounded as he turned the squelch control off, then it quietened as a carrier came in.

"Zebra control, this is India Two, do you read, over?"

Strange pressed the transmit switch. "India Two, this is Zebra control, loud and clear, over."

"Zebra, we've just spotted a youngster, early teens maybe, heading our way on a bicycle. Did he pass you? Over."

"No, India Two, he must be from the madrassa, there are no other houses in the vicinity. Ask him where he's from but don't detain him, we haven't got just cause, over."

"Roger, Zebra. Out."

Strange turned the squelch control back to normal.

"Is it a rabbit, or a rat?" Imran wondered.

"Won't be long before we find out, sir," Strange replied.

TWENTY-SEVEN

Rais pedaled around the bend, head down, watching for holes in the road. He was out of practice and the bike was too big, but he'd got it up to a fair speed.

He looked up. Fuck. A parked blue and white police Volvo. A uniformed officer leaned casually against the side of the car. A second copper stepped into the road, holding his hand up.

Rais wobbled and braked. The front wheel hit a pothole and skidded. He tried to correct it, but the forks twisted and he went over the handlebars. He bashed into the asphalt, and pain blazed through his knee and elbow.

He looked up to see a thin face topped with a police hat. A hand helped him up. Rais got to his feet with difficulty.

"Are you all right, son? You should be more careful. You haven't been riding for very long, have you?"

"No. Not ... long." Rais began to shake.

"Where are you going, lad?"

"The town. To buy a carton of milk."

"And where do you come from?"

"I live at the Grange, officer. I'll be all right in a minute." *I must get control of myself*. He bent down and picked up the bike. The front wheel was twisted out of line with the handlebars. Damn. Would he be able to fix this? The Sheik wasn't going to listen to excuses.

The policeman looked him up and down. "I'd get an anti-tetanus shot if I was you, son. You've got dirt in those cuts."

"I'll be okay. Thanks." Rais put the front wheel between his knees and pulled the handlebars. Slowly the forks straightened. It looked about right.

"You mind if I carry on?" He was getting his nerve back now. The policeman glanced at his older colleague, who was standing by the car. He nodded, almost imperceptibly.

"Go ahead. Be more careful in the future, eh? And you'd better not take too long, you haven't any lights on that bike and it'll be dark in another twenty minutes."

RAIS PULLED OFF THE ROAD INTO THE ENTRANCE TO THE DRIVE. IT WAS nearly nine o'clock. His knee and elbow felt as if they were on fire. He pressed the intercom key.

"Yes?" It sounded like Arno, Rais thought.

"It's Rais. I'm back from the shops. I had an accident, fell off. I got the milk that Zafir wanted." He had the cartons in a carrier bag, tied onto a carry-rack behind the saddle.

"I'll tell him."

There was a loud buzzing sound. Rais dragged open the left-hand gate, pushed the bicycle through, and then followed. He pulled on the gate to help the spring device close it. It was tough going pedaling the bike up the slope. The trees closed in overhead, and after the first thirty yards, the grade became so steep he had to dismount and push.

Rais got back on when the road reached the midpoint and flattened out, skirting an old lake that had long ago silted up. As he left the marshy area for the final climb, he saw Zafir approaching him from the Grange. Zafir carried one of the life-size targets from the cellar firing range. It showed a stereotypical bad guy carrying a rifle with bayonet, in green and black combat fatigues. Zafir propped the target against a tree and waited for Rais to reach him.

"Look at the state of you. What happened?"

"The bike was too big, and I haven't ridden for a while. I was trying to keep it in a straight line, and I came round the bend, and there was this cop right in front with his hand up. I grabbed the brake really hard and went over the top." It all came out in a rush.

"This cop. He ask you any questions?"

Rais thought Zafir was trying to keep his voice a bit too casual. "Just where I was going, and where I'd come from. The usual. You know, bruv."

"Yeah. What did you say?"

"Just that I was going for some milk."

"You tell them you lived here?"

What would you have said, asshole! Rais felt a flash of temper. "Well, yeah, what else could I say?"

"Nothing. It doesn't matter. Look, get yourself cleaned up. Put some antiseptic on those cuts, and change your clothes. You're a right mess. You see any other cops down there?"

"There was a car. Another copper was leaning on it."

"Uniform?"

"Yeah."

"Okay, Rais. You did okay." Zafir consulted his watch. "It's getting dark. I still have a few things to do. There's a meeting a bit later on, so don't take too long fixing yourself up."

"Okay." Rais glanced at the target. "What's that for?" Zafir's eyes narrowed, and Rais wished he hadn't asked.

"None of your damn business," Zafir said. "Finish your errand, and be quick about it."

Zafir waited for Rais to pick up the bike and start up the slope. The twilight was fading; he'd better get a move-on. The air smelled of decaying leaf mold and rotten bark. Zafir felt an affinity for this place, but he had no idea why.

He picked up the target and stepped cautiously out onto the spongy ground of the silted-up lake. It took less time than he thought to position the target, half concealed behind a shrub. He retreated to the path and went down it a little way toward the entrance gate, then retraced his steps like someone who'd be looking for trouble. They'd spot the target around *here*. Perfect.

But why did Rais ask about the target? That one would have to be watched, especially with the kuffs at the front door. No time now, though. He was late for the meeting.

Zafir carried on up the hill and, breathing heavily, came through the door of the refectory and sat down in a corner, a little apart from the others. It was a quarter to ten. Everyone seemed to be there. Zafir counted them: eleven. Would've been twelve, except for Hasan.

The Sheik came in.

"Brothers. The kuffar is watching our gate. No matter. We have struck two mighty blows already. And if it be the will of Allah, we will strike them again."

Zafir thought it would be a good idea to leave sooner than later. These donkeys could carry the load.

The Sheik related what had happened at the plastics factory, praised Zafir, and told them that Hasan was a martyr now, in paradise.

Zafir stood briefly, acknowledging the praise, but the room, the Sheik, and the other brothers flickered past like an old movie reel of another life. Unreal. Temporary.

In his mind, he stood again at the factory window, the stink of burning plastic in his nose, taking aim at the riot van. He pressed the trigger of the Winchester shotgun. The van's radiator exploded in steam. His shoulder hurt from the recoil. The shotgun barrel lifted slightly with the recoil from the magnum slug, just as he pressed the trigger again. The shot ricocheted away. He fired again and took out the driver. He reached into his jacket, pulled three more shells from an inside pocket, and loaded them into the magazine. It was a pity about Hasan, but at least Anisa wouldn't be mooning about the place looking for him.

The Sheik paused for a moment, and Zafir brought his attention back. "Zafir will give each of you a weapon. You have all fired the Zoraki pistol. You will have five magazines each, so don't go spraying bullets. There is a roster for watching the cameras."

The Sheik glanced at Zafir. "There will be a meal at midnight. For everyone. Zafir will give you your weapon and ammunition. Now rest until then."

TWENTY-EIGHT

They filed out of the refectory. Anisa glanced back. The Sheik gazed bleakly at her. How would they defend the madrassa against the kuffar?

Anisa made her way back to her sleeping quarters and lay on her bed, thoughts whirling. The air felt heavy and humid, as if an electrical storm was approaching. She had a dull ache at the back of her head. She tossed and turned for hours.

Eventually, she slept, but nightmares came. Hasan's face hung over her, smiling. Anisa reached for him, but he backed away. His face changed; his skin grew puffy, blistered; his eyes filmed over; and his mouth sagged like an old sack. A stream of maggots emerged from one of his nostrils and fell, one by one. Anisa looked down to find herself standing in a squirming nest of the things. She opened her mouth to scream, and Hasan leaned toward her, sightlessly, reached out with hands from which the skin hung in parchment wisps—

Anisa woke, panting for breath, a soundless scream caught in her throat. Her cheap alarm clock read twenty minutes before five. Unable to stand the stagnant air inside the room, she scrambled into a pair of jeans and a sweatshirt. The boards squeaked as she moved down the corridor, then a door opened. Salma looked out and smiled.

"Anisa. I didn't hear your alarm go off."

"After what the Sheik said, I couldn't sleep. Why are the cops waiting outside?"

Salma laughed. "You're half asleep, Anisa. Zafir's got something planned I'm sure."

Anisa's face darkened. "I hate him, Salma. The way he looks at me. Sometimes I see him looking at me with this snide expression, you know, like he's laughing on the inside of his face. And where is Hasan?"

"Zafir's not a nice person but he is a jihadi. We are all mujahideen now. Get some sleep." Salma turned and went back into her room.

Anisa walked the few yards to the outside door, opened it, and stepped outside. Did she feel like a mujahid? There was a faint pink glow over the trees to the east; the false dawn or the real one, she couldn't be sure. Footsteps crunched on gravel some distance away, and as they grew nearer, she thought she knew who it was.

Her suspicions were confirmed when Rais walked around the corner of the building, bent forward to counter the weight of the backpack he wore over his jacket. He stopped in front of her, mouth working as he tried to figure out what he wanted to say. Despite herself, she grinned; he was so bloody shy, it was almost painful to watch him.

"Hi, Rais. It's a bit early to be on your way to breakfast, isn't it?"

The corners of his mouth turned up. Well, that was something, she thought, he has a sense of humor.

"I'm leaving, but I came to show you this." He pulled a crumpled newspaper out of his jacket and handed it to her. "It's us. Zafir and Hasan, I mean."

She scanned the front page. The headline read: "DIRTY ATTACK: BODY FOUND." She read on, squinting to read the page under the single lamp at the corner of the wooden dorm. A body had been found at the scene. Hundreds had been contaminated. One policeman was killed, and others were in the hospital. Police were hunting those responsible.

"No. No, no, no." She crumpled the newspaper into a wad. A wave of horripilation ran through her. "Is this what happened to Hasan? He's dead?"

"Anisa, I know you haven't bothered with me. You were always for Hasan, and I'm sorry he died, believe me. Hasan was okay, not like Zafir. Something terrible is going to happen. The police are waiting outside. You have to get out." He bit his lip and looked down.

She waited, saying nothing. It was up to him. Finally, he brought his head up and looked into her eyes. "I'm leaving. I'll take my chances. I'd like you to come with me."

She looked searchingly at him. "I like you, I like you a lot, you're different from the others." She remembered the dream. "I'll come with you. Not only because I'm frightened to stay; we can help each other. We'll see how it goes, okay?"

She heard someone moving around inside, and the door opened behind her, spilling a fan of light across the ground.

"Oh, it's Rais," Salma said. She looked from Rais to Anisa, and back to him again. "I haven't interrupted anything, I hope?" Her laugh sounded brittle.

"No. Not really."

Salma was still staring at Rais. Anisa realized that Salma must have seen the backpack — and the newspaper that Anisa still clutched. Salma gave her a frozen look, turned on her heel, and went down the path that led to their communal bathroom.

"I think she realized, Anisa," Rais said the moment she'd gone.

"She'd be a fool if she hadn't," Anisa replied. "We'd better not hang around. Give me a few minutes to pack; I'll throw some things into an overnight case."

"Meet me at my hut," Rais said. "I'll wait outside for you."

Anisa gave him a brief hug, then turned and went back into the hut. Everything was quiet again. She went into her room, closed the door, then took a small overnight bag from the tiny wardrobe. There was no way all her clothes would fit into it, so she selected only the best.

She would be glad to get out of here, she thought, scanning the crude, bare plywood walls.

After she finished cramming the bag, she put on lipstick, something she'd wanted to do for a long time, an act forbidden by the Sheik.

"Painted women are the devil's harlots," he'd said.

As she picked up the overnight bag from her bed, her eyes focused on the alarm clock, and she saw with dismay that ten minutes had already passed. Rais must be going frantic. She made for the door.

Quietly, Anisa eased her way into the corridor. A narrow wedge of yellow light came from the opposite doorway. That was Salma's room. The door was open just a fraction of an inch. Anisa put her eye to the crack and peered inside. Salma's room was empty. Anisa's legs felt shaky, a sign that she'd come to believe was a portent of harm.

What was that sound? Someone shouting? No, someone screaming. It could be a cat. She suspected that it wasn't.

She fled from the hut, clutching her overnight bag, then ran frantically up the hill toward the men's quarters, keeping to the grass to avoid making noise. Thorns tore her jeans as she passed too close to the rose beds.

As she neared the small group of huts where the younger men lived, she slowed, peering carefully about. The eastern sky had paled with dawn's first blush, and the huts stood outlined in the half-light, the darker mass of the hill rising behind them. Farther up crouched the gothic manor house. Light showed in some of its windows.

The door to Rais's hut stood ajar. Anisa moved forward,

straining her ears for the slightest sound. Dew from the grass soaked her training shoes. In the distance came the plaintive call of a curlew, then far off, a cow mooed. Birds were starting their salute to the sun. Now or never, she thought, tip-toeing to the open door. Carefully, she put her head around the edge and peeped inside.

The short corridor was deserted. There were doors to the left and right, and one more at the end. Anisa slipped inside and pulled the door closed behind her. The air smelt of dust and mold. She stepped forward, wondering which of the doors was Rais's. No way of telling.

Very gently, she knocked on the door to her left, listening carefully. Nothing. She put her hand on the knob and turned it, slowly, soundlessly, until it would move no farther, then gradually eased the door open until she could peer inside. She saw a segment of the room that included a tidily made-up bed. Anisa opened the door farther. The room was deserted. A small table, two rough wooden chairs, a basic wardrobe.

Anisa closed the door as carefully as she had opened it, then repeated the procedure with the next one. Nobody. The one at the end of the corridor was a tiny washroom: a toilet and washbasin, nothing more. She felt her heart pounding as she tried the third room.

The bed was a mess. She peered inside and took in the shambles. A table lamp, on its side on the floor, shade half-crushed. A chair, also on its side. Anisa lifted her gaze, gasped, and put her hand to her mouth; the wall was splashed with blood.

Salma. It must have been her, the bitch. She must have told — who? The Sheik? Zafir?

It was getting brighter as she left the hut. The sun was probably up, though she couldn't see it because of the trees. The gravel showed parallel lines; someone had been dragged along it. Anisa followed the tracks, then lost them on a paved area. It was a circular meeting place of five paths, surrounded by a low wall of Chiltern stone.

In the middle, when she'd arrived at the Grange, a statue of Cupid stood, bow in hand as if to fire love's sweet arrow. The Sheik had torn it down, and now just a crude stump of concrete stood there.

The countryside seemed caught in a hush, and she an intruder; but no, a sheep bleated in the distance. Which path? Anisa froze. There were stains on the paving. She looked closer. Red stains. Her eyes tracked the spots and smears to the third path. Unwillingly her feet carried her to it, then up the stone stairs. This path, she knew, led to the old stables.

Her legs wobbled as she followed the gently curving path of moss-edged stones, tracking the spattering of blood spots. Anisa had never come to this part of the grounds. Ancient oaks hemmed the track on each side, their topmost branches fusing overhead as the nave of some rustic cathedral. The bleating sounded again, louder.

She rounded a curve to find that the path split into two. The right-hand branch consisted of a series of steps, descending in a long spiral into the trees. Undergrowth encroached on it, and dew-dropped ferns invaded its margins.

The blood trail continued on the left. Anisa followed. The ground rose, and she trod carefully on the slippery paving. There was a clearing ahead. On each side, the trees retreated. The stone slabs merged with the surface, finally sinking beneath the grass.

Suddenly the sheep bleated again, directly in front of her. Except this was no sheep. For a moment she failed to comprehend what she was looking at. Anisa's eyes locked on the slim frame before her. They had stripped Rais, then crucified him upside down. His feet were nailed to the lintel of the rough wooden building, his arms outstretched, his hands nailed to the frame on both sides of the empty doorway.

Pools of blood gathered underneath his upside-down body. A

wide band of gray duct tape stretched across his mouth. A spasm went through Rais, and then the bleating sound came from his nose.

Anisa gagged, barely retaining control of her stomach. She had to look away. Her bag dropped unnoticed from her nerveless fingers. Screwing up her last vestiges of courage, she went to him, and, catching the edge of the tape with her fingernails, ripped it from his mouth. His filmed eyes cleared for a moment and focused on her. Blood trickled from his mouth.

"Rais! Rais, oh—" She couldn't go on.

"Anisa," he gurgled faintly. "Too late. Get away. Get help. Help … ."

His voice died away. She looked back down to see his head hanging limply. His chest still rose and fell, but slowly.

She reached down to pick up her bag.

Zafir's voice came from behind her. "You won't be needing that."

TWENTY-NINE

Walt's mobile buzzed, waking him up from a fitful sleep in the back of the OB van. The gray light of early dawn was filtering through the windows. Eight years he'd been driving, and he knew more about electronic news gathering than any other engineer at Heartland. Should he still be doing this at thirty-eight years of age? He ran his fingers through his balding brown hair. Where was that bloody Thermos? Surely there was some coffee left.

It didn't look as if they'd be stuck at Upwood much longer. He was pleased about that. They had milked it for what it was worth. They had been the first to get shots of the disaster village. Then there'd been the riot at the tent village, and they'd been the first on the scene again, the only ones to get video of the stretchers being carried away.

Rick Hamilton, the team's reporter, was already moving around outside. He opened the rear door and said, "Okay, let's pack it up. We'll get nothing more here."

They began stowing the gear into the Nissan Navara 4WD. It

carried a Holkirk RM120 satellite uplink dish, a dismountable 4 KW generator, and had its own roof-mounted air conditioner. Walt drove most of the time, though sometimes Rick gave him a break, especially on the longer trips.

Walt's mobile played the ringtone for Beeston, Heartland's news producer. Fuck, barely after six. Did Beeston never sleep?

"Hello?"

"Walt? Something's going down."

"We're about to leave."

"No, not at your location. There's a big police operation near Worcester. Could be those people behind the radiological attacks."

"What? How do you know?"

"A friend in the chief constable's office. You don't need to know. Are you mobile?"

"Nearly. Just finishing stowing away. Couple of minutes."

"Right. It's a country house called the Grange. I'm sending you a WhatsApp with the location details. Try to find a back way in, or I doubt you'll get close. I'm sending Vicky over, Tim's driving her in the Land Rover."

Walt shoved the phone back into his pocket. "Rick — give me a hand. We need to get everything stowed. I don't care if it's messy as long as the kit isn't damaged. Something's going down, and we're going to be the first on the scene."

Walt's phone sounded a WhatsApp alert. He took it out and checked the target location. Fuck; it looked like at least a half-hour's drive. He climbed into the passenger side and dug in the glovebox until he found what he wanted among the mass of maps, tourist guides, and gazetteers: an Ordnance Survey map, scaled at one inch to the mile, covering the Vale of Evesham toward Worcester. He picked up the road and traced along it with his finger. A white road, just a track really, ran past the back of the estate, maybe a half-mile distant. It intersected with one running diagonally to the public highway on the other side. It looked as if the second white road ran from a nearby farm to the B road, with the one near the back of the other buildings — the Grange — joining it.

Walt peered at the map. Just a track, but maybe he could get the truck along it if the surface was good enough. He could almost smell it, that cubic centimeter of pure blind luck that appears every once in awhile, and either you grab it or wonder forever what might have been.

The vehicle lurched as Rick slammed the heavy door at the back.

"Secure, Walt," Rick reported.

The big diesel came to life with the first turn of the key. Walt started pulling away while Rick explained the route.

"Okay, you'll find a Y junction about half a mile ahead, you'll remember it. Take the right-hand fork and keep going, after about another mile and a half it'll widen into a dual carriageway. I'll find the fastest route with the Maps app. Just get going for now."

In less than twenty minutes they were on the M5. The motorway was quiet for once, so Walt cranked the turbo diesel up to the limit.

Walt's phone rang. He put it on hands-free. "Hello?"

It was Beeston. "Sorry for Rick, but we're replacing him. Divert to Strensham services, please, just south of Worcester. Vicky will meet you there."

"What? Why?"

"Rick'll be joining Tim Lionsey there, in the Land Rover. He's better suited to scrambling around with a hand-held."

As they headed up the motorway, guided by the female voice of the Maps app, Walt's watch said the time was ten past six. He thought about engineering issues. He'd need to align the roof antenna with the satellite and establish a link back to the studio, then set up some lighting and a fixed camera.

THE WHITE ROAD CAME TO AN ABRUPT HALT, CROSSED BY A BARBED-
wire fence with a cattle gate on the right. On the other side of the
wire, the track ceased to exist; a plowed field stretched away, already
sprouting with what Walt recognized as potato plants. "This must be
the fifth time this year that the map's wrong," Walt said.

"The farmers don't care much if it's a right of way or not. We
can't take the van through here." Walt waved his arm.

He sounded totally pissed off, thought Vicky.

On the far side, fifty yards distant, the track began again, skirted
the hill, and disappeared toward the public road three miles away. It
might have been on the moon, as far as they were concerned. The
hill was covered in secondary tree growth.

To their right, scrubby vegetation and small bushes partly
obscured small buildings of some kind. Walt wondered what the low
structures were, then spotted a couple of gravestones leaning at
crazy angles and realized it was a graveyard; almost certainly for the
inhabitants of the Grange and their retainers. Judging by the amount
of vegetation that had grown over it, the plot had been out of use for
quite a few years.

Vicky said, "So this is as close as we can get?"

"For the moment, at any rate." Walt bent down and reached
behind his seat. "I picked up some grub at the services. Two boxes of
cold pizza and a half-dozen soft drinks."

A distant thudding sound came to Walt's ears. Rotors. The sound
grew louder, and louder still, until the van vibrated with it.

Walt handed a box of pizza to Vicky. "What the hell is that?" He
lowered the window and popped his head out. A police helicopter in
yellow and blue was hovering at low altitude not more than twenty
yards distant. Its rotor wash flattened the ground vegetation and
sent litter flying everywhere. Walt saw a face peering at him from its
window.

A male voice came over a loudspeaker. "Police. This is a restricted area. Leave now. I repeat, this is a restricted area. Start your vehicle and leave."

THIRTY

They were going to catch him. Oh, God, someone had him by the shoulder—

"Come on."

D'ya wanna be in my gang?

"Wake up, sir!"

My gang, my gang, d'ya wanna be in my gang ... sir? Sir?

Strange opened his eyes, then groaned in relief. He had fallen asleep in the car. Sergeant James, an armed support officer, had hold of his shoulder and was shaking him. The last shreds of the nightmare blew away like candy floss in the wind.

"You've not been getting enough sleep, sir."

"Who is with this mess?"

"Look, sir. A girl." James let go of Strange's shoulder and pointed to a girl on the madrassa grounds. She was approaching the gate.

Strange took the microphone from its clip on the dashboard, pressed the talk switch, and spoke quietly into it. "India Two, this is Zebra. Do you read me?"

For a moment only the soft hiss of thermal noise came from the UHF, then: "India Two, Zebra. Loud and clear."

The air in the car was stale, so Strange rolled the window down. Mist pushed clammy fingers into his face, and he came fully awake. Outside, the sun showed half over the eastern horizon. The mist lay in a thin layer. Above it, in the rosy light of dawn, the country air was so clear it was almost crystalline.

"India Two, did anyone pass you on foot?" Strange asked. "Over."

"No, Zebra. No traffic through here for the last three hours. Over."

"Thanks, India. Out." Strange turned to the Sergeant. "Let's go."

They both exited the car and walked down the road. This would bring Strange within range of the madrassa's cameras, but they had already located the camera WiFi using the Gossamer and blocked it.

The girl paused for a moment in the madrassa's entrance gate, then walked out. The gate closed behind her.

Sergeant James clutched Strange's arm. "Sir! There's a wire on her! Is that a mobile she's wearing?"

It looked like she was wearing a mobile on the front of her jacket. And why was she wearing a bulky jacket on such a nice morning? A wave of cold traveled through him. Just loud enough for the sergeant to hear, he said, "Get back to the commo van. Find the officer with the Gossamer device. Tell him to locate that mobile and block it. Fast."

The young woman brought her hand up. Her fist was clenched around something, and her thumb pressed down. She looked wildly at Strange. "They ... they've ... they've crucified him! Help him. Help." Her face became a distorted mask, and she began crying.

He was perhaps ten yards distant. Well within killing range if that bulky jacket concealed an explosive vest. If he retreated, she might trigger it. Or it could be triggered remotely. Had they blocked that mobile yet? Time seemed to have slowed, each second an eternity.

"Help who?" Strange's gaze kept coming back to her clenched fist.

She took a step toward him.

"Please don't move. Stay calm." Strange took a step back. His skin was crawling as if worms were inside.

She took another step forward.

Strange desperately wanted to know how far he was from the car. Maybe he could duck behind it and use it for cover. But if he turned to look—

"Don't you understand? I need to help Rais—"

"Don't do anything silly. I'll help you. Are you wearing a vest?"

"A vest? No. This jacket. Zafir said it is full of the mother of Satan. If I take my thumb off this switch—" she waved her fist.

The mother of Satan. TATP. The tube and bus bombings. "Careful, miss. No need for us to lose our lives here. And it won't help Rais." Whoever Rais was. One of them, he supposed. But crucified?

"You did say crucified, miss?"

"Yes. Upside down."

"And what name shall I call you by?"

"Me? I'm Anisa."

Footsteps sounded behind him. Sergeant James's voice said, "Gossamer active, sir. That cell is blocked. Bomb squad on its way." The footsteps retreated again. They were leaving him on his own. No point in losing more lives than necessary. Why didn't he feel petrified? Some kind of cold logic controlled him.

"Are you going to help? If take my thumb off this switch—"

"I'll help. Just keep pressing that." Over his shoulder: "Sergeant? Get some tape. Any kind."

"My thumb is starting to hurt."

Zafir redialed. Unavailable. Redialed again. Same result. He pulled out his mobile and started the remote camera app. Anisa's phone failed to respond. He closed the tab and reopened it for the four-camera array in the folly. Same result — failure to connect.

The flint tower's base stood in gloomy shade from the closely packed trees. Roots were invading the edges of the path, cracking and lifting the old asphalt. Earwigs came from one of the crevices and marched off into the damp grass. Zafir took the tower key from his pocket. His nostrils flared as he inhaled the rich aroma of damp humus coming from the woods.

He opened the heavy oak door, crossed the circular room, and turned on a laptop. Failure to connect; the WiFi was down.

Moving faster now, clattering up the wooden stairs, he was out of breath as he reached the top. The cameras were all on, and active. But if WiFi was down, how could he see what they saw? If only he had an ethernet cable and had brought the laptop upstairs.

He peered out the slit window, hoping to catch sight of Anisa. She should have become a martyr by now. Yes, there she was. Standing in the road. She seemed to be talking to someone, but trees obscured the view. Shit. What to do?

He leaped down the steps two at a time, and ran out, slamming the heavy door behind him. As he ran down the path, he took a bunch of keys from his pocket and made for a service door at the back of the big house.

The Sheik was nowhere in sight. Zafir hurtled along the corridors, his panic rising with every step, and found the Sheik coming from his private quarters.

"Sheik! Mobile reception — jammed. WiFi jammed as well." His chest heaved as he gulped air.

The Sheik smiled at Zafir, came up to him, and placed a hand on his shoulder. Zafir turned and continued up the corridor with him, trying to calm himself.

"Zafir, do not worry. Allah will protect."

They turned right, and Zafir realized they were heading for the former chapel of the old house.

"I am going to show you something, Zafir, something that I have shown to no one." The Sheik pushed open the old wooden door, and they walked into the aisle toward where the altar had been. "Lead our brothers and sisters. Distribute the weapons. At the last, you are to gather all who will — or can — come here. Bar the door, it will stand for long enough, and then follow me with the others."

The Sheik moved to the back wall, which was lined with carved wooden panels bearing stylized representations of the saints. "The authorities would not permit the removal of this idolatry. But it has a secret." He put his hands on two of the panels, searching with his fingers.

"Look. Here and here. Yes. The heads of these two. Remember, you must press both at the same time."

There was a creaking sound and the panel swung away into what had appeared to be a solid wall. A gust of fetid air came out of the dark cavity, and Zafir wrinkled his nose in disgust. He looked down and saw a flight of narrow, steep stone steps descending into the darkness.

The Sheik chuckled at the expression on Zafir's face. "No, I didn't build it. It's an old priest's hole dating back to the time of the religious persecutions. Appropriate, don't you think?"

"Oh, yes." A bolt hole for when the shit hits the fan. "Where does it go?"

"The hole ends in the crypt underneath the old graveyard on the other side of the hill. About twelve feet down, you'll find a light switch on the right-hand wall. Just feel for it when you reach the landing. Once you get to the far end, you'll see daylight around the edges of the door. Push hard, but make sure to close it behind you. And I shouldn't take time to lift the lid off anything you might find in there." He took Zafir's hand in both of his. "I need at least a couple of hours, habibi."

He let go of Zafir's hand and stepped backward into the tunnel, placing his feet carefully on the narrow steps, then reached to one side and pressed something. Zafir backed away as the concealed door swung back into place. There was a loud click as it re-latched. He inspected the panel carefully; yes, there was a hairline crack, but it looked like part of the design.

There was no time to lose. He had to get the rest armed and into position.

THE SHEIK STOPPED ON THE LANDING TWELVE FEET DOWN THE FIRST flight. It was pitch black now inside the shaft. He felt along the wall until he encountered a rough wooden shelf, and his fingers closed around the barrel of a small but powerful halogen flashlight. The beam lit up the rough-hewn walls of the tunnel, and he quickly made out the gray electrical cable stapled to the ceiling with metal clips, ending in a galvanized steel box about three inches square, mounted nearby on the wall. There was a light switch on the front of the box and, inset flush on the side facing away, a tiny key switch.

He took his keys and inserted one of them into the key switch, gave it a half turn, and withdrew it. The steps went down another thirty feet, then he entered a large round chamber that had been part of the original refuge for dissident priests. Three large drums stood to one side. A thin gray cable came from a rough hole in the top of the center drum. The cable ran up the wall and along the roof, back the way he had come. He passed through the chamber and went down the tunnel, probing his way forward with the flashlight.

THIRTY-ONE

S trange heard footsteps, then Sergeant James's voice: "Keep pressing that switch, Anisa."

"Here's some electrical tape, sir. May I pass it to you?"

"Anisa. Stay still. This officer is going to pass a roll of tape to me. That's all." Strange showed her his empty palms.

James came up from behind and gave the tape to Strange, then retreated again.

Strange unstuck the end of the tape and pulled a few centimeters from the roll. "I am going to walk toward you. Just keep still. The sooner we help you, the sooner we can help Rais." He took a step. Another. Her arm was shaking. He prayed she could hold on. Another step. Another.

Finally, he reached her. "Anisa. I'm going to wrap this tape around your hand. Then you won't have to worry about letting go of that switch."

She held out her fist.

Strange stuck the end of the tape to the back of her hand. He pulled off a few more centimeters and took it over the top of her thumb, down, over her clenched fingers, under her fist, over her hand again, down, under — all the time very aware of the thin wires, yellow and green, that ran from her fist into the sleeve of her jacket. Very aware, too, of the mobile phone Velcroed to her, with its own pair of green and yellow wires that ran from the phone and disappeared under the collar of the jacket. He finished and put the roll of tape in his pocket.

James spoke from behind him. "Bomb squad's here, sir."

"All right, Anisa." Strange glanced behind and saw the explosives officer approaching, all geared up in his scary black protection and heavy plastic visor. "This officer knows what to do, Anisa. You'll be fine. I'm going to back away, and he'll take my place."

The expo moved up while Strange retreated to the car.

Strange spoke to Imran, in the mobile incident unit, over the police radio. "We can't go in yet, we've got an active bomb situation. Young female IC4 with a jacket. Expo is working on it."

The expo cut off one of the sleeves of Anisa's jacket with trauma shears, then began on the other.

"They must know we're outside. Let's get the drone up. And where's the helicopter?" Strange peered briefly at the sky — but no, he would hear it first. He returned his gaze to the expo. He was cutting down the back of Anisa's jacket.

The high-pitched buzz of drone rotors came to Strange's ears.

The expo spoke to Anisa. She nodded, trembling, and slowly drew her left arm out of the armhole. He cut the remaining armhole to the collar and helped her remove the jacket. It remained attached to her by the pair of wires that ran to her hand.

Anisa sat on the roadside grass next to the remains of her jacket, while the expo used a small toolkit and circuit analyzer to determine the status of the green and yellow wires. He shouted to Strange, "A bit complicated, sir. This will take a moment."

Zafir had eight Zoraki nine-millimeter pistols. Originally blank firing, they had been modified for automatic fire and could hose out an entire magazine in seconds. He gave those out, beginning with the men, kept one for himself, and gave the rest to the women. The shotgun went to Arno. He had sodium grenades by the upstairs windows of the house; the Sheik also had taken two with him.

He rallied them in the TV lounge. A jihadi video was playing on the big screen: drones dropped grenades, kuffars exploded. Zafir turned the sound low but left the video running. "Brothers, sisters, we're going to strike the kuff so hard it will be spoken of for generations to come. Take your positions — mobiles are jammed, so if the police are getting too heavy, back to the house, then join me — there's a tunnel. Do you understand? Right, then." Zafir waved his arm. "Get out there."

He followed them out of the TV lounge and through the front door, and watched as they scattered into the woods that surrounded the old house. Then he ran for the flint tower.

Imran came on the radio again. "From Indigo. Sierra? What's the situation? Is that jacket decommissioned?"

"From Sierra. Not quite, sir." Strange saw the expo shaking his head. *Shit.* "Something's wrong. I'll check."

"Fuck's sake, Strange. Don't get blown up. Air support's on its way. The drone is working — we just spotted eight of them running into the trees. And they're armed. Wait — another just came out. He's heading for that tower."

"Just a minute, sir. Back in a second."

Strange exited the car and hurried to where the expo was crouched next to Anisa.

He turned to Strange and explained, "There's a pulse signal on these wires, sir. Can't just cut them. Short or open these, we're going to be strawberry jam." Then he spoke to Anisa. "Look, love. If you cooperate we'll all be fine. Now, you don't really want to be blown to pieces, do you?"

"No, no, please get this off me, I'll do anything you want."

"All right then." The expo rummaged in his tool kit and pulled out a flat metal strip. "What I'm going to do is cut this tape here." He indicated the palm of Anisa's clenched hand. "Then I'm going to wiggle this strip in between your thumb and the plunger. When I tell you, I want you to very slowly remove your hand. But only when I tell you, okay?"

Anisa nodded. "Okay."

"And this officer," the expo inclined his head at Strange, "will tape around it, then over the top, then round it again. While I hold it." He gave Strange a look. "Won't you, sir?"

"Yes. Anisa, once you're free of the vest, walk back down the road, past my car, carry on round that bend and you'll see the incident unit. My boss is in there, Commander Imran. He needs your help. We need to know what we're facing. Have you got that?"

"Yes, all right."

Strange squatted next to the expo.

"Now, keep that switch pressed, Anisa." The expo cut the tape and peeled it back until once again she was holding down the switch on her own.

He slid the metal strip slowly between her thumb and the switch. "Now when I press against the side of the switch, hold your hand steady — here, I'll support the other side." The Expo held his right palm against the back of her hand while pressing the side of the switch with his fingers. "Good, I am going to bend this metal strip over and tape it to the switch, and as I do, I want you to remove your fingers one by one. Not until I tell you though. All right?"

Anisa nodded.

"No, don't move, please. Keep still. Now I'd like you to unstick your top finger."

One by one she removed her fingers, leaving the expo pressing the switch against the palm of her hand.

"Strange? Finish putting some more tape to hold this side of the strip, will you? I've run out of hands." The expo was visibly sweating.

Strange wiped the palms of his hands on his trousers, took the tape roll, and taped the metal strip to the side of the switch.

"Now comes the tricky part. I am going to put my thumb next to yours, press the strip down, and you are going to remove your thumb, slowly and carefully. Then I'm going to fold the strip down the other side of the switch, hold it in position, and tape it up. All you have to do is hold still. Got that?" The expo raised his eyebrows.

Anisa said, "Yes. Got it."

As he finished taping the other side of the switch, the expo glanced at Strange and said, "Sir, I'm not sure this will hold. Besides, the mobile can set this off at any moment if the blocking fails. I'm going to drop the jacket into the ditch and then we're all going to run. Clear?"

"Very clear," Strange replied.

Anisa said, "Which way do I run?"

Strange said, "Toward the car. Just go past it and keep going to the Mobile Incident Unit."

The expo looked at Strange. "Best you go now, sir. Take cover. Just in case."

"Right. Anisa, stay calm and do exactly what the officer tells you to." He hoped she would. Her face had turned the color of ash.

Strange turned, walked quickly to the car, and took cover behind it. He crouched behind one of the front wheels and peeked over the hood. The expo seemed to be removing the taped-up switch from Anisa's fist. Even from this distance, she was visibly shaking.

Anisa suddenly took off running, directly toward Strange. For a moment she blocked his view of the expo. Strange dodged to one side. The expo was lowering the jacket into the ditch.

Anisa ran past the car and continued on toward the MIU trailer, a good eighty yards farther.

Strange returned his attention to the expo, who now lay flat on the ground.

The expo still had his fist closed around the switch. He brought his left hand forward and used it to unravel the wires from the jacket. He'd got a couple of feet of wire now, and wormed backward on his belly. A bit farther. Part of a sleeve poked up above the ditch.

A high-pitched crack split the air. Instinct kicked in and Strange ducked. For long moments he lived in a world of silence. Clods of earth rained down.

He peeked over the hood. A good-sized steaming crater now punctuated the line of the roadside ditch. The expo lay halfway between the car and the crater.

Strange glanced behind. Anisa had almost reached the MIU.

Imran's voice came over the radio. It sounded strangely muffled. "Sierra? Sierra, are you all right?"

Strange mashed the transmit button. "From Sierra. I'm fine. Going to see if the expo is—"

The expo shook his head and used his arms to push himself into a sitting position.

Strange pressed the transmit button. "From Sierra. I think the expo is okay. The jacket exploded in the ditch. There's mud everywhere."

The expo was checking to see if he still had his full complement of arms and legs. He held up his gloved hand, giving the thumbs up.

As Strange climbed into the MIU, a deep thudding sounded above. It faded, then returned, louder. Strange stuck his head out the door. The police helicopter flew overhead, a couple of hundred feet up, making a loud blatting sound. It flew on and began to circle.

Imran sat Anisa down. "That was very sensible. Thank you. Now can you tell us how many are in there?" He picked up a notepad and pen.

"Eleven. No, nine, without Rais and me. Would have been ten but, Hasan—"

"We know about Hasan. He was at the factory. Who else?"

"Zafir."

"And who is he?" Imran wrote on the pad.

"He's the Sheik's right hand."

"I see. How many weapons are there? What kind?"

"Pistols. And a shotgun. Some grenades. Zafir made them. And he said he had some surprises. I don't know what."

"Quite a lad, this Zafir. And the Sheik. We met him already. Is he there, too?"

"Yes. I saw him early this morning."

Zafir took the mini-quad and its controller from a shelf on the ground floor of the flint tower. The range was only four hundred yards, but if the controller lost connection, the drone would return to him automatically unless GPS was blocked. But the police couldn't block GPS. And the frequency wasn't mobile phone, so the connection might work, even though the police had blocked mobiles; the cameras had stopped working, and the jacket had failed to detonate.

He went outside holding the drone in the palm of his hand. A deep thudding came from overhead. He peered up to see a helicopter banking steeply, moving off toward the old house, then slowing again.

Zafir pressed the start button on the drone, and it came to life with a high-pitched buzz. No time to lose. He hovered it a couple of feet from the ground and sent it along the path past the old house and down the access drive, toward the road. There, on the monitor screen — Arno, with the shotgun, on the flat roof of an outbuilding. There, and there, two more, with the automatic pistols, looking startled as the mini-quad whined past them. And here was the front entrance, the gate still secure, no police in evidence yet — other than the ones circling overhead, he reminded himself. He raised the drone and took a look over the wall. Nobody. He flew it into the road and turned it ninety degrees.

The scene imprinted itself on his mind: a parking lot of police vehicles — cars, buses, a command vehicle covered in antennae; plus two rows of officers next to the estate wall, out of view of the cameras at the entrance. Those cameras weren't working.

The mini-quad screen went blank. Shit. He waited for half a minute, but the drone failed to return. The bastard police must have knocked it out.

THIRTY-TWO

Strange's handset buzzed. He answered it.

"Strange? Can you hear me?" The voice sounded tinny and faint. It was Leavey, the minister responsible to the Home secretary.

"Yes. Just about," Strange replied.

"What's the situation up there? Commander Imran said you're dealing with a bomb?"

"We're about to go in. We intercepted a suicide bomber, a young Asian female. She says someone's been crucified on the grounds. Actually crucified. Nailed to a cross, upside down."

"Good God! And?"

"Expo partially disarmed the bomb. We separated it from the suspect, but it went off in the ditch. Expo is bruised but OK."

"You're going in?"

"Yes. Fifteen minutes."

"I'll inform the Home secretary."

"We'll bag the lot of them." Strange glanced at his watch. It read eleven minutes to eight. "I'll let you know. I'm going in with the first group."

"Good luck. Out." The connection died, and Strange put the handset back in the pocket of his waterproof waxed jacket, which strained slightly over the extra bulk of his Kevlar bulletproof vest. He checked the laces of his heavy forest boots and the fastening of his hip holster.

He turned and surveyed the road that ran past the Grange. He had one hundred and twenty uniformed officers from the West Midlands county force, in four groups.

Behind him, in disciplined formation, a group of thirty West Midlands uniformed officers waited. Three other groups waited at strategic points around the estate. Ten counter-terrorist specialist firearms officers (CTSFO) in each group carried the Sig Sauer SFX. The authorized firearms officers had Sig Sauer P229.

The "Unicorn" came around the corner and parked half on the grass. It was a squat, ugly-looking thing in black metal with thick, square plastic windows. The windshield was little more than a slit. At the front, it bore a long metal ram tipped with a square plate of inch-thick steel.

Sergeant James and one of the CTSFO officers huddled on the grass verge. They had spread a large-scale map on the ground.

"Time for the assault squad to be off, sir?" James asked.

"Right, let's get moving" Strange took out the radio. "From Sierra. Third and fourth squads, cover the rear of the property. Acknowledge."

AT THE BOTTOM OF THE HILL ON THE FAR SIDE OF THE GRANGE, WALT sat in the Outside Broadcast van gazing out the open side window across the early-morning landscape. It had been a pain driving away in compliance with the police order, but the helicopter had soon disappeared, and now he was in position again. The thudding sound of its rotors came to him from far off, drifting in and out according to the wind direction. Vicky was in the back, getting ready for her first link — assuming there would be a link. Everything seemed quiet. Someday, Walt thought, he'd get his big break. Maybe the reporter would be taken ill just as a major news story broke. Then he, Walt, would step up to the camera! No, fat chance. And Rick was really angry about Vicky replacing him.

Walt turned back to the front and saw someone standing there.

The man walked forward and moved around to Walt's side. The guy wore denim jeans, a heavy canvas jacket, and stout walking shoes, and carried a large black bag over one shoulder.

"Excuse me," the man said pleasantly, "but do you think you could give me a ride, just to the main road? I took a wrong turn somewhere, and now I'm a bit stuck for time." He smiled, deepening the lines that ran down to the corners of his mouth.

The fellow must belong to one of the walking clubs, Walt thought. "Sorry. We're not moving at the moment."

The man walked to the front, opened the passenger door, placed his bag carefully on the floor, and climbed inside. He closed the door, reached inside his pocket, and took out an automatic pistol. "You know what this is, right?"

"It's a toy. Isn't it?"

"Not a toy. Get moving."

Walt glanced at the mirrors. No sign of Rick with the Land Rover.

"Get moving — now!"

Walt put the big Mercedes in gear and moved off down the track.

Vicky's voice came from the back. "Walt? Why are we moving? I've just smeared my lipstick."

Walt reached the crossroads and slowed the vehicle to a stop. "Which way?" At that moment a loud "crump" of an explosion sounded. "What was that?"

The small window in the partition slid to one side, and Vicky's face appeared. "Walt? What's going on? Who's that?"

176

The man said, "My name is Sheik Maulan. Turn left. Get moving. Now."

"Walt? What's going—"

"Shut up, woman. And cover your face. But first, hand over your mobile phone." The Sheik put the muzzle of the pistol to Walt's head. "Drive toward London. Take the old Roman Road through Broadway and then over the hill down to Broughton. Then join the A40. You understand?"

"I don't know that way." Walt started trembling. If that had been an explosion — no, stupid thought, of course it was an explosion.

Popping sounds came on the breeze.

"I'll direct you."

"What is this? I mean, I'll do as you say, but what do you want? I don't have much money with me."

The man smiled. "All will be made clear. Allah provides."

Oh, fuck, he'd picked up a religious loon. An armed one. It was all he could do to not void his bladder.

"Just get on with it!" The soft voice turned harder, and the tip of the barrel ground into Walt's ear, as if the bastard could read his thoughts.

"Yeah, ow, okay, okay. Please, that hurts." Walt accelerated the van. Vicky should have jumped out. Too late now, they were already doing forty.

Vicky handed her iPhone through the partition window.

The man took it and said to Walt, "Yours, too. Switch it off."

Walt did so and then took the fork that led to the village of Broadway. They passed a farm tractor towing an open trailer full of hay bales, coming in the opposite direction, and the Sheik casually lobbed the mobiles into the straw as it went by.

They continued down Platt's Way, the old Roman road. Walt's thoughts churned as he tried to figure out how to escape. Flash the lights at oncoming cars? And if the cops stopped them? It seemed like an easy way to get his head blown off. And there was no traffic to speak of in this rural area.

THIRTY-THREE

"Quiet now! Spread out. Stay in line. Don't let anyone through." Strange waved his group of twenty-four men forward. He pulled his service pistol from its holster and racked it.

They maintained their line as best as they could, each keeping a distance of no more than six feet from the next officer. It was difficult ground, matted with briars. Dead branches waited to pierce the eyes of the unwary. Decayed trunks and fungal growth made the going treacherous.

Without warning, a man sprang out from a rhododendron thicket, gripping a garden rake in both hands. Before anyone could react, he brought it down with terrible force on a young officer's head.

With a crunch, the steel prongs pierced the man's skull. The young officer staggered backward, screaming like a steam whistle. His hands clawed at the rake jammed in his head, then his heels encountered a fallen log and he fell backward. He hit the ground, and the scream cut off short in a gurgle. For a moment there was a stunned silence, then two officers opened up with H&K machine carbines.

The man half-turned as if to dive for cover, but two rounds caught him in the side. The man's body spun out of view and crashed into the rhododendron.

One of the officers bent over and vomited on the ground.

Two men rushed to the first man down. His heels drummed briefly on the ground, and then he was still.

"He's gone," one of the men said, his face pale.

"Come on, get a grip! In line now!" These men looked as if they'd just come fresh from the school gates. Strange picked one. "You — check to see if that man's wearing a suicide vest." He keyed his radio. "From Sierra. Officer down. Say again, we have an officer down."

Imran's voice came over the speaker. "From Indigo. Status of the officer?"

"Deceased."

"Keep going or they'll slip past you."

One of the officers who had fired pulled a fresh magazine from his belt, slapped it into the H&K, and cocked it.

Strange glanced ahead at the others who were covering the area in front. "You, you, and you" — he indicated three men from his squad — "wait for backup. Then rejoin us. We're holding up the whole line." Adrenalin threatened to make him hyper. He looked left and right. "Move it!"

ZAFIR, IN THE OLD HOUSE, HEARD THE SHOTS AND BEGAN KICKING THE remaining brothers and sisters into action. "Come on, you lazy sods, the kuffar is knocking on the door! Here you go. Kill anything that moves. When they break through, get back here, quick as you like. We'll be out the back door and away! Stay on this side of the wire, remember, try to keep them from cutting it."

Zafir stuck a Zoraki automatic in his belt and several magazines in his pockets. He went quickly to an upstairs front room and peered carefully through the window. He could just see over the tops of the nearest trees into the glade, and halfway down the hill path. It wouldn't be long now. Far below, the last disciples were filtering into the undergrowth. He untied the black flag of Islamic State and unfurled it from the window, then settled down to wait.

HALFWAY UP THE HILL, STRANGE AND HIS REMAINING NINETEEN MEN stepped out of the trees and onto the driveway that ran from the old house to the road gate. Here the ground was so steep that the road ran diagonally up the slope. It was barely wide enough for two cars to pass. Trees closed in on each side until their branches joined overhead, and it seemed as if he, and the men with him, moved through a dark-green tunnel. Occasional shafts of sunlight pierced the canopy, leaving dancing after-images in his eyes. He felt confident, but the scene of the officer with the rake embedded in his skull still played inside his head.

The sound of the helicopter blades thudded and blatted overhead somewhere above the tree canopy.

Strange clicked on the radio. "From Sierra. Commander, does the helicopter camera have a view?"

Imran replied from the Command Unit. "From Indigo. Yes, we have it on screen, but the tree cover hides your position. Wait — air support just said that the black flag of IS has been draped from a window of the big house. Now we're sure who we're dealing with. Okay, we've got you on thermal through the canopy."

A burst of fire came from somewhere off to Strange's ten o'clock. Several more shots sounded, of heavier caliber. He pressed the talk button. "From Sierra. I can hear weapons fired."

The leader of group two responded over the channel. "From two-India. They've strung razor wire between the trees. Wait—"

Another burst of fire from the same direction, again followed by a response.

"From two-India. We shot one. Can't recover the body until we cut the wire. We're trying to find a way around."

Undertones of decayed vegetation hung in the humid air. Strange's nose twitched. He rubbed it, resisting the temptation to sneeze. The drive looped left over a ridge, then flattened out and curved around a swampy area. A World War II pillbox, a small hexagonal concrete structure, hid behind a patchy screen of bulrushes. Mold and vegetation camouflaged it more effectively than military paint. Strange remembered it from the map. He had a deep sense of unease.

Strange's point man stiffened, his left hand and arm making the unmistakable sign: Stay back! The officer flattened himself on the ground and beckoned Strange forward, then put his finger to his lips. Strange wriggled toward him through the leaf mold, thinking he'd need some new tactical gear after this outing.

"In front of the blockhouse. You can just make him out behind those bushes. Careful, now."

Strange didn't need the warning. He peered cautiously over the top of an old tree bole so that he could see across the marsh. There was the blockhouse all right, forty-five yards ahead, practically blending into the background vegetation. It had two slit windows at the front. As his eyes adjusted to the dappled light, he made out a silhouette. Part of a face, with something. It could be a rifle or a shotgun.

The point man whispered, "We'll have a hell of a job winkling them out. We could use gas."

Strange nodded. "Keep your eye on the sod."

Imran's voice came over the link. "From Indigo. Strange? Can you put the drone to good use? We're changing batteries."

"From Sierra. Yes, sir."

"From Indigo. We're having trouble on the flanks, there's wire in the trees."

"From Sierra. We'll deal with this and move up the center." Strange turned to his point man. "Lethal force is authorized; put a burst into that one." He pointed toward the half-hidden figure in the shrub.

The officer brought up his SIG516 and stitched a row of shots neatly across the bush, sending bits of shrub flying into the air. The image of a face disappeared.

Strange pressed the transmit button. "From Sierra. Sierra group, enfilade the pillbox, keep your distance, no heroics. Forty yards." He brought his hand over his shoulder in an "onward" gesture.

His men moved forward in short rushes, taking up positions up the drive to his left and into the trees on his right.

"From Sierra. Everyone in position, Sierra group?" One by one they acknowledged.

Strange waited until his men had settled. "From Sierra. Bring the ram up, we need it now."

THIRTY-FOUR

Near Snowshill, the Sheik had Walt drive off the road and into a tourist parking area. The place was deserted. The Sheik pulled some cable ties from his black bag and used them to lash Walt's wrists to either side of the steering wheel, then exited the vehicle.

The van shifted suddenly. Walt realized that Vicky had taken the chance to exit the back door — but the Sheik had felt it, too. He opened the passenger door, jumped out, and ran after her. Walt heard the shouts and a brief tussle, then the van lurched again. Someone was moving around inside the ENG compartment. His wrists hurt.

The Sheik reappeared. "This vehicle can talk directly with your studio?"

"What have you done to Vicky, you bastard?"

The Sheik backhanded him across the face.

An exquisite flower of pain burst in Walt's nose. Blood began to trickle into his mouth.

"That will teach you manners. The woman made a mistake. She won't repeat it. Now answer my question."

"Yes it can, but the antenna has to be aligned and the TWT amplifier set up. Not to mention the camera and video mixer."

"And you know how? Or you are just the driver?"

"I do know, I'm the engineer."

"And she knows how?" The Sheik pointed to the rear of the van.

Walt hesitated. "No. She's a reporter."

"What we're going to do: You are going to set up for a live report. And to make sure there are no surprises, you explain every step."

The Sheik got increasingly angry as Walt was setting up. He got as far as aligning the satellite dish and setting up the traveling wave tube amplifier before the Sheik interrupted him. "This is taking too long. Much too long. I haven't time for all this."

"Sorry. It is quite a lot to do." Not to mention that being scared rigid, Walt could hardly remember how to perform the simplest task.

"Isn't there a faster way?"

Walt thought frantically. "You threw our phones away. If we had a phone, we could use that. The studio has an IP we use for phone-in video." A thought occurred to him. "We could even use Facebook Live."

"I have a burner phone."

———

Vicky watched the Sheik enter the van and stoop close. "I'm going to untie you. Don't try anything, I will shoot." The Sheik cut the cable tie and freed Vicky's hands.

He led her outside and sat her on a folding chair, holding a printed statement. Behind her was the side of the OB van. The Sheik had hung the black flag of Islamic State across it. In front of her stood the ENG camera tripod, but no camera; just an iPhone. The Sheik had decided to use his phone and send the video directly to Heartland's IP address for news clips.

She rubbed the angry red welts on her wrists. *Oh, my God.*

"We're going to record my statement. Your life is worth less than one camel. So I won't hesitate to show your studio you, minus a head. It will make a very strong jihadi video." He opened his large black bag and pulled out a long chef's knife.

Her skin crawled. Walt couldn't help. He was in the van with his wrists cable-tied to the steering wheel. And Beeston would probably see it as a rating opportunity anyway.

"Clear?" He held up the knife.

"Yes. Perfectly clear." She felt calm. Like this was happening to another person.

He handed her a printed sheet, and she began to read it:

"You should have learned by now, that the truth of Islam does not depend upon any one individual. After me, there will be many more. You killed Anwar al-Awlaki and thought you had killed Islam. You killed Sheik Osama bin Laden, Allah have mercy on him, and you thought you had killed Islam. You captured Sheik Khalid Mohammed, but that has not shut up his voice."

Her voice shook slightly. She wondered if she was going to be killed after finishing this propaganda.

"The deen of Islam does not depend on me, or anyone. There will always be people like me, no matter how many you kuffar kill. Sharia is the law of God. The flag of Sharia will eventually fly over Downing Street."

She allowed herself to feel anger, something that she would normally avoid at all costs while reading a bulletin, and continued in a flat, emotionless voice:

"The more you fight against Sharia, the more people stand for the truth of Islam. So spend your money on the repressive police. Fight, because the more you fight, the more believers wake up. And your spending and fighting is your reward, it has brought this on you, your humiliation is not finished yet, not until the day of judgment.

"Your little island will be dominated by Islam. As the pages of history turn, your kingdom, your history will be forgotten. The future is domination of the deen of Islam to bring justice over the people in the east and the west, whether you like it or not — you shall obey."

The Sheik walked into the camera's view. He reached into his black bag and brought out the lead cylinder with its yellow radiation symbol. "This is heavy. But it keeps me safe from the Satan material. It has been in your water. It has been in your air. Where will it be next?"

He put the cylinder back inside the bag, moved out of view of the camera,

and switched off the iPhone. "Take down the flag and fold it, with respect. Give it to me." He held out his hand.

Vicky gave him the flag.

THIRTY-FIVE

Zafir sat at his position upstairs in the old house, busy with a wire that led through a front window and trailed off into the trees. Very deliberately, repeating each action in his head, he connected the red wire to the positive terminal of a motorcycle battery.

The black wire connects to one side of the light switch. Don't connect it yet. First, verify the switch is off. Yes, it's off. Right, connect it.

The other terminal, via a jump lead, connected to the battery's negative terminal, but he left it dangling for the time being. You could never be too careful.

Howling sirens and two-tone klaxons filled the air as ambulances and police arrived and departed. Gunfire cracked through the trees. Twice, he heard the deep bang of a shotgun. That would be Arno.

The police were being methodical. The brothers wouldn't hold them for long. It didn't matter now; he'd gained enough time for the Sheik, and now it was his turn. He glowed with self-satisfaction. What wonderful havoc he had created. The breakthroughs had been his. The main ideas. Not to mention his friends in Birmingham and London. And now he would teach the police a real lesson. His length of wire would trump all their high-tech phone blockers.

One of the cadres broke from the trees and made for the front door in a shambling run. Zafir lost sight of him, but after a moment heard him pounding at the front door. Zafir ran for the stairs, then leaped down them two at a time.

It was Arno, virtually unrecognizable, with his hair a tangle of briars, his face a mess of scratches and dirt. He clutched a pump-action twelve gauge in his right hand.

"Arno! Take it easy!" Zafir grabbed him by the shoulder. "We're gonna get out, but you have to help me. I want you to cover the door here, can you do that? You've still got shells?"

"Yeah. Three or four. I got one of them, Zafir!" His voice sounded manic.

"Okay. Cool down. Any more of our people show up, let them in. Put them in the windows on each side, the ones that still have shooters, I mean. The minute you see a uniform, the door gets bolted, okay? And you shout for me. I'll probably be here by then anyway. Then I'll show you the way out, right?"

"The way out?"

"Yeah. There's a back door the police don't know about. The Sheik showed me. Just do as I say and we'll be fine. Think you can manage?"

" 'Course I can."

THE CONCRETE PILLBOX SAT PRACTICALLY DEAD CENTER OF THE approach. If the line kept going, it would leave a bloody great gap in the middle, easily big enough for a small group to slip through. He hadn't enough men to set up an extended perimeter all the way around it. Strange turned to the small group of Special Branch men crouched behind him.

"Let's assume the fellow in there has a rifle or a twelve-gauge firing solid shot. The shields won't stand up to that." They nodded. "But the ram will. It's got two inches of steel at the front."

"It won't knock a hole in that," one officer said.

"Yes, I'm well aware of that. But it can get right up to the side of the building, close enough for us to lob a few CS gas cartridges inside. We'll lay covering fire on the windows with the machine pistols; that will keep his head down. Shields and vests, headgear, and gas masks. Any problems?"

"The ram, sir. The driver will have to get out the side to put the gas in. He'll be exposed."

"That's why I need a volunteer. One man to go up behind the ram, using it for cover."

The others all turned to look at the man who'd raised the objection. In a not-very-enthusiastic tone of voice, he broke the silence. "I'll do it, sir."

"Good man. Okay. When the gas goes in, Brown, Davis to the left. I'll stay dead center. You two go right. Until then we'll stay back here. Use the trees for cover."

Strange turned to estimate the number of men at his disposal. About fifteen. The ram sat back on the path. Its armored front sloped at forty-five degrees. Strange pulled his radio from an inside pocket and selected a channel.

"From Sierra. Piercer, do you read?"

"Loud and clear." The driver's voice sounded hollow, echoey.

"From Sierra. We're ready. Go, repeat, go. You've one man immediately behind you, so no reversing without warning. Got that?"

"From Piercer. Loud and clear."

The ram's diesel engine roared to life. A cloud of gray smoke came from somewhere under its rear and hung in the trees. The man crouching behind it took a handkerchief from his pocket and wiped his streaming eyes. The ram moved up the slope at walking speed until it lurched over the crest. It crept across the spongy ground, leaving deep tire tracks. There was no fire from the pillbox.

Strange took cover behind a fallen tree. The trunk had been a good four feet thick but now lay part-sunk into the loamy soil. He wondered if the pillbox might be unoccupied after all. Perhaps he was overestimating the danger? But no; he remembered what had happened at the factory.

His officers were moving around the perimeter, slipping from tree to tree, using them for cover.

Strange shaded his eyes. The pillbox sat sixty yards or so across the sunken surface of an old lake bed. Squinting, he could just make out a silhouette behind the slit window. The ram was nearly halfway across. Still no response from the building. Odd. He had a bad feeling about it.

Strange keyed the transmit button on his radio. "From Sierra. Piercer team, it's too quiet. Covering fire on the windows, please, three-round burst." On each side, his men opened up. Ricochets yowled off the pillbox, and puffs of cement dust flew into the air around the slit windows. Still no response.

The tip of the ram hit the pillbox and was stopped by the reinforced concrete. Now, go now, the control officer silently shouted, and as if he'd heard, the cop behind the ram scrambled around it. In less than a second, he was up to the base of the wall. He clutched a bulky object in his right hand. His other hand pulled something from it. Smoke puffed. The man reached up, leaned backward, then hurled the gas grenade neatly through the slit window. Dense clouds of white CS gas poured from both windows, then boiled up from somewhere at the rear.

ZAFIR SHIFTED IMPATIENTLY FROM ONE FOOT TO THE OTHER. HE watched the armored vehicle move out across the marshy area heading toward the pillbox. Officers in combat gear were grouped around the marsh. Peering down, he saw that the last of the brothers were backing toward the front doorway, their weapons extended.

Zafir squinted to the front just in time to catch a sudden movement at the edge of the trees. A man in a black combat kit. "Stop!" came a distant shout. "Armed police!"

Moments later, the harsh blast of a twelve-gauge shotgun echoed in the house, then again. Puffs of smoke came from the officer's weapon. Someone shouted down below. The officer must have been hit — he clutched himself and worked his way back into the trees. One of the brothers slammed the front door. Zafir returned his attention to the glade halfway down the hill.

The armored vehicle had reached the pillbox. Zafir laughed to see the officer behind it fiddling with something. He connected the switch to the battery's negative terminal. The Sheik said they'd be scattered to the four winds.

The man behind the ram darted out, rolled to the base of the wall just below the pillbox window, and tossed something inside. White vapor boiled from the slits and from the concealed entrance at the back.

Zafir heard muffled popping sounds as the cops fired on the windows. The police surged over the ridgeline, still shooting. Zafir gave them a few seconds, then clicked the switch and stood away from the window.

STRANGE WAS JUST LIFTING HIS HEAD ABOVE THE FALLEN LOG WHEN HIS eyes registered the sudden glare of light from the pillbox. Pure instinct dropped him back down a split second before the blast wave reached him.

A clap of sound struck him, as intense as a physical blow. The shockwave passed just overhead, causing a sudden vacuum that rolled him onto his back and sucked the air from his lungs.

A high-velocity sleet of concrete fragments, pebbles, and steel rods blew chunks off the log. Improbably, a large piece of the pillbox roof came into view, spinning like a top, rising like a giant Frisbee.

After the explosion, an intense silence hung in the air. Strange heard nothing except a high-pitched ringing. Chunks of concrete rained from the sky. He hunched next to the log and parried with his arms as chunks hit his back, his hip, his legs.

Pieces stopped falling. Strange tested to see if all his body parts were still attached. He felt as if he had just lost a fight and been given a serious kicking. His breath wheezed in his chest.

He looked over the top of the log, which had been chipped and scored by shrapnel. Around the marshy glade, trees and bushes lay in shreds. The blast had flattened most of the smaller ones. He looked downhill. His reserve force stood immobile. One of the sergeants was urging them forward. Strange could barely make out his words through the loud whistling in his head. "Up! Get on with it! Move, dammit!" Moaning came from around the glade where the badly injured had been thrown. As they came up and the younger officers saw the things that hung from the branches, some of them turned away, retching.

The ram had come to rest, minus its front wheels, nearly one hundred yards down slope, its position indicated by a trail of broken trees. There was no sign of the man who had thrown the gas grenade, just a steaming crater nine feet wide and nearly three feet deep. Jagged sections of concrete foundation projected from the torn soil. Reinforcing rods bristled from the material like mangled television antennas.

ZAFIR SAW THE FLASH REFLECTED IN THE WINDOW PANE AND THEN, A moment later, the shockwave blew the glass in. He took a quick look through the broken window and saw the ring of devastated trees around the glade. Further detail was hidden by a large cloud of dark gray smoke, rising into the air and slowly spreading at the top.

He ran down the stairs and found the rest of them in the hall. Some had been cut by fragments from the stained-glass windows on each side of the door.

"Come on! We gotta get moving. There is a way out. The Sheik showed me." He turned down the corridor, and the others followed, pressing tightly behind.

THIRTY-SIX

"It's a place for the dying," Eric Woolman said in a matter-of-fact voice.

Doctor Newton, fiddling with the television set in the resident's lounge, turned around. "Oh, I don't think that's true. Quite a few have been able to leave. The new amino-acid compounds seem to be doing a bit of good; the counts were generally lower last week."

He gave the set a firm slap, and the picture, which had been haloed in red, green, and blue, steadied to reveal a man's face set against a backdrop of the countryside. The fellow's lips moved, but the sound was turned off.

In the background, dominoes clacked and backgammon dice rattled, as several of the other residents occupied their time.

"When are they going to give the cricket scores? They're normally on at this time," the doctor complained in a mild tone.

Woolman looked at him with a certain amount of compassion. They'd lost themselves, he thought. The doctor wasn't contaminated but had lost his wife and his way of life instead. He wondered which hurt the most.

There were just twenty-nine of them left. Fifteen more lay

nearby in a general hospital. Tubes ran in and out of their bodies, respirators helped them breathe, and life-support monitors beeped quietly as the jagged green lines traced the pulses of their lives. *If you could call it life*, reflected Woolman gloomily. He watched the man on the screen mouthing his dumb show, but his thoughts were elsewhere.

Just after the riot at tent town, the authorities converted a small hotel and moved the Upwood villagers in. Now it was really more of a specialized hospital, except there were no doctors other than Newton; only nurses, who administered the daily care routines, the dosages, diets, and supplements. Every day, a special vehicle came to take away body waste, anything that had been in contact with the patients.

Most of them didn't care to go outside, though they were allowed to. Woolman had taken part in one or two little expeditions. Memories they invoked pained them like open wounds. On London's crowded pavements, the throng had parted before them, flowed into the road, or moved into shop doorways. A couple of hundred years earlier, someone would have preceded them with a bell, shouting "Unclean, unclean!" It was like the treatment accorded to lepers.

Woolman could understand it. The remaining patients were oblivious to their condition. Hair in tufts on those who still had any, great pits in bodies where surgeons had dug out tumors and pustules, and skin growths like strangled weeds hanging from their faces. He watched the doctor fiddling with the TV. Still they hadn't put on the cricket scores. What was this rubbish that had taken over the channel, he wondered.

"Turn the volume up, willya, Doc?" he called.

"—more than one hundred and fifty men involved in the operation. A steady stream of ambulances is arriving and departing, and two fire engines are parked on the access road. Automatic weapons fire is coming from the estate. The police have confirmed that armed officers are involved."

The picture cut to a scene of two people, jackets pulled over their heads to thwart the cameras, being led from a police van into a building.

"Raids are taking place in London connected with the mass poisoning attempt in the North of England. At this time the authorities will not comment as to whether there is any connection with the armed siege in the Midlands."

The announcer put his hand up to the side of his head, listening intently, evidently to some comment from his control room.

"We have a live news report of the siege coming in from our helicopter on the scene." The announcer turned slightly in his seat, and the picture cut to a scene of treetops, a gray ribbon of a road in the background, with vehicles parked along it, looking like toys in the distance.

The airborne reporter's voice spoke over a background of whistling turbines and rotor-blade chatter.

"This is Robin Adams reporting live from the Grange estate near Worcester." In the distance, the tree line stopped and an island of green grass could be seen. A doll's house stood in the center of the grass, surrounded by a cluster of structures like a child's blocks. Tiny dots moved near the main structure. The camera zoomed, and the doll's house grew into a stately residence. Paths led to and fro; a broader road wound away into the trees. The dots became ant-like people. A ragged circle of them retreated across the grass, toward the house.

The camera zoomed even further, then stopped, evidently at the limit; the picture danced and wobbled. Those retreating toward the house seemed to dance and wobble, too.

"The operation started at first light when a teenage girl surrendered to the police. She is now helping them with their inquiries. Local people say that the Grange, a stately house dating from the seventeenth century, was bought by a controversial religious leader more than a year ago. This is believed to be the same person who appeared on this channel within the last half hour reading an Islamic State manifesto. Several of his followers are resisting the efforts of the police to execute a search and arrest warrant."

Figures appeared from the edge of the trees on the far right. One fell backward. One of the ragged figures also fell, crumpling in slow vertical motion, and was dragged back into the doorway by two of the others.

The reporter's voice rose in excitement: "We appear to be witnessing an exchange of gunfire here ... yes, a man is down ... a police officer also appears to have been shot. ..."

Woolman glanced behind him. The five residents at the back of the lounge peered intently at the television set. Two of them were on their feet.

"Well, there go the cricket scores," Doctor Newton said.

THIRTY-SEVEN

Vicky struggled with the cable ties that cut into her flesh as she leaned away from the Sheik on the van seat. Behind her, Walt was setting up the equipment for the direct link back to the studio. The Sheik seemed to think that Heartland's main studio was in London, not Birmingham. Why else drive to the capital? In fact, the London studio was little more than a video suite.

"Is everything ready?" the Sheik asked.

Walt turned to him. "Yes. This is the camera, here. The microphone's attached. I've mounted it on this stand, but if this clip is undone, you can walk about." Walt pointed to the camera, then to a selector on the tiny control desk inside the door. "Turn this to the first position and the camera picture — and sound — will come up on one of the monitors in the studio control room."

"Very good. Sit on the floor at the back." The Sheik twitched the gun toward the back of the van. "Right. Stretch your hands out. Yes, like that."

The Sheik secured Walt's hands to metal anchors on each side of the rear doors so that Walt sat in the center of the gangway with Vicky just to one side.

"Now sit quietly. Remember my jacket is lined with the mother of Satan explosive." The Sheik stepped back and lifted a lead cylinder from his bag. "There's more here, and I can detonate it at any time, but the explosives are a gift for London; a reply to the gifts you British send my people in drones." He retrieved his gun and slid a round into the chamber. "I don't want to waste them on you, so move in a way I don't like, and I'll shoot you instead."

HEARTLAND'S NEWS CONTROL ROOM WAS CRAMMED. ONE MONITOR had the aerial view from the helicopter, another had a view of the police roadblock. Hetherington, the program director, and Beeston, the producer, were jammed into a corner at the far end. They spoke in low voices.

"You can't put that lunatic on air, Beeston. The IBA won't permit it. We'll be sanctioned and you'll be lucky if you end up producing the epilogue."

"It's news. And it ties in directly with that—" Beeston flung an arm out, indicating the aerial view. Armed police surrounded the old house. Officers hid, crowding behind nearby structures — low stone walls, wide trees, and outbuildings. Smoke drifted across the lawns, and gunfire rattled from several directions.

"If you were to take full responsibility—" Hetherington said.

The engineers stared at their equipment as if they were not listening. One of them turned around and remarked in a matter-of-fact voice, "Three minutes to commercial break, Mr. Beeston."

"And thirteen minutes to the deadline for Vicky Wallis and Walt, Mr. Hetherington," Beeston said urgently.

"All right. Run it. We'll catch it from all quarters afterward, justified or not, so I'll say just one thing. I want it to be great television. The sort of television that wins awards. A BAFTA for sure." Hetherington looked around the control room, then fixed his stare on the producer.

"Whatever it takes, Mr. Hetherington," Beeston said. Hetherington turned on his heel and left the control room through the airlock door. Beeston picked up the nearest telephone and dialed nine for an outside line, then Strange's direct line. The duty officer answered.

"This is Andy Beeston at Heartland Television. Can I talk to Chief Inspector Strange, please? It's a life or death situation." He tapped his foot impatiently against the side of the desk. Time was running out.

"I'm sorry, sir. The inspector is on an investigation. Can you tell me what this is about, please?"

Shit, Beeston thought. Bloody shit. The clock said seven minutes left. "In that case, send assistance. Two members of my staff were abducted, and they're making a broadcast in precisely" — he checked the clock — "six and a half minutes."

THIRTY-EIGHT

The residents' lounge had filled up rapidly as word spread. Seventeen of the Upwood villagers were focused on the television set, while several more, who couldn't find room, had taken over the set in the nurses' day room. The volume was on high.

"The Islamic State students have barricaded themselves into the house, and the police are closing in. One or two students, probably armed, are believed to be holding out in an old World War II concrete blockhouse in the woods." The beat of helicopter blades could be heard under the reporter's voice. "This is Robin Adams, reporting live from the Grange near Worcester, for Independent Tele— Jesus Christ!"

The residents gasped and craned forward as the camera on board the news copter showed a hot blue and yellow flash toward the center of the woods. The trees bowed as if pressed down by the hand of an invisible giant. A pall of dark gray smoke rose above the trees. Out of it, a large circular shape emerged, spinning crazily towards the aircraft. The view tilted sharply as the pilot took evasive action.

A splitting crack followed, and then the picture tumbled crazily, showing sky, clouds, treetops, and sky again.

Eric Woolman turned to Doctor Newton."My God, did you see that?"

Newton could only nod as a babble of remarks broke the silence in the room: "maniacs," "religion and politics, as bad as each other," "bloody hell." Then Doctor Newton raised his voice and said, "Quiet, I can't hear what's happening!"

The picture cut back to the news studio, showing an announcer sitting at his desk, hand clamped over the device in his ear, listening intently. Then he faced the camera, breaking in smoothly, "We're sorry to interrupt the live coverage, due to an explosion at the Grange estate, a madrassa in the West Midlands. Our news helicopter has been forced to land to check for damage after being hit by flying debris."

He continued. "Police have confirmed they are seeking this group for an incident that occurred several weeks ago in the North West. They are believed to be responsible for contaminating the village of Upwood with a radioactive isotope in an arson attack that caused a number of deaths."

The atmosphere in the room became as brittle as dry ice. The residents looked at each other and then back at the television set. The announcer listened intently again to his earphone, then peered at his monitor, mounted at the side of his desk and out of direct view of the camera. He returned his focus to the front.

"News has just come in that the leader of the group, who calls himself the Sheik, is in London at an unknown location. He is apparently demanding a live interview on Heartland Television and is holding two Heartland employees hostage."

A neon light started blinking on a telephone in front of the announcer. He picked up the phone, but the sound was muted. The silent conversation lasted only fifteen seconds. "Due to broadcasting regulations, we will not be able to screen the live interview with the religious leader. Now, we will return to the scene at the Grange."

"Change the channel," shouted a voice from the back of the room. "Try Heartland, it's their reporter." A mutter of assent filled the room, and the doctor changed the channel with the remote. The scene cut to a narrow view of the outside broadcast vehicle taken from a small ENG camera. Two hostages sat, bound hand and foot, on the tailgate. In the foreground stood a man wearing hiking gear.

Chairs scraped as the villagers stood up. They were all on their feet now. "Let's get the bastard," Woolman shouted. "A trial's too good for him!"

THIRTY-NINE

S trange drew his legs up underneath him and rose to his knees to see over the log. Steam was rising from the bomb crater. Someone put a hand on his shoulder and mumbled something.

The chief inspector leaned forward and cupped a hand behind his ear. "You'll have to shout — there's a loud whistle in my ears."

"I said, are you all right, sir?"

Strange patted his hands over his body. "Everything seems intact."

"Sir, you're bleeding from your left ear."

Strange put his hand up to feel. Yes, sticky. "I've got to get moving." He made to get to his feet, but the sergeant stopped him.

"Sir, Superintendent Atherton has taken command. Commander Imran has requested military intervention. We've at least five dead, plus injured. You're to wait for medical assistance, they'll be here in a minute."

"With respect, Sergeant, fuck that. Help me up. I'm going to get the twat responsible for this."

"Sir—"

"No arguments. Give me a hand."

Standing up took more effort than Strange expected, as if his lungs weren't working properly. He couldn't get enough oxygen. His radio was making a strange crackling sound. He clicked the mic button. "From Sierra. Reporting back on duty."

Nothing. The crackling sound continued. "From Sierra. Please report my signal." More crackling. Useless.

An ambulance was backing up the drive, its engine revving. Another followed. The first ambulance parked half off the path. As it came to a halt, a paramedic flung the rear doors open and collected a scoop stretcher from a side compartment. A second paramedic followed. They headed toward an officer who lay groaning nearby. But there was no time to waste. Strange looked uphill. The line had advanced ahead of him. No officers were visible except the injured, the dead, and Sergeant James.

Shots cracked in the distance. Pistol fire, by the sound of it. The unmistakable bang of a shotgun. Twice more. A sudden racket of small-arms fire of mixed caliber. Where was his pistol? Ah, there. He hadn't lost it.

"Let's get on with it, Sergeant. Use your radio to report that I'm back on duty." Strange began moving uphill on rubber legs.

The slope flattened out, at the same time as the trees thinned, so as he came over the peak, the edge of the trees lay some sixty yards in front, and beyond, he caught glimpses of sunlit grass.

Strange waited for Sergeant James to get off the radio.

"Sir, Commander Imran says you are to wait here. You are not — he said absolutely not, sir — to join the assault team."

"All right. But I want a view of that house."

He crossed the open ground to a parking lot where Atherton seemed to be holding his men back, using the trees for cover. A lawn separated the woodland from the old house.

Suddenly, three blasts of a whistle sounded.

"Go, go, go!" Atherton stood up and waved his arm.

Strange fingered his pistol. But no, he was in no shape to join the assault.

The helicopter began to hover above the treeline. Strange guessed that at least one sniper covered the house.

Sergeant James put his radio to his ear.

The officers at the edge of the trees began running across the lawn. Some had remained in cover and were firing rifles and carbines at the windows.

The assault line reached the house. Riot guns hurled gas grenades through the windows. The men nearest the house hurriedly donned their masks.

James cupped the radio to his ear. "They're going in now, sir."

A three-man squad charged the door and reached it without injury. Two more loud bangs sent crows squawking into the air. The door sagged. They kicked it in and disappeared from view.

More officers rushed across the lawn and vanished through the door. From inside came the sound of firing.

"What's happening, Sergeant?" Strange asked, itching to join in.

"Nobody inside, sir. They're holed up in the chapel, at the rear."

The metal sound of a police loudspeaker came from the house. "Armed police. Come out! You are surrounded." After a few moments, the loudspeaker sounded again. "Armed police. I say again: Come out now! Put down your weapons."

"They're breaking the chapel door now, sir." Sergeant James's brow furrowed. "They're in."

Strange wondered why he'd heard no more shooting.

"Sir, there's no one inside. Suspected bomb — our men are pulling back — oh, my God!"

A black fountain of earth erupted from the rear of the old house, rising and spreading. A split second later, the house sagged back-ward, then blew into fragments.

The ground thumped Strange hard under his feet. He shouted, "Take cover, Sergeant!" and dodged behind a tree.

The blast wave hit his ears. For several seconds, the blast echoed from the landscape as if the ground were breathing it back out.

A chimney pot hurtled from the sky with an ominous "thrumm" and hit the ground nearby, sending ceramic shards flying.

The airborne cloud of soil slumped down. A column of smoke and flame replaced it.

"Oh, fuck, fuck, fuck." Strange sat with his back to the tree. Debris was still coming down. He sneaked a look. The helicopter was circling where the house had been. A crater had swallowed the structure. Huge cracks ran out across what had once been a pristine lawn, now all heaved up.

"Sergeant. Contact Commander Imran, please. Suggest to him that I resume command. And get me a radio, please."

STRANGE, WITH SERGEANT JAMES IN TOW, ARRIVED AT THE ESTATE gates to find they had been taken off their hinges to better allow access for emergency vehicles. Ambulances were arriving. Strange and the sergeant walked to the MIU trailer. An ant's nest of activity surrounded it. As they approached, Commander Imran flung the door open and stepped down.

"Strange! It's a wonder you weren't blown to pieces. I'm glad you followed orders and didn't go charging after the superintendent. He and his men are gone, along with the chapel, most of the house, and part of the hill. A huge bomb. But come inside and sit down. Look at you, you're bleeding from the ear. We'll get you into an ambulance."

A cop appeared at the door to the MIU. "Commander, it's the air unit. They've spotted someone leaving from the rear of the property."

"I'm not getting in any ambulance," Strange said as he spotted a police Land Rover Defender parked on the verge and pointed to it. "Sergeant James! Are the keys in that?"

"Strange! Get yourself into an ambulance. You're not fit for duty."
Imran shook his head.

———

STRANGE FOLLOWED IMRAN UP THE FEW STEPS AND INTO THE MIU
trailer. A hive of activity. That electronic and plastic smell. All the
workstations were in use.

Imran pointed to three officers. "We've begun the after-action
review. We need to talk to you, but now you need to get to casualty."

"Sir, are they all dead? What about Sheik Maulan? Him, too?"

"Ah. No. Sit down for a moment and I'll explain."

Strange sat on one of the folding chairs.

"Sheik Maulan has escaped. Just a minute before you got here,
Heartland TV called to say one of their reporters and an engineer
were abducted."

Strange suddenly felt freezing cold. "One of their reporters.
Which one in particular?"

"Vicky Wallis."

Ice seemed to coat Strange's throat. Why Vicky? Why all this
carnage? His thoughts began to spin out of control.

"Where? Do we know where?" he said.

"Maybe. We've tracked the phones. They are all switched off, but
you know that doesn't matter. Two of them are in the Cotswolds
and not moving. But the third is on the outskirts of London."

"Sir—"

"Before you say anything, Chief Inspector, the answer is no. Now
get yourself into an ambulance." Imran turned away and gave his
attention to an officer who had just come in.

Strange shook his head — and immediately wished he hadn't. He
went to the door, opened it, and climbed down the short set of
aluminum steps.

Sergeant James was standing there. "It didn't go too well, sir?"

"What do you mean, Sergeant?"

"I can see it on your face, sir. Is there anything I can do?"

"Yes. I need to get back on this, but first I need to get fixed up. Can you drive me to Accidents and Emergencies?"

"Which one, sir?"

"The Queen Elizabeth in Brum."

FORTY

"Wait — look!" Doctor Newton reached into the corridor and grabbed one of the patients by the arm, a big swarthy fellow called Ed Crowell. Crowell yelled in pain and lashed out with his free hand.

"Sorry. Sorry, I forgot." Newton cursed himself. Crowell's arms and upper torso were a mass of painful boils that were intractable to treatment. The man was rapidly becoming a walking colony of staphylococcus aureus.

"What is it?" Crowell snarled. Three of the others had stopped because of the commotion.

"Look, there—" Newton pointed at the TV screen. The helicopter was back in action again, circling the house at a discreet distance. A pall of smoke lay over the house, red flames flickering in its depths. Behind it, a crater had appeared in the hillside, about halfway down. The police stood in a circle around the property, watching it burn. At the bottom of the hill at the front, a fire appliance moved slowly through the gates.

"It's all over for them," Newton said. "It's over. Can't you see that?" God, let it stop now, he prayed. Crowell turned, and Newton recoiled at the expression on his face.

"No, it fuckin' well isn't, Doctor," Crowell spat. "The bastard who started this is still running around, spouting off his bloody mouth on the telly. Well, we'll close it for him."

"Look man, you don't know how to find him. He could be anywhere."

Now another voice replied. Eric Woolman, the cynic. He carried a serrated kitchen knife in his hand. "Oh, we'll find him, Doctor. There's nothing they can do to us that hasn't already been done. We'll start at the TV studio."

Without more ado, he turned and marched purposefully toward the front door. The others followed him. They were carrying a variety of implements: knives, a chair leg studded with nails, a heavy chain. The mob went down the hall out of his sight. A few moments later he heard the door slam. He went across the room and picked up the telephone. Was this an emergency call? He wasn't sure. Best not make a fuss. He decided to look up the number of the local police station in the directory.

———————

PASSERS-BY RECOILED WITH CRIES OF DISMAY AS THE ARMED PATIENTS poured out of the door of the converted hotel brandishing their weapons. A red double-decker bus was just pulling up to the curb. Crowell ran to the driver's door, bounded onto the running board, and yanked the handle. The driver turned. He was a big fellow with Rastafarian dreadlocks crammed tightly into a white felt hat. His face was struck with disgust and disbelief as Crowell's pustulated features hung over him.

"There's been a change in your route. It's now an express service. D'you know where the television studios are?"

"Which ones, mon? There's Television Centre, White City … must be a dozen at least."

"Heartland. Christ man, haven't you heard the news?"

"News? I drive this bus, mon, I don' listen to the bloody news. Now get off before I call the police," the driver blustered.

Crowell laughed, produced his knife, and waved it in the driver's face. "Listen. I don't give a shit. Just do us a little favor and nothing's going to happen to you, see? Just drive us to Heartland right now and then let us off. Okay?"

The driver eyed the knife, then the armed mob behind Crowell. "Okay, mon. Anytin' you like."

As the driver turned the first corner, Crowell saw that the five or six passengers that they'd thrown off the bus now stood in line waiting for the next one to arrive. He turned to the driver.

"Look at that. Business as usual, eh! Don't worry, feller. We're not maniacs. We've just got some unfinished business. You do your bit, we'll do ours, and then you can go about your life as usual."

"Sure, mon. Jus' a normal day in London town."

FORTY-ONE

Strange expected to join the queue when he arrived at A&E, but a separate section had been set up to deal with the casualties arriving from the madrassa. He had barely sat down before he was being triaged.

A nurse cleaned the blood from the side of his head and his ear. He could now hear on that side again, but in a dull way, and he had an earache.

A doctor examined him with an otoscope. "You have a perforated eardrum. The injury is severe; it would be better to schedule you for surgery."

A nurse handed Strange's triage notes to the doctor.

"And you've got a concussion. And general contusions. You're suffering from shock. I'm surprised you are still walking around."

"Doctor, I need to continue walking around, as you put it. I'm still on duty." On duty, perhaps, but itching to get after Sheik Maulan and Vicky.

"I'll discharge you, but against my advice. At least I can prescribe something for the headache and earache. You'll need antibiotics for the ear. ..."

Strange took an Uber to his apartment.

He put a frozen meal in the microwave and stripped off his personal protection kit. While the meal was heating, he turned on the shower and laid out a change of clothes. Heartland TV was running continuous coverage. He got into the shower and, protecting his ear from the water, sponged himself down with water as hot as he could stand, discovering bruises everywhere.

Out of the shower, he dressed, put on a shoulder holster for the pistol, gobbled the meal, took the antibiotics he'd been prescribed — he'd already downed the painkillers at the hospital — and grabbed the keys to the Jaguar.

His mobile phone rang as he was on his way out. Sergeant James.

"Sir? I was waiting for you to be discharged, but you slipped past somehow. Where are you?"

"I'm just leaving my place. That bastard has got Vicky."

"Sir, I'm still on detached duty, responsible to you. Where are you?"

"Edgbaston."

"I can be there in ten minutes, or less on blue lights. Commander Imran told me under no circumstances to allow you to drive."

"Hmm." Strange glanced at the keys in his hand. The Jag was a difficult car on a good day. The sergeant had a point. Besides, the police car had all the gear. "Right. No need for blue lights, but get here as fast as you can."

James parked the car on the double yellow lines outside Heartland's Birmingham studio. Even before the car stopped completely, Strange leaped from the door and took the steps two at a time into the foyer, brushing aside the security guy.

The receptionist looked up as he came charging in.

"I need to talk to Beeston. Now. Police business."

"I remember you, Detective Chief Inspector." She picked up the phone. "Mr. Beeston, please. Oh, Freddy, is that you? I have Detective Chief Inspector Strange here." She listened for some moments. "I'll tell him." She put down the phone. "Freddy will be here in a moment."

When Freddy arrived, he had none of the banter of Strange's first meeting with him. "Mr. Beeston is reviewing the video in an editing suite. Please follow me."

They were replaying Vicky's video, making notes.

Beeston turned to Strange. "We've scraped the location from metadata. It was sent from a parking lot in the Cotswolds. Well off the beaten track. Roughly halfway to London."

"Please explain."

"This wasn't a proper outside broadcast. Maybe he didn't trust the engineer. It was made with an iPhone. The file was uploaded to our tips web account."

"You've informed our office, I take it?"

Beeston looked down at his feet. "Not yet. We only just now had a close look at it."

Strange thought his head might explode. Oh, for fuck's sake. These idiots.

"And it's Vicky's phone. We bought it. All our news staff have high-end phones, a lot of reporting—"

"Yes, I know. For God's sake, call our office right now with the phone number. We can track it even if it's switched off."

If anything had happened to her, he'd not rest until—

His mind was a maelstrom of conflicting emotions: fear of losing her, despair that he already had, the hot anger of the terrible revenge he'd exact, frustration.

Freddy turned to Strange. "That Sheik, he took her with him. Please bring her back."

The intercom buzzed. It was the Pinkerton security man.

"There is a message from a Commander Imran. Would Chief Inspector Strange call him immediately?"

Strange used the telephone in Beeston's office to get a bit of privacy.

"Strange. What the hell d'you think you're doing, man? You're supposed to be recovering in the hospital, not gallivanting around a television station."

Strange managed a couple of words.

"The minister wants to know where you are. The hospital has made a complaint about you discharging yourself against doctor's orders. West End Central has taken over the case, in London. And we've had a report from them that the vehicle has been found."

"The van, sir?"

"Outside the Baker Street tube station. There was no one in it. The newspaper seller outside the station says he saw a man in hiking gear going into the station. He didn't remember whether there was a woman with him or not."

"I'm on my way, sir," Strange said immediately.

"On your way? What d'you mean? It's—"

Strange put down the phone.

FORTY-TWO

Halfway to London, on the M1, a line of thirty-ton trucks struggled up the inside two lanes, while light vans and slower-moving cars played tag in the third lane. The road had been widened to four lanes because of the long, steep hill, but Strange and Sergeant James were now stuck behind four cars, balked by an elderly Peugeot that evidently was unable to live up to its driver's expectations.

"They'll probably fire me for this, you know. I should never have let you talk me into it," Sergeant James remarked.

"Ah, shut up and put your foot down. Look, you've dropped below eighty again," Strange said.

"It's the hill, sir. And the traffic, too many slow trucks."

"Why doesn't that idiot get out of the bloody way?" Strange exclaimed, leaning forward in his seat. He grunted in pain, bit his lip, then settled himself gently back again.

"Careful, sir," James said.

Strange changed his attention to the car radio. He fiddled with the buttons, trying to bring a station in, but all he got was the whining sound made by the car's alternator; buzzes; and clicks.

"I can't get a damn thing," Strange muttered.

"I know, sir," James said, not for the first time. "It's faulty."

The Peugeot driver finally gave up the struggle, and the four cars that had been trailing along behind it surged forward. James wasn't slow to take up the challenge. As they crested the top of the slope and started the long run down the other side, he had the speedometer needle hovering around the hundred mark.

"I hope I don't get a ticket, sir," James said and grinned.

"It's a police emergency." Strange hoped the car had been serviced recently. It would be bad to blow a tire at this speed.

The M1 spat them out onto the North Circular Road. Strange drummed his fingers on the armrest. "North West to Brent Cross flyover. Then South on Hendon Way to the Finchley Road. Blue lights."

Near the reservoir at Cool Oak Lane, Walt was sitting on leaf litter with his back to a tree. His arms, awkwardly bent backward around the trunk, hurt badly. The Sheik had dumped him here and tied his wrists together with audio cable before driving off with Vicky.

Walt's voice was hoarse from shouting for help. The skin on his wrists was raw, but he kept rubbing the microphone cable back and forth against the rough bark of the tree. He knew he must be somewhere in northwest London. Before the Sheik left, Walt had plucked up the courage to ask him where he was taking Vicky.

The Sheik thought for a moment. "Maybe we'll visit the Queen." He laughed. "Hot dust will fly!"

As soon as the sound of the exhaust faded, Walt started rubbing the cable. It had taken him half an hour or more to work his way through the insulation. He redoubled his efforts, face screwed up against the pain. There! A strand parted. One by one, the cores of the multi-conductor cable gave way. Finally, he gave a heave and the remainder of the insulated sheath snapped. Walt inspected himself. Blood was streaming from his wrists.

Slipping and stumbling in the wet grass, he made his way through a thicket at the top of the slope. A chain-link fence. Blocks of apartments. Nobody about. The fence had been torn open a little distance away. Was this a bad part of London? One of the gang places, where people got stabbed all the time? What the hell to do? He checked his pockets, but he already knew what he would find. No phone, wallet, or money. Empty.

He pulled at the broken fence and squeezed through. A parking lot. For the tower blocks, he assumed. He looked around. No one in sight. No, wait — movement, over there. It looked like a storage area for garbage bins, with a large one parked in it.

A man's head and shoulders popped up from the garbage bin.

Walt walked over. "Excuse me? I need help. Do you have a mobile?"

The man flapped his hand and said, "Dispari, dispari."

A homeless person. Useless. Walt continued on past the entrance to the block, down a pedestrian path, and into the street. He walked on another twenty yards to a crossroads. To his left, more tower blocks. To his right, traditional London semi-detached houses. A man was washing his car in the driveway of one of them.

Walt walked to him. "Excuse me."

The man looked up. White, mid-fifties perhaps, balding. "Something I can do for you?"

"This will sound crazy. I just need to use a phone. I was mugged. The guy took my phone and wallet. Look—" Walt held out his lacerated wrists.

"You're in a bad way, mate. It's not a phone you need, but an ambulance and the police."

"Y-yes." Walt began shaking uncontrollably.

"Come inside. The missus will make you a cuppa, and I'll call the police. I've always wanted an excuse to do that."

FORTY-THREE

The walls of the Baker Street tube station carried mosaics depicting scenes from the Sherlock Holmes books. Vicky wished the fictional detective was able to help her now. The platforms were crowded and yet she felt totally alone with the tall man in the walking jacket. She sensed eyes upon her, but when she sought them, her fellow passengers were reading the advertisements on the tunnel walls, or studying their newspapers, or peering toward the tunnel mouth as if they could spot the next train coming. The Sheik had her by the elbow, his grip like a vice. He'd warned her: One shout, one false move, and he'd shoot her through the head. What happened after that would be, for her, academic.

A gust of warm, funky air billowed from the mouth of the tunnel. The rails began to hum and creak, then the blunt nose of a Circle line tube train butted from the tunnel mouth. It was followed by a string of carriages almost too long for the platform, going rat-a-tat-tat, rat-a-tat-tat, like a clockwork toy running down, as the train drew to a halt. The crowd pushed and shoved, maneuvering so as to be next to the doors when they opened.

The Sheik tightened his grip to the point where she felt sure he'd cut off the circulation in her arm. Gordon Strange, where are you? He must be somewhere in the Midlands.

The station's public address system came to life. A metallic voice rang down the curved platform. Echoes came back from all directions, mangling the message. She could only make out bits and pieces.

"The next train … terminate … Mile End. Normal service … be resumed … change at … ." The PA clicked off, then on again, and the message repeated. It made even less sense than before. People milled about; some stood where they were, some sat down on the few seats available, and others were determined to board the train.

Air smelling of smoked fish puffed from the release mechanisms, and the doors slid back. The passengers trying to get off fought their way onto the platform, while those waiting crowded in on each side.

The Sheik propelled Vicky forward. Her foot nearly went through the gap between the train and the edge of the platform.

A man in a pinstriped suit with an umbrella said, "Do you mind?"

The doors started to close, then opened again; Vicky was crammed into the corridor. She grabbed a roof strap with one hand; the other was starting to go numb. There was a sharp pain in her ankle. Again the doors tried to close, yet opened again; some idiot must have his foot in the way, thought Vicky, then she realized it was hers. She pulled it inside, allowing the doors to close.

Over the loudspeakers, a voice announced: "This is a Circle line train via King's Cross St. Pancras and Liverpool street."

The train lurched, then slowly gathered speed into the tunnel.

The lights went out, flickered for a moment, then came back on, as the carriage passed over a live rail junction. A hand from one of the tightly packed travelers briefly caressed her buttocks. She glared around, wishing she could burst into tears, feeling embarrassment, fear, and anger all at the same time. The carriages rocked as the train negotiated a bend, the wheels squealing in protest. Festoons of yellowed lamp bulbs trailed along the tunnel walls, a green signal light flashed by, and then the wheels squealed again as the brakes went on. The tunnel walls brightened as the train entered the next station. Vicky glanced upward at the Circle Line map, fixed on the curved bulkhead above and to the right of the door. They were coming into Great Portland Street station. The Sheik, standing like a statue next to her, stared impassively.

The doors opened with a hiss while the train was still coming to a complete halt. This platform was even more crowded than Baker Street. Vicky wondered just how many more it could hold before people fell onto the rails. The crush became even greater. Finally, the doors hissed shut, then they moved off. The train entered the tunnel again, its wheels grinding. It rounded a curve and slowly gathered speed on the straight, the wheels going tickety-tack, tickety-tack.

Half the passengers got off at Euston Square. Hardly anyone got on. The Sheik stayed in the doorway even though a few seats had become available. Vicky started thinking morbid thoughts again. To distract herself, she counted the stations on the map, going around and around. There were twenty-six stations on the Circle Line. It didn't help. It was like trying hard not to think of something.

Christ, where are we going? she wondered. All the way around the Circle Line?

Euston Square came and went, followed by King's Cross with a tidal wave of passengers. Vicky's feet were getting sore. As the train entered Farringdon, there were plenty of empty seats, but still, the Sheik stood in the doorway, his face set like stone.

A cold wave passed through her, making her shiver for a moment. What was that expression her mother used to use? "Someone's walking on your grave." She'd always thought how illogical that was since you hadn't been buried yet.

FORTY-FOUR

The double-decker bus pulled up outside the doors of the building that housed Heartland TV's London studio. Eric Woolman jumped off, followed by Ed Crowell and the rest of the Upwood village victims.

Ed turned as the last man got down.

The driver lowered his window and stared back at him. "Hell an powdahouse, mon."

"Thanks for not causing a fuss." Ed followed Eric up several steps and into the office building. The rest stayed on the bus.

Eric Woolman, a barrel-chested man with sandy hair, approached the security counter. Pustules were taking over Eric's face. The skin on one side of his nose had cracked open, exposing a raw pink.

The guard got up from his chair. "Just a minute. You can't come in here." He put his hand on a can of pepper spray.

Eric was practically at the counter. The guard took a step backward.

"I'll call the police."

"Oh. You haven't called them yet? Good!" He pulled a length of

225

chain from his waist. "Better not think of using that spray. My friends would get mad. We just want to talk to your program manager, or producer, or whatever you call it. Nothing violent."

On the wall, a large TV monitor showed the studio video feed. The view was a road junction near the Grange estate. Ambulances were lining up. The picture cut to an aerial view. A section of the hillside had collapsed; the raw red clay looked like an open wound in the grassy slope.

Eric pointed at the screen. "It's about that. We're the people from Upwood village. Remember? There's not many of us left. But we will be enough."

"As long as you behave yourselves, I'll find out."

The guard spoke into an intercom. "Front desk. I've got some visitors here, they want to know the whereabouts of Sheik Maulan."

A voice came from the intercom. "What visitors?"

"They say they are the survivors from Upwood village."

A reply came. "Tell them, then. And ask if they will do an interview on camera."

The guard turned to Eric Woolman and said, "The police just left. They said Sheik Maulan is on the London Underground. And the producer would like to interview you on camera for the news."

"Any other time. Not now. Where on the Underground?"

"They found our van abandoned outside the Baker Street tube — the Circle line."

Eric said, "Not that far. We'll take the bus."

"Right." Ed turned and made his way out. The bus still sat there, the engine ticking over, and the rest were still sitting inside, but the driver had run away.

FORTY-FIVE

Strange and Sergeant James were nearing West End Central police station when Strange's police radio came to life. It was Commander Imran.

"Strange? Where the hell are you?"

Strange clicked the transmit button. "London, sir. Chasing Sheik Maulan." This was worrying. He couldn't disobey a direct order to return if his boss told him to.

"You're out of the area. That's handed off to Metropolitan now."

"Yes, sir. I really feel I have something to contribute."

"Not to mention he has a hostage, eh, Strange?"

"Yes." Strange had an empty hollow feeling in the pit of his stomach.

"I'll save you the time of reporting to West End Central. He's in the tube. Spotted on the Circle Line by the CCTV. The only reason the tube is still running is not to cause panic and get the public out of the way. And she's with him."

"Where on the Circle Line, sir?"

"Was Baker Street, but the CCTV shows them getting on to a train bound for Liverpool Street. The service has been suspended there, but they could get off at any of the stations in between. Wait—"

Strange said to Sergeant James, "Head for Liverpool Street, Sergeant, blue lights and siren."

Imran came back on the radio. "I've had a word with the PPS, and you're seconded to Metropolitan Anti-Terror Group for the purpose of this investigation only. You will remain responsible to me but temporarily detached. Sergeant James is the liaison with MATG. Got that?"

"Thank you, sir. I'm on my way."

FORTY-SIX

Rattling and squealing, the tube train burst out of the tunnel mouth into Liverpool Street station.

An announcement came from the loudspeakers: "This is Liverpool Street. Change for the Central and Hammersmith & City lines and National Rail services." The doors puffed fish air and opened. The Sheik propelled Vicky out and onto the platform. Not many people got off.

The doors hissed shut behind her, then the train pulled away into the tunnel. Vicky heard humming and clicking sounds from the public address system, then a man's voice announced: "We regret that due to technical reasons, service has been suspended. Please leave via the nearest exit. Do not remain on the platform. Service is suspended."

Vicky twisted her head to watch the carriages pull out. Blank windows blurred past; the train was deserted. When she turned again, she noticed a man leaning casually against the tiled wall at the far end of the platform. He was about twenty-seven years old and had a narrow pointed face and a shock of red hair. He wore faded blue jeans and an equally faded ski jacket.

The Sheik stared at him.

Something rattled overhead. She looked up and saw the noise was coming from letters rotating on the signboard. As she watched, the letters settled down into a message: "ALL CENTRAL LINE TRAINS CANCELED UNTIL FURTHER NOTICE."

The Sheik sucked air sharply through his teeth.

Vicky looked down the platform again, but the red-haired man had disappeared.

"What are you looking for?" the Sheik said in a tone that made her shiver.

"Nothing," she replied in a small voice.

<hr />

STRANGE AND SERGEANT JAMES WERE NEARING MOORGATE TUBE when the radio broke squelch, this time with a new voice, female. "From Superintendent Alison. Sergeant James please."

James picked up the microphone. "James here."

"From Alison. Sergeant, the tube is closing, there's no point in you trying to use Moorgate station. We have them on the CCTV at Liverpool Street, and one of TFL's plain-clothes detectives just spotted them on the Circle Line platform."

Sergeant James glanced at Strange. "By road, sir? Just a few minutes, I think."

Strange was already pulling the information from the GPS. "Keep north on Moorgate, then right into South Place and then Eldon Street, keep on into Broad Street … ."

By the time he had finished, James was slowing for the right turn at the Helicon building. The traffic lights were on red, but with the blues and siren going, James made the turn and accelerated hard, passing the junction with Dominion Street and flying through the traffic-calming narrow section. As they passed Wilson Street, the road became one way, and two lanes wide, into Eldon Street. They were stopped halfway by a cab. James bullied it out of the way. Into Broad Street, too fast around the one-twenty-degree right, then left into Liverpool Street, taking the bus and bike lane with the siren barking loudly. To the right, opposite the clock tower and right next to the tube station, a pedestrianized path offered a place to leave the car.

"Sergeant, tell ATG we'll leave the car outside the tube. The keys will be behind the sun visor. Have someone pick it up. We've no time to find a parking spot."

James picked up the microphone.

Imran called Strange. "You're to wait at Liverpool Street, there's a team assembling there. Remember, you're seconded; you're to comply with the Met."

FORTY-SEVEN

The anti-terror team entered through the Liverpool Street portal and gathered on the mezzanine. The officer in command, Superintendent Javid, introduced Strange to his fifteen-man team. Strange knew none of them and, minutes later, found he'd forgotten most of the names.

Liverpool Street above-ground rail was still running normally, but the sliding doors to the tube had closed, shutting off passenger access to London Underground.

The PA system announced, "Please do not leave luggage unattended. Unattended luggage may be removed and destroyed by the security services. London Underground is closed until further notice."

Strange wondered if there was a special reason for Maulan's arrival at Liverpool Street. "Sergeant James. The ventilators for the tube system. They exhaust to the open air, don't they? If you get close to them you can smell that tube smell. The fans must be pretty big. Maybe he plans to use them to spread that radioactive dust? How many levels are there here at Liverpool Street?"

One of Javid's men overheard him. "There's four lines here, sir —

four different levels to worry about — the Central, Circle, Hammersmith & City, and Metropolitan lines."

"Could he get at the ventilation system? Surely those areas are all under lock and key?"

"He's got the best key there is: a weapon. The LT staff will have keys to get into all those places. All he has to do is put a gun to someone's head. If he's carrying that stuff, we'll have to take him before he gets a chance to use it."

"I thought the system had been evacuated."

"Passengers, yes, sir. Still quite a number of LT people though. Takes a while to shut down a system this complex."

Javid said, "We're going in now. Other exits have been sealed off."

Strange made sure he was one of the first through the doors.

FORTY-EIGHT

Teacher headed for the first set of escalators. They were
still a few yards from the top when they saw the Sheik and
Vicky near the bottom.

The Sheik had his right arm around Vicky's neck. Strange drew
his pistol. He was torn between wanting to put a bullet into the
Sheik's head and fear for Vicky.

"I wouldn't do that if I was you, Officer Strange," the Sheik called,
his voice clear and mocking. "Yes, I recognize you from your visit.
You wouldn't want me to explode, would you? This woman, it would
be a waste." Strange backed away; the team, too.

Vicky was half sobbing, half grunting, fighting to get her breath
with the Sheik's arm across her throat.

The Sheik shoved her forward, keeping her in between himself
and Strange. He pulled something from his bag. It looked like a
tennis ball. He forced Vicky sideways, crab-like, until they were at
the top of the down-going escalator. He backed onto the escalator,
and they started descending, but they had hardly begun to move
when he pulled his arm back to throw.

Strange remembered what Anisa had told him, about Zafir and homemade grenades. He shouted, "Back! He's got a grenade!"

The team scattered. Strange ran as if his feet were hardly touching the floor.

The Sheik lobbed the grenade. It hit the floor but failed to explode. A loud fizzing sound came from it, then white smoke — no, steam. It rolled away toward the newsstands, fizzing and spitting.

Then with a loud bang, the grenade exploded, scattering blazing yellow fragments in all directions. Racks of newspapers in the newsstands caught fire. Billows of dark gray smoke coiled across the ceiling. The smoke alarms went off.

Strange looked toward the second escalator. The Sheik and Vicky were nowhere to be seen. The smoke was getting thicker, and flames erupted from the kiosk. Shouts came from behind. He turned. Burning yellow fragments had struck two of the team. The stuff had set fire to their uniforms, and they didn't seem to be able to put it out.

A third officer yanked a fire extinguisher from the wall and sprayed his mates. Strange began coughing; he pulled his radio from an inside pocket and pressed the talk switch.

"From November Two. November Two. Fire—" A loud hiss came from the speaker. "Bloody tunnels," he muttered. He scuttled toward the escalator, bent double, coughing.

FORTY-NINE

Eric Woolman decided he'd act as self-appointed conductor. The others pointed out that the buses were all driver-operated nowadays, but Woolman didn't care. Crowell turned around and bellowed from the cab:

"Shut up, will you!" Woolman left off ringing the bell and shouted back, "Head for the Mile End Road."

"I've always wanted to drive a bus," Crowell said, pulling away from the curb without bothering to check the mirror. "Especially a double-decker." Horns sounded as cars swerved out of the way.

After two miles of traffic chaos, the red double-decker pulled up outside the Baker Street tube station. The mob found a metal trellis gate pulled across the front entrance. A porter stood just inside next to a blackboard that bore a message in large yellow chalk letters: "NO TRAINS UNTIL FURTHER NOTICE." Underneath, as if an afterthought, someone had added: "The Management Regrets Any Inconvenience."

"Hey, you," Crowell shouted, "open this fucking gate."

"Can't you read?" the porter, a dignified middle-aged man, said in a cockney accent. He pointed to the sign.

"Sign or no sign, we've got business in there!"

"I'm sorry," the porter said, folding his arms. "The station is closed until further notice."

"Where's my chain?" Crowell demanded, twisting round to see the others.

"Still on the bus," Woolman's voice replied from the back of the pack.

"Okay, mister. We'll see," Crowell said. He spun on his heels, then walked to the bus. Crowell picked up the heavy length of chain from one of the seats, got out again, then bent down at the back of the bus to peer underneath. There was a tow hook behind the bumper. He hooked one end of the chain over it and walked back to the station entrance. Now he was really enjoying himself, and he smiled at the porter as he passed a loop of chain through the trellis, then fastened it back on itself.

"Hey, what are you up to? Stop that, or I'll call the police!" the porter said.

Crowell looked at him, and an even bigger grin split his face.

"Oh," he said. "You haven't called them yet?" Almost in unison, the rest of them shouted, "Good!"

The bus was still idling at the curb. Crowell climbed back into the cab and moved the gear selector to first. He rammed the accelerator to the floor, and the engine roared. The double-decker was still only doing ten miles an hour when the chain tightened, but it pulled the gate outward like a broken concertina. The fastenings gave way with a rending sound, sending pieces of broken brick and twisted metal flying.

The porter was still standing inside the gates, staring at the remains, when they shouldered him out of the way and clattered down the steps past the deserted ticket office.

"Hey. Hey!" He shouted after them, but they paid no attention.

Eric Woolman watched the other villagers clustering around Ed Crowell, gesturing and arguing. He felt a terrible sense of loss at what they had so recently been: ordinary folk, going about their ordinary lives in a little place that had been trying to become a small town. Ed had been the respected leader of the village's troop of boy scouts. Only a thin skin, easily shed, distinguishes a human being from a brute.

The empty platform stretched away on both sides until it met the mouth of the tunnel. The world above existed in a different time and space, not merely a flight of stone steps and a set of metal gates.

A hollow murmuring was in the air; maybe it was their own voices echoed back at them from the tunnel. Maybe it was something else. It was hard to say. A train stood at the platform as if waiting to take on passengers who had forgotten to wake up that morning. As one day or another, soon enough, some of them would fail to wake up. *I'm becoming maudlin. Well, I'm their leader, not Crowell. It's time to take back the reins.*

"You did okay driving the bus, Ed," he said. "D'you reckon you could handle that?" He pointed towards the tube train.

FIFTY

A babble of messages came from the loudspeaker in the mobile communications vehicle parked outside Liverpool Street. The inspector from West End Central had agreed, with reluctance, that Strange could take command of the hunt again. He had the Liverpool Street plans spread out in front of him.

"It's a rabbit warren. Look at these connecting tunnels. How deep do they go?"

"The Central Line is deep. That's not all, sir." A London Transport maintenance supervisor stood beside him peering down at the diagram. "There's stuff down there that doesn't appear on this map." He pointed a finger. "Round about here, there's an entrance to the government system that was set up during and after the Second World War. They say that it goes seven miles, with branches running under the Mall and right up Horseguards Parade, even under Whitehall."

"Could he get into that?"

"Not without oxy-acetylene. I've seen the doors, they're steel."

"Keys?"

"Not even the station master has them."

Strange felt relieved to know that.

"Anyway, we spotted him on the CCTV going into the Metropolitan line eastbound tunnel."

Sergeant James stepped through the door and said, "Sir. The teams are in position. We're ready to go."

"Let's not underestimate the bastard. And I want him alive, is that clear? I don't want any nasty surprises later. Make sure all the teams understand that."

"They do, sir. It was part of the brief."

Strange got up from the desk and turned toward the door. The LT supervisor made as if to follow him, but Strange put his hand up to say no. "Best wait here. He's very dangerous."

"I know everything about the system. I'd like to do what I can."

"Okay, but remember: Stay back, and do exactly what you're told, for your own safety."

A small fire truck was parked in front of the station. The full-size vehicles had already left; it hadn't taken them long to deal with the fire, but a filthy smell of charred insulation and plastic hung in the air. Pools of water lay everywhere.

A cordon of uniformed policemen was holding back not only curious onlookers but an insistent group of news people and their engineers, brandishing ENG cameras, boom microphones, and other paraphernalia. A civilian police engineer was setting up mobile connections. A cable ran into the station entrance and disappeared down the stairs.

Strange, James and the supervisor went past the still-smoldering remains of the kiosk. Sergeant James was carrying a small backpack by its straps. In his other hand he toted a combat shotgun. Their feet crunched in the wet debris.

The cable ended in a tangle of equipment on the Metropolitan eastbound platform. A bi-directional antenna hung over the edge, pointing into the mouth of the tunnel. Radio waves tended to reflect off metal objects, such as the rails and cables, so with luck, the relayed signals would reach at least a few hundred yards into the tubes. The main purpose, though, was so that Strange could keep in contact with the other teams.

Two men, Morrow and Brown, crouched at the side of the tunnel entrance. Each wore a Kevlar bullet-proof vest over his street clothes. Brown was an expert firearms officer, brought in from Bethnal Green police station as backup. Morrow hunched against the wall holding an H&K automatic in the two-handed police style.

Brown was cautiously peering around the tiled edge of the brickwork into the tunnel. He wore an image intensifier. The goggles gave him the appearance of a horned insect. That seemed perfectly in tune with the surroundings.

Strange spoke into the radio, "All squads hold position. We're going into the eastbound Metropolitan line, at Liverpool Street."

Brown turned to Strange, "Nothing moving sir, but I can't see very far; the tunnel curves to the right."

"Okay, let's go. Me first, then Morrow, then you, Brown, and Sergeant James. Keep to the left wall. Any trouble, get to the right wall and you should be out of sight." Strange pulled his weapon, retracted the slide, and checked there was a live round in the chamber.

Strange moved cautiously into the tunnel mouth, holding the pistol extended before him, then crouched down and moved crablike to the left wall where he could see past the curve. He gestured to the others that they should stay close to the right wall, then began inching his way forward. Ten yards … twenty … there were no lights ahead, he was staring into a pool of blackness, but knew that he would still be outlined by the dim illumination coming from the station. He scuttled over quickly to the others.

"Either there's a lighting failure or the bastard has broken the lamps. Brown will have to take point. We've got flashlights with us, but using them will be a dead giveaway."

BROWN TURNED A SWITCH ON THE NIGHT GOGGLE SET AND RE-SEATED them over his eyes, then moved cautiously to the left side. He moved slowly at first. He turned to Strange and whispered, "Johnny did break the lamps, but I can see better than he can. First stupid thing he's done. By the way, the curve is straightening out — I can see at least a hundred yards now."

He continued carefully along the wall. Strange held on to Brown's shoulder with his good hand. Morrow followed, then James brought up the rear. Suddenly Brown stopped, brought his hand up, and played with the controls on the goggles.

"Peculiar," he said. "It's growing brighter, but—"

Before Brown could comment further, a trembling came through the ground, then a twittering and creaking in the rails. Brown twisted his head around; a flood of radiance came from behind them, though the source was not apparent yet.

Brown shouted: "Strange! There aren't supposed to be—" then the blunt nose of a Circle line train came into view with headlights blazing. It wasn't more than a hundred yards behind them.

Brown, cursing, pushed the night goggles up onto his head. The train was almost on them. Strange, Morrow, and James ran frantically down the tracks, toward one of the safety alcoves in the walls. Too late, Brown turned to follow them.

IN THE DRIVER'S CAB, WOOLMAN SPOTTED A FIGURE FLATTENING himself against the wall. He grabbed Ed Crowell's arm.

"Look!" he shouted. The speed indicator hovered around twenty miles per hour. Crowell had only taken the motor control lever to the second detent. He was still getting the hang of it.

"Yeah! I'll get the bastard!" Crowell reached for the motor lever and pushed it to the end stop. Steel squealed against steel as the power came on.

"No, no, for Christ's sake, it's not him, it's a track worker or a copper!" Woolman shouted.

"How do you stop this thing?" Crowell reached for the lever again.

Woolman watched in horror as the man on the track dived toward the rails. The train passed through the space where he'd been standing. If it ran over a man, you'd never feel it, he thought, no more than if you stepped on an ant.

The train carried on, Crowell messing with the controls. They passed an alcove in the wall. Woolman caught a glimpse of white faces smeared with grime, three men crammed into the tiny niche.

"More of them!" he said.

"I think I've got the hang of it now," Crowell replied. "I'll bring it into the next station."

As soon as the rear of the train cleared the niche, Strange, Morrow, and James leaped out. Strange saw no movement from Brown, who was lying prone between the rails. In the fading illumination of the train's rear lights, he looked like a casually discarded clump of rags.

Morrow got to him first, reaching out a hand; but just before Morrow touched him, Brown groaned and put his hand to the back of his head. A wave of relief washed through Strange. Morrow pulled his flashlight from a pocket and turned it on. Brown's police cap was torn, and blood trickled from under it.

"Are you okay?" Morrow asked.

"I ... think so," Brown replied in a shaky voice, feeling the back of his head. "Must have been something hanging down below the train.

Caught me a right wallop. Lucky I missed the live rail or I'd have been toast by now."

THE SHEIK WAS REGRETTING HIS DECISION TO MOVE INTO THE TUNNEL, but he'd had little choice in the matter. It was costing him time to smash the lights behind him, although he'd found a long-handled track pick in one of the alcoves — that had made the job a lot easier. In the distance, he made out a faint glimmer of light that meant he was getting near the next station. He marched Vicky in front, with her arm twisted behind her back. They had just entered the final straight section when he felt the rails beginning to sing under his feet.

Nervously he glanced behind him, but the bend in the tunnel wall limited his vision to a hundred yards or so, at best. He hadn't seen or heard a train in, what was it? Must be nearly an hour, he estimated. The bloody police, that's who it must be. There was an alcove on his right; he ducked into it, dragging Vicky after him.

"Stay still, you bitch!" he growled into her ear, reaching inside his robe and pulling out the pistol.

Yes, here they came. The train wasn't going very fast; in the dim lighting he made out white faces, peering from the window of the driver's cab. Well, he'd teach them a lesson. He reached round the edge of the alcove and leveled the gun at the window, then squeezed the trigger, just as Vicky brought her hand up and pulled his arm down.

The shot went wild. Cursing, the Sheik reached into his bag again and brought out another of the homemade grenades.

"I'VE GOT THE HANG OF IT NOW," SAID CROWELL CONFIDENTLY, THEN spoiled the effect by adding, "I think."

"Well, watch it," Woolman said. "Don't overrun the next station. It's the end of the line! We can't be far away." He peered over his shoulder and saw the carriage corridors behind them twisting and turning like a snake as the train came around the long curve. When he turned to the front again, he wondered for a moment if his eyes were playing tricks with him.

Ahead in the darkness, a bright yellow flare lit up the tunnel walls. The track was on fire — no, the sides of the tunnel were also ablaze with yellow flame. Crowell let go of the controls and leaped for the door into the passenger carriage.

The deadman's handle triggered the brakes now that no one had control, so the train slowed rapidly and stopped short of the alcove.

FIFTY-ONE

"What the hell was that?" Strange asked. They'd heard the blast shortly before smoke drove them out of the tunnel to Liverpool Street. The station had been evacuated and closed to the public.

"Maybe the same thing as he used on the kiosk, sir," Morrow said.

Strange spoke into his handset. "From Sierra. Foxtrot, this is Sugar; do you read me?"

"From Foxtrot One. Loud and clear." Foxtrot team was in the next station, Aldgate.

"From Sierra. Foxtrot One, any sign of fire at your end?"

"From Foxtrot. Yes, sir. There's smoke coming out the tunnel. Not much, but it's building up. What's happening at your side?"

"There's a fire about a hundred yards in. A train came through, bloody nearly turned the lot of us into mincemeat."

Brown nodded his head in fervent agreement, then winced in pain.

The voice from the other station squawked: "Ah — we couldn't warn you in time. Sorry. It's the people from that converted hotel.

246

The hardcore from the army camp near Upwood. They hijacked a bus, raided a studio, and pulled down the gates at Baker Street. There was a train parked in the station, and they made off with it."

"Great. So now we've got a bunch of civilians in here as well?"

"They're after him. The Sheik."

"The smoke drove us back out the tunnel again," Strange said. Suddenly he had a thought. "Are you carrying oxygen?"

"No sir, we've got a tear gas projector and gas masks, though. The masks might be of some use in smoke."

"Right. We'll get oxygen from the brigade here; they're upstairs still damping down. Then we'll see if we can put that fire out. Keep a close lookout at your end — the smoke will drive him in your direction. As soon as we've cleared the fire, we'll come at him from both sides. For God's sake, be careful, or we could end up shooting at each other."

Sergeant James came down the platform with two firefighters in full protective gear. The firefighters each had large carbon dioxide extinguishers under their arms and carried oxygen masks. James carried two more of the breathing sets. One of the firefighters approached Strange.

"Better let us deal with it, sir. If you'll just let us have one of your men to make sure it's safe."

"No. We're dealing with a psycho here, I'm not letting you take the risk. Show us how to use the oxygen masks and we'll deal with it."

The radio came to life again. "Sir, we've—" it was Foxtrot team again, but then the voice cut out. Sounds of a struggle came over the channel.

Strange thumbed the microphone key. "Foxtrot, Foxtrot. What's going on up there?" There was silence for a moment, and then a new voice came on.

"You police in the other end—" Strange didn't recognize the

voice. There was some muttering going on in the background, but he couldn't make out any of the words. *Who the hell was—*

"Yeah. You police. This is the village social club." They started laughing.

Strange's cheeks flushed with anger.

"We've got our own bit of religion for that bastard, mister detective. It's called an eye for an eye, a tooth for a tooth. Your team here is," again a pause, "helping us with our inquiries!"

The laughter came again. As soon as the carrier went off, Strange pressed the transmit key.

"This is Detective Inspector Strange. If you've assaulted police officers, you'll face the consequences. And don't take the law into your own hands. It's a job for the police."

"Don't worry, Inspector. Your men have agreed to cooperate. They have a few bruises, is all. We're not scared of you, or that bastard the Sheik, or whoever he really is. There's nothing more anyone can do to us. Death would be a release."

The radio went dead. Strange called them on the channel, called again and again, but it was no use. *Vicky, Vicky*, a voice wailed in his head. He turned to the others. "Let's get on with it. Before they do."

They went in using their flashlights, but even the powerful LED beams didn't penetrate very far in the foul smoke. The fire had burnt itself out, though, and gradually the air began to clear; a draft from the far end carried the fumes past them and away. They passed the place where Brown had fallen between the tracks. The night-vision goggles were gone.

"Great. Fucking great," Strange muttered to James. "Now the Sheik's got the night-vision kit. Well, we can play, too. Foxtrot team has a set. ... Oh, shit, I forgot. It's probably the village mob."

Strange jacked the portable phone into the line-side socket in the alcove and pressed the call switch. The circuit was dead. "Damn. Signal cables must have burned up. Useless." He turned to James. "Get back down there, please, Sergeant. Relay a message from the platform to Foxtrot. Tell them to start toward us, night-vision kit if they still have it, armed and ready. We'll trap the bastard somewhere between us. He can't look in both directions at once."

Strange sat in an alcove until James returned. There was a variety of junk in the safety alcove: a half-used can of grease, a spool of black signal wire, some bags of nylon self-locking ties, a battered spade. On one side lay a broken thermos flask and the remains of a sandwich. Strange nudged the sandwich with his foot, and the biggest cockroach he'd ever seen made a run for it. "You're under arrest!" he muttered, bringing his foot down, but it surprised him by taking to the air, flying off into the tunnel. He hoped it wasn't an omen.

They saw the beam from James's flashlight reflecting off the walls shortly before he arrived.

"They're starting at six-fifteen exactly, sir. But the mob from the village has already disappeared into the tunnel." Strange checked his watch; it was twelve minutes past.

"Who's Foxtrot? Remind me."

"Couple of chaps from Bethnal Green, sir. An old-time sergeant, he was around at the time of the Kray brothers, and a newly promoted inspector. Oh, and a rookie PC fresh out of training."

"Christ, is that the best we could manage? What's the sergeant's name?"

"Blake, sir. Training instructor on the firearms range. Qualified on Heckler & Koch machine pistol, Heathrow airport duty."

Strange grinned. "You're a mine of information, Sergeant James."

"Well, we've passed a few favors from hand to hand, sir." He was straight-faced. Strange wondered what the favors were but knew better than to ask.

"I don't think the inspector will have anything better than a pistol, and as for the rookie—"

"A peg, if he's lucky."

"That's about it, sir. The sergeant will keep him well back, I should think."

They inched along, a pair on each side, the point men flattened along the curve of the wall, arms outstretched, pistols aimed ahead. It was arguable which team first became aware of the other. Blake was the point man for Foxtrot squad, and he spotted light being reflected off the tunnel walls, while Strange swore that he'd heard them moving first.

They met opposite one of the workmen's alcoves. Strange was baffled and angry.

"Where the fuck did they go? This is ridiculous. The sod can't have dematerialized and walked through the wall. And what the hell happened to that mob from the hospital?"

The old sergeant — though he couldn't have been much over forty-five, reflected Strange — shrugged. He had a large bruise over his cheekbone and traces of dried blood under his nose.

"No one got past us, sir. Not from your direction. I'll swear to that. Sir, that mob — they were armed with all sorts of makeshift stuff. No guns, though. There were six or seven of them. They pushed on down the tunnel. They wouldn't stop, and we could hardly shoot them. Though it might have come to that if they'd tried to take one of the weapons from us."

He had a Heckler & Koch machine pistol slung over his shoulder, a webbing belt around his waist carrying extra clips. Strange eyed it.

"What kind of load are you carrying, Sergeant? Don't you think that weapon's a bit excessive in these tunnels? If you let go with that, chances are one of us'll catch a ricochet."

A grin split the sergeant's weathered features. "No, sir. These are low-powered specials, only half the usual charge. They'll still stop a man at forty yards, but not much more, and any ricochets are too slow to do much harm."

"You checked all the alcoves?"

"We looked in each one, sir, but we didn't have time to stop and search them for evidence."

"Okay. Here's what we'll do. Back out the same way, but this time I want every square inch checked. Look for manhole covers, inspection plates, anything like that. This fucker's like a cockroach, but I don't think he's got wings."

FIFTY-TWO

"You took a chance with that bloody sergeant, Billy," Ed Crowell said in the darkness.

"Yeah. I thought we might be able to persuade them to let us have a pistol or something. You're right, though. I think he'd have used it on me. He wasn't scared."

They clustered in a small group around a circular opening in the tunnel wall. The grating that had covered it lay broken on the floor. Eric Woolman was wearing the night-vision goggles but hadn't got the hang of them yet.

"Right. Everybody here?" Woolman said.

"I fuckin' hope so," someone else replied. "Whose bright idea was it to come in here without so much as a light?"

"I've got a cigarette lighter," someone replied. Woolman thought it sounded like Tony Emerson.

"Keep it for emergencies. We've got three ends of candle from that alcove down there. Anyone else? Matches?" Woolman asked. They dug in their pockets. Altogether they had two cigarette lighters and their phones.

"You ready, Eric? Them goggles workin'? All I can see is black spots on black." Ed Crowell seemed eager to get on with it.

"Yeah, better now."

"Good. And keep quiet," Crowell demanded.

Woolman put his head and shoulders into the tunnel. "It's narrow and low." He moved up to the opening, rested his left hand on the ground, used it to pivot forward, and pulled his body in so that he could proceed on his hands and knees.

He shuffled forward slowly, listening to the muffled curses from behind when one of them banged his head or scraped an arm.

The walls closed in until they were scraping shoulders against the rough surface, then widened out again. The sounds of their breathing, coming back at them from the walls, became a guide to their surroundings.

Woolman stopped abruptly. Phosphorescent light reflected from some kind of chamber. He looked down. A jumble of footprints entered it. Some were a man's, judging by the size; others were smaller. They looked fresh, deeply printed in dust so thick that it resembled gray snow.

Woolman entered the chamber and, holding the small of his back and grunting, stood, half bent over, listening intently. He peered about through the goggles. They painted the scene in a ghostly green radiance. Brighter patches showed here and there where patches of photo-luminescent lichen grew on the decayed masonry.

From far away came a sound of brick scraping on brick, then a faint scream.

The chamber had two exits, and they had only one set of night-vision glasses. He scanned the floor: more footprints, and the trails led into both passages.

Maybe the bastard had entered each one, then walked backward out of it again to confuse his pursuers. Maybe they went in a circle. He'd have to choose one or the other.

What did you do to find your way around a maze? He tried to remember. Yes, that was it. One way, at least. You kept to the left and trailed your hand along the left side of it. Or the right. Same principle. That way you couldn't get lost.

"Right," he muttered, turning around. "There are two tunnels. He could be in either of them. We'll have to split up. I'll lead into the left tunnel; you'll have to use your phones as flashlights in the right tunnel. Bloody watch out."

FIFTY-THREE

It was Morrow who first spotted the narrow tunnel. "Look, sir, there!" He used the LED beam like a pointer. A broken, rusted metal grille lay on the ground nearby. "It's been moved recently. You can see the fresh marks."

He switched the white light off and brought out a small black-light. It showed luminous patches on the low edge of the narrow opening. "Skin, I think, sir."

Please, God, not hers, Strange thought. "Got the tunnel map?"

"Brown has a copy, sir."

They wasted several minutes trying to find the side shaft on the map. It didn't exist, at least as far as London Transport was concerned. Strange called in the Foxtrot team. They clustered in a group in the middle of the tunnel next to the shaft.

"Right. I'm asking for two volunteers, it looks like it's going to be cramped in there. The others will split up. According to the map, there's another tube line next to us, the Metropolitan, and yet another next door, the District. And the Central line is somewhere below. Maybe this access shaft leads into one of them. Now, we've got those sealed off at each end as well, so I don't expect he'll get out

255

this way, but just in case, I want you to check it out. See if you can locate the other end of this access from there. You're not to go in without backup. Armed officers only. But don't forget — I want the bastard alive. If at all possible, that is. If you put a bullet into him and his jacket explodes, you'll kill the hostage and yourselves and contaminate everywhere."

All of them stepped forward, as Strange had expected; even the rookie PC. Hoping to make a name for himself and quick promotion, Strange thought irritably. The last thing he needed was a spotty young constable. He grinned sourly to himself; his days as an equally young and spotty PC seemed to belong to another age, as foreign as the gothic squalor of these subterranean passages.

"Morrow, Blake. You'll join me. Sergeant James, take the constable here with you. You know what you have to do. I want the inspector here with Brown in case our man gets around us somehow and comes back this way."

He shone the flashlight's halogen beam upward and saw a low, sharply curved ceiling above. The brickwork was different from the stuff they'd been used to: smaller, irregular, uneven. Handmade? Most of the mortar pointing had dropped out, and everywhere it ran with condensation and seepage. The air stank of decay.

Strange got into the small tunnel, bent practically double; the ceiling was no higher than four feet. Morrow and Blake followed him. After a while, they came to a place where the tunnel split in two directions.

Strange's voice sounded hollow in the odd acoustics. "There's footsteps in both branches. Fresh. It looks like the villagers are hot on his trail." It felt as if they were about to enter the Silurian epoch.

Brown and Morrow nodded. Their faces looked cadaverous in the reflected light.

"Sir, I think I can hear something," Morrow whispered.

Morrow must have damned good ears. Strange heard only the pounding of his own blood. Or was it? Careful not to scrape his head against the ceiling, he went a few yards farther into the tunnel and stopped again.

Morrow moved up until he was cramped in beside him. "There, sir," he whispered. "Can't you hear it?"

It wasn't his heart he could hear, although the rhythm could have been the same. A distant muffled pounding, traveling partly through the gelid air, partly through the ground, so that the echo gave a trip-hammer effect. It was as if two machines hacked at the walls some-where in the distance. The sound stopped while they were crouched there, although it seemed to persist for long moments in Strange's mind. He turned to Morrow.

"How far, d'you think? Care to make a guess?"

Morrow reflected for a few seconds. "Hard to say, sir, the differ-ence between the speed of sound in air and in brick. Can't be nearer than eight hundred yards, though. Sound travels a long way in these conditions."

"True. And it travels from us to him as well. We'd better be as quiet as we can. Let's go. Blake, you take the point. And remember, we don't want to give them any warning up there. Go by flashlight only for now, and take it easy!"

"Ready, sir?"

"Okay."

They turned off their lights.

Strange counted the steps, walking with his left hand on Blake's shoulder. In a similar fashion, Morrow had a finger looped around Strange's belt. Not a single photon penetrated from the outside world. Lichens, growing sparsely on the rotting brick, gave off a faint chemo-luminescence, though this was barely detectable by unaided eyes. Occasionally they flinched as their heads brushed into hanging stalactites of anabiotic fungus.

The passage started to broaden, and Strange could move up prac-tically alongside Blake, his pistol aimed in front, although the black-ness was still impenetrable. The roof was now nearly seven feet in height; their backs complained as they straightened up after the long time spent hunched over. Blake stopped Strange with an outstretched hand and spoke directly into his ear.

"Have to use the lamps. The walls branch away on each side."

"Okay. I can't hear anything now. You?"

"No, nothing," Blake whispered. He turned around. "Lights on!"

They stood in a circular arena, some ten or twelve feet wide. There were two exits. Footprints went into each. There seemed to be more of them leading into the branch on the right.

"Maybe it's a ventilation shaft," said Strange. He shone a lamp upward but couldn't see the roof. "I'll take the left branch, you take the right, with Morrow. Best of luck." We'll need it, he thought, hoping that his hadn't already run out.

"Yeah. You, too. If I'd known when I got up this morning—"

"Don't give me that, you love it, you old bastard."

Blake grinned at him in reply.

Strange crabbed forward, keeping as flat against the wall as he could. He should have brought adhesive tape to secure the light under the pistol barrel.

The trail of footsteps continued in the dust. The Sheik or the villagers? Both?

A stray draft of air whispered past, and the short hair on the back of his neck stood up.

A glimmer of light showed ahead. Footsteps. Someone was padding toward him. Strange froze in place, gun out, covering the corridor. Ah. It was Blake, with Morrow following.

"It's circular, sir," Blake said. "The two passages join up again. Up ahead there's a door. Looks like someone's gone through it. Thought we'd wait for you."

Strange followed Blake and Morrow up the tunnel, which was in a disturbing condition of decay. They found the door. The LED torches revealed a subterranean mingling of weird colors decaying in rotten beauty. Here and there the bricks had finally succumbed to the pressures of the dank earth beyond, which had spilled out, forming small mounds like molehills. The door had once been plastered over, but the plaster had broken up into a network of fissures like some incredible marine delta. A huge incredibly rusted padlock with a broken hasp lay on the floor, along with a broken track pick.

FIFTY-FOUR

Eric Woolman stood with the others in a dank room beyond the heavy iron door. It was so dark that his eyes struggled to make out anything — the darkness itself filled with mottled patches as if his visual imagination was inventing its own details. He could see, though, outlined against the blackness, that at the far end a low arch in the rotting wall led to yet another underground chamber. It seemed to be a way off. A glimmer of light flickered within.

Woolman sidled forward in the dark. The others followed closely. He crouched down and peered through the arch. The space beyond seemed huge. A tiny flame wavered, making a small circle of light — a candle? Shapes moved in the shadows. A female voice, half stifled, said, "Let … me … go!"

Woolman whispered to the others, "We've caught him. No quarter. Let's finish this."

Carrying their improvised weapons, they entered the chamber.

Strange peered through the partly open door, but the space beyond was so dark that he couldn't make out anything except a dim radiance from somewhere ahead. Blake and Morrow crouched behind him, weapons ready. An unpleasant smell came from within. Strange had encountered the odor before: three years ago, at a neat little house in South London, a murder inquiry. The bodies in the cellar had been partially mummified.

He grimaced in disgust, reached into a pocket, brought out his handkerchief, and tied it around his mouth.

Shouts echoed from somewhere ahead. Strange pulled out his flashlight. Might as well use it, rather than run full tilt into something nasty. He inched through the door and clicked the switch.

The beam shone out, and he caught his breath. On both sides, rough-hewn biers had been let into the walls: skeletal remains, desiccated bodies, decayed rags of clothes. They came from a time of rats, fleas, and buboes. A time when carts rolled through the streets collecting bodies; a time when the cry "Bring out yer dead" echoed from the walls of Whitechapel.

Strange shone the torch on them. The mummified faces still preserved the grimaces of these victims of the Black Death.

They ran forward with weapons ready, sweeping the flashlights from side to side. The chamber was twenty or more feet in width. Rough columns of lath and plaster supported the ceiling at intervals of eight feet or so. The bodies were tightly packed. In some places, the fabric had collapsed, leaving human remains scattered on the floor or protruding gruesomely from the wall. The ceiling bulged downward under the pressure of God knew what.

Strange stifled a shout as something brushed against his face. He looked up. Here the ceiling was cracked and broken, with mummified limbs, bones, and rags of clothes dangling down. Ahead there was a low archway, perhaps four feet high. A fan of yellow light glimmered from it across the bone-rubbled floor.

Strange, followed closely by Blake and Morrow, ran to the

archway and hunkered down, peering around its brick edges. Strange placed his flashlight on the ground, shining inside. He could barely see the Sheik because of the group of villagers surrounding him. And Vicky? It was difficult to see.

"Now's the time," he muttered, then dived through the doorway, the pistol held out before him. Morrow followed close on his heels.

"That's enough," Strange shouted. His voice echoed back from the seeping walls. The circle of villagers turned their heads to see who it was. "This is a matter for the police. Sheik Maulan — release the woman and I'll guarantee safe custody out of here. You're coming with us."

FIFTY-FIVE

They stood around him like hounds around an animal at bay. The ceiling was lower in this chamber, no more than six feet. Ed Crowell, who was six feet and an inch, stooped awkwardly. Their headroom was invaded here, too, by parts of those buried above in another layer of the catacombs.

Against the wall, Vicky gagged with disgust. Her hands were pinioned over her head by a strip of her skirt. The other end was lashed tightly to a rusted metal railing that stuck out of the ceiling.

The Sheik had used her own pantyhose to bind one of the cadavers tightly to her. She cavorted slowly in an obscene waltz with the mummified figure, her bare legs pale in the torchlight, sobbing as she tried not to vomit. Its face grinned into hers in a skeletal rictus, and its arms draped over her shoulders in a parody of a dance. One of the hands fell off.

The Sheik stood facing the seven villagers. In his right hand, he held a pistol; in his left, he clutched the lead cylinder.

"Bastard!" Tony Emerson spat. "You did this to us. Now it's your turn, you filth!"

The Sheik laughed unpleasantly. "It's time," he agreed. "Time for you, too."

He laughed again. "It's time." He took the top off the lead cylinder and let the lid drop to the floor.

"This is Lot's wife. She will be turned into a pillar of salt." Spittle flew from his mouth.

"She has done nothing to harm you." Strange said. "Let her go. Safe custody out of here. I guarantee it." It sounded as convincing as the guarantee on a five-dollar watch.

Ed Crowell turned with a sneer on his lips. "You?" he said. "You'll guarantee nothing. He is ours now."

The Sheik waved the container. "This is the power of the atom. I need no more guarantee than it provides. Here, take the woman. You're all going to die." He reached out and gave the knot a twist. The piece of the dress came free. He brought his foot up and gave Vicky a shove that sent her, still united with the decayed body, staggering toward them.

Strange jumped forward and grabbed her as she teetered on the edge of falling. He pulled a Swiss army knife from his pocket and hacked at the nylon pantyhose. The body came free, and Vicky pushed it from her in violent revulsion.

Strange, supporting Vicky, and his men backed out of the room. There was no way this could end well. They had Vicky, and that was enough for now.

"Come on. Can you walk?" he said to Vicky.

"I think so," she said in a shaky voice.

A sudden roar of voices came from the room they had just left. A harsh screaming started.

"Quick. He's wearing a suicide vest. Let's get out of here," Strange said.

A voice called from the room: "Coppers! Get out. The stuff in the cylinder — it's all over us."

Strange called back, "Stay put. We'll get a team in here. We'll get you out."

"We've had enough. Now we're covered in this shit. Don't forget to shut the door behind you. Don't look back. I'll count to twenty."

Strange and his group exited the room, and Strange jammed the door back into the frame and wedged it in place with the track pick. "Back the way we came, and hurry!"

They made it into the circular chamber when a loud "crump!" came from behind them and the floor jumped under their feet. A roar of falling bricks was followed by a cloud of dust. A jagged crack opened in the ceiling and widened as they watched.

"Run!" Strange waited until the last of his men was clear, then followed, coughing in the choking dust cloud.

EPILOGUE

Strange was sitting in Commander Ashraf's office rubbing his ear with the palm of his hand. The tinnitus came and went; rubbing made little difference. Sometimes, when he concentrated, the noises abated, but then he would realize how deaf that ear was now, since the explosions.

He was meeting Vicky later. She wasn't the same Vicky that he'd first met.

Ashraf tapped the table with his fingernails, bringing Strange's attention back. "Rather convenient for the government. The tube cave-in, I mean. Buried the radiation. And plague pits aren't popular. Nobody wants that dug up."

In a parking lot above the last resting place of the village survivors and Sheik Maulan, the ground had slumped. The site had been roped off, excavated, and backfilled.

"Yes, sir. But I wanted to see him in court. A lot of good men lost their lives that day. And there's not a single one of the scum left to put before a jury."

"The house was erased from the map. One of the chimney pots was found half a mile away in a haystack." He flipped pages in a folder. "Seven of them were in there, gone up in bits. We'll never know if that was deliberate or a trick that Sheik Maulan played on them." He steepled his fingers and grimaced. "We lost eleven. And twenty-seven were injured."

Strange couldn't think of a suitable response, so he kept silent. He couldn't help thinking, though, that if he hadn't been in command, it could have been worse.

"If it hadn't been for the wind changing and blowing the smoke cloud out to sea, imagine the contamination from the factory fire. And we, the authorities that is, were far too slow to respond."

"I couldn't agree more, sir." The scene flashed into his mind unbidden, unwanted, Hasan's body, the top of the skull missing, brain exposed. That bloody useless Carragher, sending in a riot van. The army should have dealt with it from the word go.

"As for the village. It will eventually be decontaminated. A long process. Nearly two hundred poisoned, twelve dead at the camp, plus those who died underground with Maulan; many of the rest still in care." Ashraf looked up from the page. "How's your lady friend, the reporter?"

"Back at work. Getting counseling. It's difficult. Being with me reminds her of what happened. It's like that for me, too. I'm not sure it's going to work. I'm seeing her later."

Ashraf closed the folder. He stared at Strange for a moment, as if considering. "My marriage wasn't on solid ground before this started, and now it's broken. My wife, she's first generation. Devout. Me, not much. My daughter prefers a secular life. It has been difficult."

Strange knew. There had been the occasional drinks in a pub. And he'd never seen Ashraf stop work to pray. The job had always come first. That was one of the things he liked best about his boss, the job being above everything else. "I'm sorry. My own daughter isn't speaking to me, either. My ex has packed her off to boarding school, and — well, the girl thinks I've betrayed her."

"I'm not sorry." Ashraf glanced at the wall clock. It read six forty-eight. "Let's finish this later." He picked up the file and locked it in the secure cabinet. "Oh, by the way. You're taking over here tomorrow."

"Sir?"

"And you're going to get a medal. For your prompt actions. And in exchange, you will keep your mouth shut. We lost a lot of good men. The public no longer trusts us. It could have been a lot worse. Heads must roll, and I was the officer responsible. The details will never be made public, Strange. You, your team, and Ms. Wallis are the only ones who know. You're going to be asked to sign the Official Secrets Act."

"I already have, sir."

"Again. And with specific relevance to what happened in the Underground. There'll be an inquiry. You won't be asked any dangerous questions. The government has been caught with its pants down."

"I see, sir."

"One last thing. You'll be contacted. I'll give you the keywords. To do your job properly, you'll need outside resources."

THAT EVENING, STRANGE PICKED UP VICKY AFTER SHE FINISHED HER work at the studio. He drove them to a balti restaurant on Ladypool Road. Strange ordered the chicken and mushroom balti, and she had the lamb korma.

He broke off a piece of naan bread and offered it to her. "How are you feeling now? Any better? Is the counseling doing any good?" He was also in counseling; he blamed himself for what had happened around the pillbox.

"A little. It's the dreams. I wake up screaming. But taking pills isn't going to help."

"I can't forget what happened to my men. I've been to their funerals. I caught the looks from their wives. If I'd—"

"Stop blaming yourself. It could have been worse. Whoever left the radioactive source in that hospital is really to blame. Without that, none of this would have happened."

"They'd have improvised something else, I'm sure. I keep going over the events again and again. Each decision. Each failure to make a decision." One of the coffins had been buried empty. No trace had been found of the volunteer officer who had thrown the CS canisters into the pillbox.

"And now? Where are we? The two of us?"

"I've been promoted. I'm taking charge of the Midlands anti-terror group. But I'm not sure I want that."

She leaned forward and took his hand. "Do it. There'll be no one better."

"But I thought—"

In the immediate aftermath, she'd said that she regretted dating a copper. The words burned him.

"I've changed my mind. You're a real hero. My hero." She dropped her fork and knife, reached across the narrow table, grabbed his face, and planted her lips on his.

THE END